Praise for *Who Left That Body in the Rain?*

"*Who Left That Body in the Rain?* charms, mystifies, and delights. As Southern as Sunday fried chicken and sweet tea. Patricia Sprinkle's Hopemore is as captivating—and as filled with big hearts and big heartaches—as Jan Karon's Mitford. Come for one visit and you'll always return."
—Carolyn Hart

"Ms. Sprinkle has created an heirloom quilt. Each piece of patchwork is unique and with its own history, yet they are deftly stitched together with threads of family love and loyalty, simmering passion, deception and wickedness, but always with optimism embued with down-home Southern traditions. A novel to be savored while sitting on a creaky swing on the front porch, a pitcher of lemonade nearby, a dog slumbering in the sunlight."
—Joan Hess

"Authentic and convincing. This series is a winner."
—Tamar Myers

Thoroughly Southern Mysteries

WHO INVITED THE DEAD MAN?
WHO LEFT THAT BODY IN THE RAIN?

WHO LEFT THAT BODY IN THE RAIN?

⊰ A THOROUGHLY SOUTHERN MYSTERY ⊱

Patricia Sprinkle

A SIGNET BOOK

SIGNET
Published by New American Library, a division of
Penguin Group (USA) Inc., 375 Hudson Street,
New York, New York 10014, USA
Penguin Group (Canada), 90 Eglinton Avenue East, Suite 700, Toronto,
Ontario M4P 2Y3, Canada (a division of Pearson Penguin Canada Inc.)
Penguin Books Ltd., 80 Strand, London WC2R 0RL, England
Penguin Ireland, 25 St. Stephen's Green, Dublin 2,
Ireland (a division of Penguin Books Ltd.)
Penguin Group (Australia), 250 Camberwell Road, Camberwell, Victoria 3124,
Australia (a division of Pearson Australia Group Pty. Ltd.)
Penguin Books India Pvt. Ltd., 11 Community Centre, Panchsheel Park,
New Delhi - 110 017, India
Penguin Group (NZ), cnr Airborne and Rosedale Roads, Albany,
Auckland 1310, New Zealand (a division of Pearson New Zealand Ltd.)
Penguin Books (South Africa) (Pty.) Ltd., 24 Sturdee Avenue,
Rosebank, Johannesburg 2196, South Africa

Penguin Books Ltd., Registered Offices:
80 Strand, London WC2R 0RL, England

First published by Signet, an imprint of New American Library,
a division of Penguin Group (USA) Inc.

First Printing, December 2002
10 9 8 7 6 5 4

Copyright © Patricia Sprinkle, 2002
All rights reserved

 REGISTERED TRADEMARK—MARCA REGISTRADA

Printed in the United States of America

PUBLISHER'S NOTE
This is a work of fiction. Names, characters, places, and incidents either are
the product of the author's imagination or are used fictitiously, and any resem-
blance to actual persons, living or dead, business establishments, events, or
locales is entirely coincidental.
   The publisher does not have any control over and does not assume any
responsibility for author or third-party Web sites or their content.

THANKS TO . . .

Judge Mildred Ann Palmer, Magistrate, Burke County, Georgia, who inspired the series, hosted me while I did research, and helped with details about MacLaren's role as a magistrate. Because of Judge Palmer, MacLaren lives.

Curtis St. Germaine, Chief Magistrate of Burke County, and deputy clerks Cynthia Lewis and Nicole Hammock, for their patience with my many questions about details relating to their work.

Our cousins, Mary and Dan McKenzie, who answered numerous questions about owning a motor company in a small Southern town. I assure them and our mutual relatives that neither the motor company nor the characters in this book are based on Dan, Mary, or McKenzie Motors.

Joe Sklandis, who filled me in on the automobile business from a salesman's point of view, and Chris Potts, who explained how to detail a car.

Composer Betty Carr Pulkingham, who suggested appropriate hymns for the imaginary St. Philip Episcopal carillon in Hopemore.

Lucia Ravelo, who polished up my Spanish.

Ellen Edwards, my editor, who greatly improved the manuscript, and Nancy Yost, my agent, who cheered and encouraged me.

Most of all, Bob, who, as always, provided support, a sounding board, and, this time, the ferret.

Where the book is accurate, these folks deserve the credit. The errors are my own.

CAST OF CHARACTERS

MacLaren Yarbrough: amateur sleuth, Georgia magistrate, co-owner of Yarbrough Feed, Seed and Nursery

Joe Riddley Yarbrough: MacLaren's husband, a former magistrate, co-owner of Yarbrough Feed, Seed and Nursery

Clarinda Williams: Yarbroughs' long-time cook

Ridd: Yarbroughs' older son, high school math teacher and small farmer

Martha: Ridd's wife, emergency room supervisor
    Cricket (4) and **Bethany** (16): their children

Walker: Yarbroughs' younger son, insurance salesman

Cindy: Walker's largely ornamental wife
    Jessica (11) and **Tad** (9): their children

Fergus "Skye" MacDonald: owner of MacDonald Motors in Hopemore and friend of the Yarbroughs for thirty years

Gwen Ellen MacDonald: his wife and friend of the Yarbroughs since she was a child

Laura MacDonald: their daughter, vice president of MacDonald Motors

Skellton (Skell) MacDonald: their son, would-be playboy and unwilling manager of the family used car business, Sky's the Limit

Jimmy Bratson: assistant manager at Sky's the Limit Used Cars

Ben Bradshaw: service-department manager at MacDonald Motors

Nicole Shandy: receptionist at MacDonald Motors, claims she is Skye's secretary

*   *   *

Hubert Spence: Yarbroughs' nearest neighbor

Maynard Spence: Hubert's son, curator of Hope County
   Historical Museum

Selena Jones: his fiancée, later his wife

Marilee Muller: a plain little girl from Hopemore who
   grew up to be a television celebrity

Humberto Garcia: newcomer to Hopemore who opens the
   town's first Mexican restaurant

Emerita Garcia: Humberto's wife, co-owner of their
   restaurant and cook

Rosa Garcia: their daughter, who teaches the Yarbroughs'
   granddaughter Jessica

Charlie Muggins: Hopemore police chief

Isaac James: assistant police chief

⇥1⇤

Only one of us committed murder that particular Friday, but a lot of folks were out of sorts. Maybe it was the weather. February in Middle Georgia is generally mild, but as we drove home that noon for dinner, heavy gray clouds hovered overhead and the air was uneasy and restless.

Clarinda was banging dishes around, fixing to have a conniption. She's been keeping house for us for over forty years. I know her moods.

I set my pocketbook on the counter. "Who put ants between *your* sheets?"

She jerked her head toward Maynard Spence, our nearest neighbor. He sat at our kitchen table with his long gold ponytail gleaming in the light and a fool's grin on his face. "Hey, Mac." He hoisted a mug. "Where's Joe Riddley?"

"Talking to his dogs in the pen. What are you doing here?" I bent to pat my beagle, Lulu, reassuring her I'd returned home yet again in one piece. "Don't you have things to do?" Maynard was getting married the next morning.

"Clarinda and I were checking on a few last things for the rehearsal dinner tonight." He hauled his tall frame erect. "But it is time I got moving. I've got to collect my tux and Selena, then we have to drive all the way to Milledgeville to visit her great-grandmother. She's too frail to come to the wedding, so Selena's promised we'll get all dressed up and take pictures with her."

Clarinda rested both hands on her stout hips. "Miss Mac-Laren, did that boy just say he's gonna see his little bride in her dress before the ceremony?"

"It won't be the first time," Maynard said, further rocking her boat. "I helped design the dress."

"I'll bet she's gonna be real fashionable," Clarinda muttered to Lulu, "for eighteen fifty." Maynard had a master's degree in art history from NYU and was curator of our Hope County Historical Museum. He did sometimes tend to prefer the past to the present.

He laughed and gave me a quick hug. "See you tomorrow. Don't forget, I want you to sit on the pew with Daddy. You're the closest thing to family I've got."

"We'll be there," I promised.

"See you tonight, Clarinda. Sure hope you're speaking to me by then." He went out the door at a fast lope, stopping on the porch to greet Joe Riddley.

Before I could ask Clarinda again what was bothering her, my husband ambled in with Joe, his scarlet macaw, on his cap. We had inherited Joe the previous October from a man who died in our dining room.* Joe slept in the barn, where we kept camping gear, the fishing boat, and lawn and garden equipment, and Joe Riddley carried him back and forth to the office every day. His favorite perch was on Joe Riddley's red-billed cap with "Yarbrough's" stitched in white letters across the front to advertise our store, Yarbrough's Feed, Seed and Nursery.

Joe Riddley knuckled Joe gently so he'd fly to the curtain rod above the sink, and hung his cap on its hook by the kitchen door. "Hey, Clarinda," he said mildly. "Have a good mornin'?"

*Who Invited the Dead Man?

Clarinda grunted. "Not so's you'd notice." She continued to bustle about the kitchen huffing and puffing and making a lot of clatter without doing much else as far as I could see. Our whole dinner seemed to consist of one pot.

Joe leaned down and turned himself almost upside down, peering at her. Then he called "Sic 'em. Sic 'em." When she ignored him, he righted himself and turned to preen a feather on his back. That parrot was a lot of trouble, but even I had to admit his scarlet breast and rainbow back and tail made a gorgeous display against our gray wall.

Lulu danced around protesting that parrots didn't belong in the house. Joe taunted her with more squawks, safe since she couldn't fly. Clarinda banged flatware on the table, her chocolate-brown face pinched and martyred.

"Hush!" I yelled. "All of you, hush. What is the *matter* with you, Clarinda?"

Clarinda heaved a sigh that nearly dropped her sizeable bosoms to her kneecaps. "You aren't gonna believe what Maynard has gone and done. Here he is getting married, you know—"

Joe Riddley gave a snort of impatience. "Of course we know. Have we talked about a blessed thing since Christmas except that precious wedding?" He was still recovering from getting shot in the head back in August.* By now he could talk plain unless he was tired, remember most things, and walk unaided, but his sweetness and light tanks weren't always full.

"Hush," I told him. "I want to hear what Maynard's done."

Maynard had lived down the road from us all his life, a pallid gawky child who whined a lot, emphasized words in a strange way as he spoke, and loved history and art in a small town that preferred golf and football. To tell the truth,

*But Why Shoot the Magistrate?

I hadn't been real fond of him back then. I'd felt more charitable when he'd given up a good New York museum job the year before and hurried home when his widowed daddy had a heart attack. I'd been impressed with the way he nursed Hubert back to health. And I'd grown really fond of him while he was helping me do a spot of detecting right before Joe Riddley got shot. I'd even introduced him to his bride-to-be, Selena. And I had to admit that the pale boy who left home several years before had come home a downright handsome fellow. I didn't even mind his earring anymore.

Nobody had expected Maynard to stay in Hopemore once Hubert was on his feet. But here he was, a year later, still taking some of the load off Hubert at Spence's Appliance Store and spending the rest of his time revitalizing our once moribund Hope County Historical Museum. Last fall he'd supervised a crew in renovating a Victorian house in town where he and Selena would live. Currently he was fixing to open an antique store in one of Hopemore's three antebellum mansions up on Oglethorpe Street, near the courthouse square. It appeared to me if anybody deserved praise it was Maynard.

Also, Clarinda loved him like he was her own, and if you don't believe that, you've never witnessed the relationship that can grow up between a lonely little boy and his neighbors' cook.

Joe Riddley looked up and said to Joe, "Hey, bird, maybe he's decided not to go through with it. I couldn't blame him. A man never knows what he's getting in for, tying himself down for life. The woman might turn into somebody he hardly knows. Take Little Bit, here—"

I gave him a light swat. "You already took me, forty-three years ago, for better or worse. You got the better and I got the worse."

"Sic 'em, sic 'em," Joe advised again.

Clarinda glared up at the parrot, her own feathers equally ruffled. "Don't you poop in my clean sink, bird."

"So what has Maynard done?" I was tired of waiting to find out.

She rested her fists on her wide hips again. "Gone and spent money on a new sports car. I told him and told him his Saturn would do fine until they put something by, but he wouldn't listen. Says Mr. Skye gave him a real good deal, and it's a honey of a car. I'd like to honey him. It's pride; that's what it is. Nothin' but pride, and he's gonna marry that sweet child with a load of debt on him." She thumped bowls down on the countertop in a way that made me nervous for my crockery.

"He's twenty-seven," I reminded her, "and he inherited a good bit of money from his uncle in Atlanta. He knows whether he can afford a new car or not."

She ladled something into the bowls and huffed several times, making it clear that working for somebody as unreasonable as me was the greatest imposition in the world.

At the sink, Joe Riddley soaped his hands for a second time and rinsed them good. "Maynard's smart. Valedictorian of his class in high school and got a big scholarship to NYU."

"How can he remember that when he can't remember he already soaped his hands?" I asked Clarinda, but she didn't crack a smile.

Joe Riddley reached for a towel, dripping water all over the floor. "Ought to make good money on that antique store, too, and Selena's a nurse. They'll pay off that loan. Stop your worrying. What did he get?"

Clarinda took a skillet of cornbread from the oven and banged it down on a trivet in the middle of the table. I sighed. We'd probably have a new dent. Our table has been in the family for three generations, and is what dealers like to call "distressed."

Clarinda pursed her lips to show she'd rather certain words didn't have to pass through them. "Blue BMW convertible, or so he says. 'Co'rse, I haven't seen it. He didn't want to dust it up, coming down your road. Said he's leaving it in town until after the ceremony."

"The way you talk," I told her, "folks would think we were hicks living in the middle of nowhere." Instead, we were college-educated, reasonably prosperous store owners living at the end of a good gravel road. We're half a mile from the highway and less than a mile from Hopemore, county seat of Hope County, located in that strip of Georgia between I-20 and I-16. Joe Riddley's great-grandfather built our house right after the War (if you have to ask which war, you weren't born in Georgia), and none of his descendants has ever felt a need to lay asphalt—although I sometimes think we could have paved it in gold and saved money, with all the gravel we've put down.

However, since the road does get a tad dusty in dry spells, and that particular month *had* been dry, I decided not to fuss. What was bothering Clarinda most was not Maynard's new car, but Maynard's departure from next door to his own house in town, and his upcoming switch of allegiance from her to Selena. That's why I offered her a little comfort. "His Saturn might not make it all the way to Disney World. It's getting pretty old, and it's been giving him trouble." I went to wash my own hands, sending a warning glare up to Joe about messing in my hair while I was under him. "What if they broke down between here and there?"

She heaved another enormous sigh, but I could tell she was a tad mollified. Like I said, the woman and I know each other. She set steaming bowls on the table. "I hope y'all are planning on goin' to that openin' tonight, 'cause I just made corn chowder, squash cornbread, and canned tomatoes for your dinner."

"What opening?" Joe Riddley held my chair, then took his own.

I buttered my cornbread and sneaked Lulu a bite. "The new Mexican restaurant, remember? They're having a fiesta tonight with a live band, a dancer, and all the food half price. I ordered a lot of plants for them and promised we'd be there."

Joe Riddley gave me a puzzled frown. "How come you had to order plants? We got plants."

"He wanted hibiscus, palms, and cactus. Kinds they have in Mexico, I guess." Yarbrough's Feed, Seed and Nursery has a store in the middle of town and a large nursery outside the city limits, but we don't have many calls for tropicals in the middle of winter. "He ordered so many," I added, "that I don't see how he can fit them all in and still have space for customers."

"Y'all need anything else?" Clarinda demanded. When I shook my head, she plodded off to the den, where she'd rest while we ate.

Joe Riddley chewed his corn chowder as if he had something on his mind. "I'll be underdressed. I don't have a sombrero." The old familiar twinkle danced in his eye.

I reached over and patted his hand. "So long as you don't start dancing on tables, hon, we'll be fine. It's your turn to say the blessing." While he prayed, I sent up a silent thanks of my own that I was slowly getting my old Joe Riddley back.

We met when I was four and he six, and had been together ever since. While I don't often go around saying so, I've always thought him the handsomest man in Hope County, with a tall, lanky frame he inherited from a Scottish grandfather and high cheekbones, dark eyes, straight dark hair, and a copper tinge to his skin he got from a Cherokee grandmother. But the past six months had stretched both our patience real thin while he coped with a mind and body that didn't always function the way they should. Folks who haven't lived with somebody after a brain injury will thankfully never know what they have missed.

He'd scarcely said "amen" when Clarinda yelled, "Miss MacLaren, Judge Stebley called and said you don't have to worry about tomorrow—he'll fix things so you can go on to the wedding." She waited, then yelled, "Did you hear me? I said—"

I heaved a huff of my own. "I heard you," I yelled. Clarinda has always refused to take meals with us, but she insists on joining in on our conversation from the den and making us shout back at her.

Joe Riddley raised one eyebrow. "Did she say the judge is postponing your arrest until after the ceremony?"

I gave him a sour grin. "Sure sounded like it, didn't it?"

What the message Clarinda took really meant was, I would not be on call the next day. I'm a magistrate in Hope County, and Judge Stebley is the chief magistrate. Joe Riddley was a magistrate for thirty years, and Judge Stebley appointed me to serve in his place after he got shot. And no, neither of us is a lawyer. In Georgia, chief magistrates are elected and the rest are appointed from the general population. I was honored to be asked, and figured it was because I'd gone to magistrate's school with Joe Riddley and watched what he did for so many years. Our younger son Walker, however, let the air out of my balloon. He claimed I got appointed to save the county money: they could reuse the old Judge Yarbrough sign on our office door.

Having passed on Judge Stebley's message, Clarinda settled herself into the recliner with a maximum number of grunts, preparing to take a little snooze. She would eat her own dinner in queenly leisure after we went back to the store. But first, she had one more question. "You hear from

Ridd and Martha today? They definitely gonna be here tomorrow?"

"Yeah," I called back, slipping out of my shoes and rubbing my feet on the cool floor. "They'll fly up to West Virginia tomorrow afternoon."

"That's good. That's real good." Her chair squeaked in contentment. "So long as you're sure."

Our son Ridd and his family had changed their annual Presidents' Day weekend ski trip for Maynard's wedding, but he'd teased Clarinda he couldn't get new plane tickets. Clarinda wasn't going to believe they were coming to the wedding until she saw them in church.

Joe Riddley shouted back to her, "None of us is gonna miss that wedding. Bethany is a bridesmaid, Little Bit here is running the reception, and Cricket's carrying the rings. It's a dadgummed family affair."

So, of course, was the murder.

◊ 2 ◊

Joe Riddley's silver Lincoln was getting a tune-up, so he was riding with me that day. The clock on the courthouse tower boomed one as we neared our store. He touched my hand. "Go by the motor company. Skye might have my car fixed, and I want to help Maynard pay for his car as a wedding present."

"Your car isn't ready until four, and I gave Maynard and Selena a gorgeous tea set."

Joe Riddley didn't say a word.

The new carillon in the Episcopal church steeple started playing a spirited rendition of "Hail to the Lord's Anointed." I like chimes, but those were driving me around the nearest bend. "I wish they'd adjust those things," I complained. "They're twice as fast as they're supposed to be. That song sounds like Jesus is racing into town."

Joe Riddley still didn't say a word.

"If we stop by Skye's, we'll be late getting back to work," I warned.

His jaw set in the stubborn look that had become so common since he got shot. "That tea set's your present. Helping to pay for the car is my present."

"After forty-three years, we're into separate-but-equal in the realm of wedding presents?" Even as I asked the question, I was turning my green Nissan toward MacDonald

Motors. There was no use trying to reason with him in that mood.

Hopemore had three car dealers: Hopemore Nissan and Volkswagen, MacDonald Motors for Fords, Mercuries, and Lincolns, and Sky's the Limit Used Cars. All three were owned and operated by Fergus "Skye" MacDonald and his two grown children, Laura and Skellton. Skye had come to Hopemore straight out of college to marry Gwen Ellen Skellton, whose daddy owned the Ford dealership. In twenty-eight years Skye had built that one dealership into an automobile empire. The MacDonalds were easily one of the richest families in Hope County. They were also one of the closest. When Skye referred to them as the "MacDonald Clan," he wasn't joking. Even now that the children were grown, the MacDonalds worked together and vacationed together. Laura lived in an apartment over their four-car garage. When Skell came home from college and rented his own apartment, they were all surprised. Gwen Ellen was especially hurt—she'd talked to an architect about building Skell a small house in their huge backyard.

Gwen Ellen and Skye were among our best friends. We belonged to the same clubs and business organizations and went to the same church. Skye sold and serviced our cars and business trucks, and they used our lawn service and bought more plants from us than any other family in town. We went out to eat together at least twice a month. Only Clarinda really understood our relationship. To their faces she called them "Miss Gwen Ellen" and "Mr. Skye," but privately she referred to them as "Miss Gwen Ellen" and "Miss Gwen Ellen's husband."

Gwen Ellen was born when I was fourteen, and I babysat her until I went to college. After Joe Riddley and I got married, she used to stay with us when her parents went out of town. Joe Riddley started calling her "Baby Sister" when she was ten, and sometimes he still does. She was a sweet and pretty child who dawdled over her meals and happily put on whatever clothes her mother laid out for her, right through high school. Some people are born dashers and some dancers. Gwen Ellen lived at a slow waltz.

She grew into a beautiful young woman with soft eyes as dark as her hair. Spiteful people claimed it was her daddy's contribution to athletic scholarships, not grades, that got her into college, but she didn't go to college for an education. She was a princess seeking a prince to inherit her daddy's realm. She was delighted to come home after her sophomore year to marry Skye and settle down as a wife and mother. She told me once, "I am so lucky. I've always had everything I wanted."

We helped a tad. Joe Riddley got Skye into Jaycees. I sponsored Gwen Ellen for Junior League and the Garden Club. We served as honorary aunt and uncle to both their children. They even named their first child for me—although I persuaded them to call the child Laura instead of MacLaren. I figured MacLaren MacDonald might be too much of a good thing for a Georgia girl.

Now forty-seven, Gwen Ellen remained beautiful and still moved at a languid pace reminiscent of mythical days when Southern women had scads of servants and hours to dress. But don't think she was useless. She was as soft and powerful as a gentle flowing stream. She single-handedly got our Junior League to adopt a new literacy program and our Sunday school class to take a mission trip to Africa that resulted in a program to send medicines and medical equipment to a hospital over there. When her son wanted to play cello, she showed up at school board meetings with gentle but firm requests until they voted to put orchestras in each of our middle schools and the two county high schools. Then she got after all her friends—including us—to donate instruments for children who couldn't afford them. At Gwen Ellen's insistence, MacDonald Motors still sponsored an annual county orchestral concert, even though Skell had been out of high school six years. She also volunteered at the local hospital, working with oncology patients with a gentle compassion they found restful. A woman once told me her mother had literally refused to die until after Gwen Ellen's weekly visit.

Where Gwen Ellen was soft and gentle, Skye was a bundle of energy and enthusiasm for any project that attracted his attention. A tall, beefy man about to turn fifty, with thinning yellow hair and soft golden fuzz on his arms, he had a friendly pink face, laughing blue eyes, and a contagious laugh. When Skye bent and picked up a grumpy child, you could guarantee that child would be giggling within a minute. He served as an elder in our church and chaired the administrative committee, spending hours of his own time taking down the heating system to see why it wasn't working properly, or climbing onto the roof to check for loose shingles.

He also adored his wife and treated her like porcelain. He insisted that she have a full-time maid and often went home to eat lunch with her. He once fired a salesman who used profanity in her presence. He didn't expect her to be brilliant or versed in international affairs. It was enough that she created a restful home, raised their children well, and was her own graceful self. Every woman in town was a bit jealous of Gwen Ellen, including me.

The MacDonalds' whole life had been a placid sea across which a beneficent sun had sprinkled diamonds—except Gwen Ellen worried constantly about their children. Just two weeks before, we had roomed together at a church women's retreat, and in one of those late-night conversations that are the real reason most of us go to conferences anyway, her voice came sadly through the darkness between our two beds. "Laura's never going to find a husband working in that office all day, and Skye is on Skell's back about something all the time. No wonder Skell hates the motor company."

Fighting to stay awake, I ignored her longtime fears for Laura and focused on the issue dearer to her heart. "What would Skell like to do instead of work in the business?"

Poor Skell, he'd hoped to become a concert cellist until college music professors informed him he had a mediocre talent, at best. After that, his dad told him to major in business so he'd know how to run the motor companies. Not until graduation did Skye discover that Skell had majored in Spanish instead. "Which he needs like a third head," he'd told us angrily.

"Skell doesn't know what he wants yet," Gwen Ellen had admitted drowsily through the darkness, "but he'll find something. He just needs a little more time. He's only twenty-three." At twenty-three she'd been a mother and Skye had been working for her daddy. At twenty-three Joe Riddley and I were already learning to run his family business. I didn't say any of that. Even good friends don't criticize each other's children, particularly the baby.

My mind was on Skell when I pulled into MacDonald Motors' parking lot that Friday afternoon. I wasn't exactly questioning the ways of the Almighty, but it seemed to me a shame that Skell had been born to prosperous parents. Joe Riddley and I both thought he could benefit from a little adversity. Currently, he was little more than a playboy dabbling at running the family used-car lot, knowing his daddy and big sister would rescue him if he got into trouble.

We went in the front door instead of directly to the service department, and saw Skye ushering a woman out of his office in the back left corner. As always, he wore his trademark "Skye blue" oxford cloth shirt, a rumpled khaki suit, and a tie in the navy-and-dark-green MacDonald plaid.

I was more interested in his companion. "Isn't that Marilee Muller?" I asked softly.

Joe Riddley stopped drooling over a new white Thunderbird and turned to drool over Marilee. She was worth at least a small drool—she'd come a long way in the thirty-five years since she was born in our Hopemore hospital. She'd been a scrawny little girl in Walker's class with fat beige pigtails and such a big overbite that the boys called her "Beaver." Nowadays, her hair was fluffy and blond, her teeth straight and white, her mouth a shiny bow, her skin tan even in February. Instead of lanky she was willowy, instead of skinny, slender, instead of friendly, enchanting. Marilee Muller made me wonder what a makeover could do for me.

I hadn't seen her in the flesh for seven years, since she and her husband (now her ex) moved to Augusta. We watched her, however, almost every night on an Augusta television affiliate, because Marilee Muller, a child without the sense to come in out of the rain, had grown up to forecast the weather.

She crossed MacDonald's showroom trailing glamour, intent on whatever she was telling Skye, one arm tucked through his elbow. When Skye looked up and saw us, though, he dropped her arm and came right over to give me a hug. It's easy to appreciate a man like that.

"Hey, Joe Riddley, Mac. You all remember Marilee Muller? We're both Southern alums, and they've asked us to put a committee together to raise some funds."

Joe Riddley, Marilee, and I exchanged the kind of greetings people use when they don't know each other well, haven't seen each other for years, and figure they aren't likely to see one another again in the foreseeable future.

Marilee reached out again to take Skye's arm, but Joe flapped his wings and squawked, "Back off. Gimme space."

She stepped back with a nervous laugh. "I'd better be going," she told Skye. "I do want a decision today, though. Will you call me, or shall I call you?"

"I'll call you," he promised. "I need to talk to these folks right now, but I'll get back to you later this afternoon."

"Okay." She paused as if expecting him to say something else, but when he turned to Joe Riddley she gave me a dazzling smile and hurried out. As she crossed the parking lot to a red Jeep Cherokee, she clutched her coat to her throat. The wind was picking up and had a raw edge to it.

"I'm trying to sell her this car"—Skye patted the T-bird—"but she wants me to come down too far on the price. I'll have to see what I can do." He grunted. "I give to charity same as anybody else"—actually, he gave more than most folks—"but my business is not a charity."

"We know what you mean," I assured him, following him to his office.

The entire wall behind his desk was covered with family pictures, certificates, and plaques he had received for community service. That was one difference between Skye and Joe Riddley: Joe Riddley kept his award certificates and plaques in a file drawer at home. "If you get one more award, you're gonna have to get a bigger wall or take down some of the family," I teased.

"I'll build a bigger office." He waved us to his two visitor's chairs and settled into his own big leather one. It creaked under his weight as he shifted a crystal bowl of yellow roses and rested his forearms on his desk as if we were the most important thing on his calendar that afternoon. "Now, what can I do for you folks today?"

I let Joe Riddley do the talking. This was his visit.

He still wasn't well enough, though, to do two things at once. Before he spoke, he deliberately lowered himself into a vacant visitor's chair and took off his cap. As I moved unopened mail from the second chair, I couldn't help noticing that the top letter was from a dude ranch in New Mexico, addressed to Mr. and Mrs. Fergus MacDonald and beginning, "We sure hope you folks enjoyed your stay." Skye and Gwen Ellen traveled so much I couldn't keep up with all their trips. She had given up a ski week in Colorado after his business meeting in Denver just to attend that church retreat. "I've been to Colorado," she'd told me, "and besides, we're going to Norway in the spring. Won't that be nice?" I handed the mail to Skye and repressed a sigh. Would Joe Riddley be well enough to travel again in the foreseeable future—like sometime before I had to go in my own wheelchair, pushing his?

Skye dumped the mail onto his credenza while Joe Riddley explained, "I came to see if my car is ready. Ben said he might get it done today." Ben Bradshaw was Skye's head mechanic. "I'd like to have it for Maynard's wedding."

"We *could* go to the wedding in my car," I pointed out so Skye wouldn't feel pressured. However, he and I both knew Joe Riddley loved that car and hadn't been driving again very long.

"Let me check on it." Skye called the service department. "Ben? Joe Riddley's here about his car. How soon will it be ready? . . . But he said . . . Wait a minute. I'll come back there." He hung up and stood. "Give me a minute. You all want a Co-cola or anything?"

For those who don't know, Co-cola is the colloquial Southern name for what the rest of the world calls Coke.

"We're fine," we assured him.

That was only true in my case until Joe hopped onto my shoulder and pooped. "You filthy bird," I scolded him. "Now I've got to find the ladies' room and wash."

Joe bent over and peered into my face. "Not to worry," he assured me. I glared. He gave a maniacal laugh that our grandson Tad had been teaching him, and hopped onto Joe Riddley's shoulder.

I wasn't real fond of that bird. I only tolerated him because Joe Riddley adored him and because Joe had done as much to heal Joe Riddley's brain as the doctors and physical therapy.

"I'll be right back." I went to find the ladies' room and left Joe Riddley stroking Joe's stomach to show him that one of us, at least, still loved him.

The ladies' room was down a dim hall next to the service department. As soon as I got there, I heard Ben Bradshaw's voice, faint and aggravated. "I said I'd *try* to get Yarbrough's car done today. Right now, we've got four other cars on the racks, including the white limo. Maynard Spence reserved it for their bridesmaids and it needed new shocks after those kids rented it last week. We ought to be able to get to Yarbrough's later, though. Tell him to check with me around eight-thirty tonight."

"Whose jalopy is that on rack two?" That was Skye.

"José Perez's. His brakes are shot, and we put it right up, because he needs it so he can get to work by three."

"You put a Mexican's jalopy ahead of my best friend and good customer?" Skye's voice rose with his temper. Joe Riddley said Skye had the shortest fuse in Hopemore. I personally wondered why he'd never had a heart attack, the way he carried on when people crossed him. "Take it down. Joe Riddley wants his car by four."

"Yarbroughs have two cars," Ben argued. "José and Marguerite don't have any other way to get to work."

"They'll find a way if they have to. Go ahead and do like I said. You can fix that piece of junk tomorrow." I didn't hear Ben's answer, but I heard Skye real clear. "You still work for me, remember?"

Ben was a good mechanic, but I'd seldom heard him use more than three words at a time. Joe Riddley must be right that he was just shy around women. He didn't mind talking straight to Skye. "Sure I remember, but I also remember that you made me manager back here, with full authority. That's what you said—full authority."

"You have full authority, so long as you don't step over the line."

"Full authority means I decide which car gets fixed when. You don't need to keep coming back here to tell me my job. I know my job. I also know José Perez came in this morning with shot brakes, and he needs brakes worse than Judge Yarbrough needs his car."

Skye's voice went low and deep. "Listen to me, boy, and you listen up real good. Joe Riddley Yarbrough is a close and personal friend. You bring Perez's car down from that rack and get Yarbrough's fixed by four. Then you finish the rest of the work we've promised for today. When all that is done, you fix the Perez brakes. You hear me? I don't want any gaff."

"I hear you," Ben said, "but I don't like it. Am I the manager out here or not?"

"You're the manager until I say different."

"Or until I say different."

"Don't you threaten me, boy."

"I'm not threatening you. But I am warning you that if you pull this again—"

"Don't say something you'll live to regret, son." The door slammed.

I felt the building shake as Skye lumbered past the ladies' room on his way back to his office. Ben's mutter was so faint I almost didn't hear it. "Someday, man, you are going to go too far, and somebody's gonna throttle you."

❧ 3 ❧

By the time I got back, Skye was telling Joe Riddley about land he'd found for a project called Hands Up Together. The two of them wanted to buy undeveloped land and hire a contractor willing to let young men who'd just gotten out of jail apprentice with his various crews. They'd learn skills while building their own lodge. Afterwards, some might continue in the building trade while others could learn to farm or work in local businesses to learn skills like auto mechanics in Skye's service department, landscape maintenance in our nursery, or appliance repair at Spence's Appliance Store. The scale was small and local enough, it might just work.

"This place is right off Warner Road," Skye was saying as I came in. "Six acres with a pretty little pond, in easy walking distance—hey, Mac. Your car will be ready by four."

So help me, I could not think of a thing to say.

"There's one other thing." Joe Riddley remembered without any prodding from me. "I hear you sold a car to Maynard Spence this morning. BMW convertible?"

"Sure did. It came up this morning in a batch from Orlando. One of the sweetest used cars we've ever had. I thought about keeping it for myself, but Gwen Ellen might think I was having a midlife crisis." His chuckle was so infectious we laughed, too.

"Clarinda didn't say it was a used car." Joe Riddley reached for his checkbook. "Maynard's got more sense than she gave him credit for. I want to pay down the principle a bit, as a wedding present. Can you arrange that?"

"That's a fine idea." Skye picked up the phone again. "Laura? Joe Riddley and Mac are here wanting to pay down the principle on that BMW Maynard bought, as a wedding present. Can you help them with that?"

He hung up. "She'll be right here to take care of you. Doesn't it seem like just last week she was a kid in pigtails, swinging by her knees? Now she practically runs the place."

That was no surprise to anybody. Laura MacDonald had always preferred running with boys and hanging out at her daddy's office to playing dolls.

"If she was a boy," Skye said for the umpteenth time, "I'd leave her the whole shebang."

"You still could," I pointed out, also for the umpteenth time. "It's the twenty-first century."

"I guess." Skye rubbed his nose and looked thoughtful, but I didn't figure he was fixing to call his lawyer. He couldn't fathom that Laura might prefer running a business to running a home.

Yet, good old boy that he was, he still couldn't help bragging, "Remember how little she was when she sold her first car? Nine, hanging around here doing homework. Jack Stubbs, the accountant, came into the showroom to browse while his car was getting fixed, and Laura informed him he could save money by buying a new car. When he laughed, she marched back to the service department, pulled his records for the year, and calculated what he'd averaged each month and what he'd have to pay for a new car with the trade-in. She was right—he'd save money buying a new car. He was so impressed, he bought a car and told her she could have a job as soon as—oh, here she is now."

He was mistaken. I didn't recognize the young woman who pranced over to his desk on long legs that ended in black sandals with thick soles. She wore a mere sliver of a black skirt, a pink long-sleeved T-shirt that seemed at least a size too small, and such a quantity of silver bangles, I wondered how she could type. Eyes like blue marbles sparkled beneath a mop of blond curls. "I finished those letters, Mr. MacDonald." I didn't like the familiar way she said his name. "And I brought in my pen for you to use, but you can't keep it and lose it."

The view as she bent over to lay down her papers made me speak quickly to distract Joe Riddley. "Did I get all the parrot doo out?"

He peered at my shoulder. "Looks like it."

"Not to worry. Not to worry," Joe advised, then squawked and flapped his wings.

The young woman squealed and moved around the desk away from him. "He won't hurt you," I assured her.

Skye scanned the first letter and sighed. "There's still errors, sweetie. In the first paragraph, it's t-o-o, not t-w-o, and in the second, it's supposed to be o-f, not o-f-f."

"I tried," she complained prettily.

"Try a little harder." He made corrections on the next two letters as well and handed them back. "Here. Go do them right."

"Yessir." She flounced to the door, then came back, bracelets jangling, and put out her hand. "My pen, please."

He told us sheepishly as he returned it, "I'm the worse pen loser you ever saw. Laura claims I chew and swallow 'em."

"You lay them down and forget where," the young woman teased. She paused at the door to promise, "I'll get the letters right this time." Skye laughed.

Joe Riddley said thoughtfully, "She looks like she'd be a pleasure to have around."

"Nicole's hopeless," said a deep voice at the door. "She can't spell or type, and her computer skills aren't worth a darn. But she is great with customers." Laura MacDonald strode forward to greet us. "Hello, Mac, Joe Riddley, bird." She reached up and stroked Joe's scarlet breast.

I considered it a mystery of the universe that Laura had turned out so well, because she grew up under the disadvantage of being the plain daughter of a beautiful mother. She'd inherited Skye's prominent blue eyes, broad shoulders, and long legs—she stood six feet in low heels. Her hair was blond like his, but long, thick, and heavy. When she was small, Gwen Ellen made her wear it down her back. Finally she gave in to Laura's pleas—"It's hot, Mama"—and plaited two fat braids. They only emphasized the child's big nose, broad forehead, and strong chin. On Skye the features looked good. On a child, they were a disaster.

But Laura's looks had never bothered Laura the way they bothered her mother. I had watched Gwen Ellen agonize during Laura's preschool years when thoughtless strangers looked from mother to daughter and said, "Boy, she sure must look like her daddy." I had witnessed Gwen Ellen's heartache when Laura had no date for various dances. I had cheered as Laura led her high school soccer team to the state championships her senior year—and I had watched Gwen Ellen wistfully eyeing the cheerleaders. My son Ridd, who coached the soccer team, bragged, "Laura's a born leader. She grasps what has to be done, knows what each player can do, and deploys them to the best advantage." But that didn't take the briers out of Gwen Ellen's socks. She still believed cheerleaders grew up happier.

At twenty-six, Laura had the confidence that comes with an MBA and had grown into her features, but she looked older than she was. Maybe it was a few too many pounds on her big frame. Maybe it was the careless way she pulled that mane of hair back at her neck and fastened it with a plain steel clasp. Maybe it was the fact that she didn't bother with makeup except for a quick brush of blush on her cheeks. Maybe it was her comfortable gray wool slacks, white oxford cloth shirt, navy blazer and sensible navy pumps. Or maybe it was her air of utter competence that let you know you were dealing with somebody who knew what she was doing.

"Let's go back and see what we can do for you."

We were following her out when Skye called, "Laura? Did you change that radio ad?"

His voice was stern, but she didn't seem bothered by it. "Yessir."

"I thought so. I heard it this morning. I didn't approve the change and I don't like it. Change it back."

"Advertising's my department, Daddy, and the other ad was blah. We need to reach younger customers."

I heard his fist hit the desk. "I've told you and told you not to okay anything without running it by me."

"You were in Denver when they needed the okay. I kept trying to reach you, but couldn't, and they had to have an answer. We can talk about it when it's time to look at next month's ad." She stepped out of his office and pulled the door closed behind her.

"Come back here when I'm talking to you," he roared. Laura gave us a tolerant smile and ignored him. On our unhurried way to her office she stopped twice to answer questions from salesmen and once to help Nicole reset a computer toolbar she'd deleted in error.

Laura worked across the showroom, on the short hall that led to rest rooms and the service department. As we reached her door, Skell dashed up the hall from the service area. Five-foot-seven and as dark and handsome as his mother was dark and beautiful, Skell looked real natty in an expensive brown tweed coat, brown slacks with a razor-sharp crease, and gleaming brown wing tips. His face, however, was flushed with anger and his eyes glittered. Without even greeting us, he demanded, "Where's Daddy? I gotta see him real fast."

"In his office." Laura wasn't the least bit flustered by him. The two were so different, no stranger would have guessed they were related.

He made a beeline for his daddy's door, frantic as a cat whose kittens have been moved. We heard him shout, "Did you sell a BMW off my lot this morning?" Then the door slammed. The only thing Skell inherited from Skye was his temper, and Skell's temper had gotten steadily worse since he'd joined the business two years before.

Laura's office was very like her, a simple room with practical working surfaces. She did have, however, a very fine painting hung over the desk, a bronze sculpture of swinging children on her credenza, and an expensive black leather briefcase tucked down beside her desk. Laura might like things simple, but she did not like cheap.

While she was pulling up Maynard's records on her computer, Joe Riddley growled, "It's high time Skell got over the fact that he's never gonna reach five-eight and will never be a world-class cellist."

"Shush," I told him softly. Then, seeing that Laura had heard every word, I added, "It's partly our fault—Hopemore's I mean. We bragged on him so much when he was little, we raised his expectations too high."

Laura gave me a rueful smile. "He'll be all right. How much did you want to pay?"

While she took Joe Riddley's check, gave him a receipt, and credited Maynard's account, I kept thinking how much handsomer Skell would be if he got rid of that balky mouth.

After we finished our business, Joe Riddley needed to

visit the men's room. "You get back to work," I told Laura. "I'll go sit in a new car and enjoy the smell."

When I got to the showroom, Gwen Ellen was knocking at Skye's office door. She was petite and elegant in a green tweed suit and short brown boots. We don't often need boots in Georgia, but Gwen Ellen bought a lot of her clothes in New York.

Before I could call out a greeting, Skye opened the door. "Hey, honey. Come in and wait a minute. Skell was just leaving." She went inside, and Skell and Skye both came out. Skye spoke in a tone any parent would recognize, the ultimate warning: "You want that car back, call Maynard and make him a deal. But it better be a good deal, you hear me?"

Skell clenched his fist and jabbed the air once, then stormed out. Neither had noticed me.

"Oh, Mr. MacDonald." Nicole waved a sheaf of papers. "I have those letters done right. You want to sign them?"

"Sure." Skye lumbered over and bent over her desk. She looked up at him and said something I didn't catch. He laughed and reached out to jerk one of her curls. "Third time's the charm, honey."

What are friends for if not to save you from indiscretion and sexual-harassment lawsuits? "We're done, Skye," I called.

He turned. "You can't leave without saying hello to Gwen Ellen. She's in the office." He held out one arm and draped it around my shoulders as we walked back together. "Honey, look who's here. Mac and Joe Riddley came by so they could help Maynard pay for a new convertible he bought. It's their wedding present."

Gwen Ellen turned from Skye's desk with her slow smile. Few women can pull their hair to a soft knot at the nape of their necks and still look beautiful. On Gwen Ellen, the style always looked dainty and sophisticated. "What a nice idea." She tucked a letter into her bag. "Are you all going to the new Mexican place tonight?"

"Yes, are you?"

Skye answered for her. "Wouldn't miss it for the world. Shall we share a table?"

I grimaced. "We're joining Walker and his family."

"Oh." Gwen Ellen knew I didn't exactly enjoy the company of my younger son's wife.

Before we could say more, Joe Riddley came up behind me and asked, in a tone that let everybody know he'd been waiting ages, "You ready to go?"

"We'll see you there." Skye walked us to the door and gave me a parting hug. "Tell Maynard I hope his honeymoon is as great as that new car."

None of us had an inkling that in twenty-four hours our attention would have shifted from a honeymoon convertible to a murder.

ໃ 4 ໃ

The courthouse clock chimed seven that evening as Joe
Riddley and I climbed out of his car in the parking lot of
what used to be a steak house chain restaurant. The threatened rain hadn't arrived, but the air was damp. Lively
music of guitars and fiddles collided in the parking lot with
the distant Episcopalian chimes. A flashing sign in green,
red, and purple, depicting a cactus wearing a sombrero, announced that this was now Casa Mas Esperanza.

"Why didn't they write it in English?" demanded Joe
Riddley. He was a tad fussy, because I'd made him put on
nice clothes.

"It's a Mexican restaurant. House of More Hope."

"Why didn't they just say Hopemore House and get it
over with?"

"It doesn't sound as good. Be good, now, Mr. Grumpy.
You promised."

He grunted.

A clever architect had transformed the place by covering
plate-glass windows with high narrow arches, facing the
roof with barrel tiles, and painting the building adobe tan
with brown trim. "That's what they did with all those
plants." I pointed to hibiscus and palms set in colorful pots
to line the inside of a low stucco wall that formed a new
patio adjoining the building. In each corner stood tall cacti

in big bright pots. Strings of colored bulbs gave a festive air. A pergola of dark wooden beams jutted from the side of the restaurant, and confederate jasmine planted at each corner would eventually climb the supports and cover the beams to form a shady bower.

Joe Riddley scratched one cheek and contemplated the small jasmines. "Shoulda used kudzu," he concluded. "Coulda covered the whole shebang in a week."

For those who don't know, kudzu is a vine imported from China back in the nineteen-thirties, reputedly to prevent erosion in the South. Or maybe it was a Yankee plot to bury us. It can grow a couple of inches in one hot summer day, and sends out sneaky climbing shoots that envelop whole forests. Nobody—and I do mean nobody—plants kudzu.

I rubbed my cheek on his sleeve, delighted with that glimmer of his old sense of humor, and thought how good he looked. He might not have a sombrero, but he had a lovely alpaca sweater with llamas knit in rows. Walker's family had given it to him the previous Christmas, and its natural shades of tan and brown set off his coloring real well. But one can only admire one's husband out in damp night air so long. "I'm getting chilly. Are you ready to go in?"

He turned and strode toward the door so fast I had to hurry to keep up.

We had to wait a minute or two before we could be seated, so I took the time to admire what the Garcias had done. The walls were now pale gold and hung with colorful serapes, black sombreros sparkling with tiny mirrors, and large oil paintings of what I supposed were Mexican scenes. Judiciously placed potted plants gave privacy and softness to the large room. Crepe paper flowers in red, turquoise, orange, and yellow adorned each table, and bright piñatas hung from the ceiling. At a small stage near

the front, a three-man band in black and silver was playing
Mexican music while a woman in a long rainbow skirt and
a red blouse danced and clicked castanets.

"They've got a good crowd," I told Joe Riddley, who
wasn't paying me a speck of attention. He was waving to
Isaac James, our assistant police chief, who seemed to be
enjoying his dinner across the way with his wife and little
boy, and at newlyweds Jed and Meriwether DuBose, holding hands in a corner. Police Chief Charlie Muggins had his
head bent too close to his plate to notice us, but as I turned
away from his polecat features, I couldn't help thinking, as
I often did, what a shame it was that our city fathers had
brought in Charlie to head up our police department instead
of promoting Isaac, who was a far better law officer, merely
because Charlie was white and Isaac black. We still had a
ways to go.

But we now had a Mexican restaurant. It isn't every
month that a new restaurant opens in Hopemore, and we'd
never before had what our weekly newspaper called "an
ethnic dining experience." I was surprised not to see any
Mexicans among the diners, because the face of Hope
County, like the face of most of the South, was changing.
Farmworkers who used to pass through town each growing
season were beginning to stay, and we regularly heard the
staccato syllables of Spanish in our schools and stores.

Humberto Garcia, our host, came to greet us with a smile
full of strong white teeth. "I am so pleased to see you,
Judge. Your plants have transformed this place." His dark
eyes glowed with happiness. Mr. Garcia was not much
taller than me and a bit pudgy, but his eyes were warm and
friendly, and he wore the wisp of mustache under his nose
with distinction.

"If the food is as good as the place looks—" I began.

"It will be. My wife, Emerita, is a magician in the

kitchen. Let me find you a table." He scanned the room, rocking slightly.

I saw Walker waving. "That's our son. He's saving us places."

The room thrummed with music as we joined Walker, Cindy, and their children. Jessica, eleven, has the same honey-brown hair and light brown eyes her daddy inherited from me. Tad, nine, has Cindy's black eyes, but his towhead is a throwback to her big blond father.

Tad pointed to the vacant chairs. "Men at one end, women at the other."

I sat down a trifle nervously. Cindy and Walker were very different from us or from our son Ridd and his family. Cindy grew up near Thomson, Georgia, in one of those big white houses with columns some people think all Southerners live in. They had fox hunts and elaborate parties, and she and Walker lived the life to which she was accustomed. They were renovating a huge, expensive house at a cost that sometimes sent Joe Riddley to the medicine cabinet for antacids at night. They leased an Infiniti for Walker and a Lexus SUV for Cindy, bought their clothes in Atlanta, and drove their children to Wellington Academy rather than sending them to public schools. Cindy had a maid three days a week and spent most of her time playing golf or tennis, volunteering in a variety of organizations, cooking gourmet food for elaborate parties, or running fairs and special events at her children's school. They preferred planned visits to casual drop-ins, and since they didn't come to church or belong to our clubs, we seldom ran into them.

Frankly, where Cindy was concerned, that suited me fine. A little of Cindy went a long way. She was so lean, sleek, and elegant, I always felt old, plump, and dowdy around her.

That night I had on a bright shirt we'd bought on a Caribbean cruise, and red pants. My mirror had told me I looked real festive, but one look at Cindy, in slim black slacks and a white silk blouse, and I felt like a tongue-tied frump. It wasn't her fault. We were just oil and water.

Still, I reminded myself that night, Cindy had her virtues. If she hadn't worked hard with Lulu after Lulu got shot, that beagle wouldn't have become the fastest three-legged dog in Georgia. Cindy also told us what to feed Joe when we inherited the parrot. Because of all that, I made my lips turn up in a smile and leaned over to say, "Honey, you look gorgeous."

She slid nacho chips and salsa my way, her smile bright and nervous. "Thanks. Like my new haircut?" Dark and shining, it had been shaped to fall straight from a side part and curve under her ears.

"Very chic." I heaved a silent sigh. I knew Cindy must talk about something besides clothes and hairdos with her friends, but in the fourteen years since Walker first brought her home, that's all the depth we'd ever attained.

At their end of the table, the men started talking basketball, which was almost as exciting as haircuts and clothes.

While I stowed my pocketbook under my chair so it wouldn't trip anybody, Cindy added, brushing back her shining hair, "I went to that new salon that's opened out near us. You ought to give them a try. They work wonders."

She hadn't needed to say that. She knew Phyllis had done my hair for over thirty years. However, I swallowed words I might later regret and gave her what I hoped was another friendly smile. "I'll keep that in mind. Sorry we're a little late. Joe Riddley wanted to wear blue slacks with that sweater, and it took me a while to change his mind. Have you ordered?"

"Yes, ma'am. Walker went ahead and ordered two specials for you all. We figured you'd be here before they came. I hope that's what you wanted."

I also hate being called "ma'am" by a grown-up. With all

the words I was already swallowing, I might not need to eat.

"What's the special?" Joe Riddley asked.

"A burrito, an enchilada, a taco, yellow rice, and guacamole," Tad answered him.

He frowned across the table at me. "Do I like all that stuff?"

"You're going to love it," I assured him. When he turned back to Tad, I confided to Jessica and Cindy, "We don't know an enchilada from a burrito, but Mr. Garcia says his wife's a great cook." I reached for a nacho and dipped one corner in the salsa. Finding it wasn't hot enough to make my eyes water or my nose run, I took a bigger dab on my next bite. By the third bite, I figured I was eating salsa like a Mexican.

Across from me, Jessica's pale cheeks suddenly flushed and her brown eyes grew wide beneath her straight brown bangs. "Look, Me-mama, my teacher."

"Don't point," Cindy warned.

Jessica darted a quick sideways look across the room. I followed her gaze and saw a young woman in an elegant black dress with a long, full skirt. Her long dusky hair was bound with a black velvet ribbon, and she carried her head like a queen. Cindy had said Jessica adored her, and no wonder. The woman wasn't much taller than her students and had a small pointed chin, enormous black eyes, and slim high-arched eyebrows. She moved as gracefully as a small cat, approaching Humberto Garcia while there was a lull at the door. He greeted her with a happy smile, circled her waist with one arm, and gave her a squeeze.

"Her name is Miss Garcia and her daddy owns this restaurant," Jessica informed me happily. "Isn't she simply beautiful?"

"She certainly is. Is she a good teacher?"

"The best I ever had." Jessica dipped a nacho in the salsa and nibbled it. "She even makes math interesting."

Just then I saw Chief Muggins throw a dollar on his table and head for the door. Mr. Garcia stepped behind the cash register. Chief Muggins held out his money to the father, but kept his eyes on the daughter. *You old lech,* I thought. *You're older than her daddy and ugly, to boot.*

He sidled closer to her as he spoke. She moved away. He threw back his head and laughed. Mr. Garcia frowned and spoke to him. Chief Muggins laughed again as he took a handful of matches from the bowl on the counter and swaggered out.

Just then a waiter in tight black pants and a black shirt trimmed in silver braid slid our meals before us. "The plates ees hot," he informed me with a flash of white teeth.

"Do you know which is what?" I asked my grandchildren.

Of course they did. Cindy's children started eating international foods in the womb. "This is an enchilada," Jessica informed me, "and this is a burrito."

"And this is a taco." Tad picked up his and added, "Anybody knows that, Me-mama." He tried unsuccessfully to take a bite without dropping anything out.

Jessica wrinkled her nose in distaste. "You're so messy."

"Am not. You're a brat."

While they wrangled, I dug into my food and looked around. Marilee Muller sat with another woman at a table along the far wall, and I was tickled to see people pretending not to be impressed to be eating with a celebrity. Marilee caught my eye, smiled, and waved at me. I waved back and pretended not to be impressed she knew me.

Eventually Miss Garcia worked her way to our table. "Hello. Are you having fun?"

Jessica turned scarlet with pride and embarrassment. "Yes, ma'am. We sure are."

Miss Garcia gave me a questioning look. "Is this your grandmother, the judge?"

"Yes, ma'am."

I tried not to feel hurt that Jessica didn't sound as proud of me as she'd been of her teacher. After all, grandmothers are around every day. An exotic teacher is a rarity.

Miss Garcia bent toward me. "My mother wants to speak to you. Just a moment." She hurried toward the kitchen. In a minute she was back with a short round woman. Mrs. Garcia beamed down at me, hands clasped on her stomach.

Miss Garcia shoved her forward a bit. "She wants to thank you for the potted croton you sent as a gift with the other plants."

I smiled at the older woman, who looked about my own age, and wondered how much English she understood. My Spanish sure wasn't adequate to explain that while they hadn't ordered any crotons—tropical shrubs with leaves that develop brilliant colors in sunlight and muted ones in shade—I had hoped they would enjoy one for their home. "It's for your *casa*," I said slowly and distinctly. "Welcome to Hopemore."

Mrs. Garcia bobbed her head, still beaming. "Thanks so much. I've always loved crotons, particularly the ones that turn maroon and gold. I didn't know they'd grow here." Her accent was pure California.

Jessica had turned stiff and pink with joy that her family was getting so much attention from her teacher. I turned bright pink to match, so embarrassed I didn't know what to say. Cindy saved my bacon. "Aren't crotons wonderful? I have several varieties in pots on my deck."

"In my last house, I also had different varieties," Emerita told her. "I was real sad to leave them, but I never imagined they'd grow here."

"We have to take them in if we get frost, but most of the

time I leave them outside," Cindy assured her. "They just need a sheltered place."

"What colors do you have?" The next thing I knew, my swanky daughter-in-law and Mrs. Garcia were discussing crotons like bosom buddies. Why hadn't I ever talked plants with Cindy?

Miss Garcia bent for a private word in my ear. "You could not have pleased her more. *Mami* loves plants. Did you see the patio? She planned the whole thing and persuaded *Papi* to let her finish it for opening night, even if it is too cold to sit out there yet. She said people will remember and come back when it gets warm."

I hoped she wouldn't be offended, but I had to ask. "Why aren't any Mexicans here? I'd have thought they'd be flocking in."

Her laugh was soft and pleasant. "Mexicans like to eat late. The place should be lively for quite a while." She looked up and drew a quick breath, but I saw no cause for alarm. It was not Charlie, but Isaac James paying his bill and standing to one side to let the MacDonalds enter.

I know it's not polite, but I stared at Gwen Ellen. She'd cut her hair. Slightly longer than Cindy's, it also hung straight from a side part to cup her jaw. She looked several years younger. She also looked pale and peaky. Her nervous stomach must be acting up again.

Laura and Skye were with her, but not Skell. They worked their way through the crowd, stopping for Skye to speak to somebody at almost every table. When he got to ours he gave everybody a wave. "Howdy, folks. Lookin' great tonight." He gave Rosa a wide smile. "Great place you all've got here. Hope the food's as good as everything looks." He clapped Joe Riddley on the shoulder. "We've got that property sewed up. I talked to the owner after you left."

Gwen Ellen threw me a wan smile, but she looked like

she might throw up if she opened her mouth to speak. Skye really shouldn't have brought her out, feeling like she did.

Miss Garcia touched her mother's arm. "We need to get back to the kitchen before Carmen burns someone's dinner." She turned and glided away.

Emerita slapped one cheek with her fingers and her eyes widened. "Talking about plants, I forgot the kitchen. I hope you enjoy your meals." She bustled out at her daughter's heels.

Across the room, Marilee Muller was giving the air little jabs, trying to attract Skye's attention. He finally noticed and gave her a smile, but when she beckoned him over, he called, "Our table's ready," and steered Gwen Ellen to her chair.

Marilee's smile stayed on her face, but her eyes grew stormy. Skye must not have given her the deal she wanted on that car.

Gwen Ellen's chair faced mine, and what I saw worried me. Her face was pale, her eyes huge and distracted. Even though she smiled when she saw me looking at her, her expression was anxious and strained. Since Skell wasn't with them, I wondered if he was still mad at his daddy. Their quarrels always made Gwen Ellen sick.

The MacDonalds' food had just arrived when Nicole, from MacDonald Motors' front desk, waltzed in on those impossibly high-soled sandals. Her coat hung open, and in honor of the occasion she'd put on a long red dress. In the glow of all the colored lights, her hair looked like spun glass.

Mr. Garcia bustled over to explain that she'd need to wait for a table, but Laura saw what was going on and went to bring her to their table. Skye beamed. Gwen Ellen gave her a wan smile of welcome. From then on, Nicole took over the conversation, talking and waving her hands like she was trying out for a part. Whatever she was saying must have been funny, because Laura and Skye laughed and even Gwen Ellen smiled—although she looked like she wished she were home.

Her face brightened, though, when Skell rushed through the door and paused to search the room with his eyes. Whoever he was looking for, it wasn't his family, because his gaze passed them and roamed on. Then he waved Mr. Garcia aside and crossed the room.

As he stood beside his father talking and waving his arms about, all he needed was a thunderbolt or two in his fists to be the spitting image of a small Greek god. Whatever Skye said didn't make him any happier, and he waved his arms some more. Laura watched the two of them, her eyes grave. Nicole puckered her forehead, but kept a saucy smile ready to bring out each time Skell looked her way. Gwen Ellen looked like she might throw up.

Skye motioned for Skell to get an empty chair and add it to the table. He did, but perched on the edge and kept talking. He reached for a nacho and nibbled it, but dismissed his mother's offer of food from her plate. Something Skye said made Skell look our way, jump up, and hurry toward our table.

"Do you all know where Maynard is? I've been looking for him all afternoon."

Joe Riddley was about to shake his head, so I answered. "They went to Milledgeville this afternoon, to visit Selena's great-grandmother; then tonight they had the rehearsal at St. Philip Episcopal, and Clarinda is catering a dinner at their new place afterwards."

"That's Miss Marybelle Taylor's old home?"

When I nodded, Skell looked at his watch and wiggled like he was standing on hot coals in his bare feet. "You think they'll have gotten back to the house yet?"

I checked my own watch. It was approaching eight. "Possibly."

He headed toward the door without saying good-bye.

Because Skell was in such a hurry, he didn't see Miss Garcia coming his way, carrying a tray of drinks to the musicians. He hit her broadside. She gasped and staggered. Her tray clattered to the red floor tiles. The glasses fell, soaking her skirt, and shattered.

"I'm sorry." Skell grabbed her shoulder to steady her. She twisted away and stepped back, red to her hairline. "I didn't mean . . . I wasn't looking . . ." Equally red, Skell couldn't seem to finish a sentence.

"It is all right." Mr. Garcia hurried over and caught his elbow. "She is not hurt. Rosa, fetch more drinks." She hurried back to the kitchen.

"I'll pay for the glasses," Skell said, his eyes on the door that still swung behind her.

"It is nothing. Don't worry." Mr. Garcia snapped his fingers and a waiter glided in to clean up the mess.

"Thanks," Skell told him. "Please tell Rosita again I'm real sorry."

As he hurried outside, we heard the distant rumble of thunder.

﹩5﹞

Rosa didn't come out of the kitchen again, so in between talking with Cindy and Jessica, I amused myself watching Marilee glower at Skye. He had no clue, of course—he'd had the good sense to sit with his back to her—but he did go over and speak to her before he paid his bill. He looked pleasant enough, but she pouted as she watched him leave. Since Joe Riddley was still eating slowly in those days, we were just starting our dessert when the MacDonalds headed home.

We were almost home ourselves when the cell phone rang in my pocketbook. I carry it so deputies can get me at all times, but in a town the size of Hopemore, the thing is more nuisance than needed, just one more weight in a pocketbook that is already too heavy.

Clarinda's voice filled the car. ". . . over here about to cause trouble. You all need to get over here before somebody gets hurt."

"Where are you?" I demanded. "Maynard's?"

"Yeah. The rehearsal went long, and they just got here a few minutes ago. Now Skell's come in sayin' Maynard has to give back that car and buy another one. Maynard says no way; it's the one he wants. They started out polite, but now they're yelling. They gonna fight if somebody don't step in. You gotta come."

"Call the police."

"And spoil this nice party? You know Chief Muggins. Now that he knows Maynard's got a little money, he'd come himself instead of sending a deputy. Then he'd hang around here moochin' himself a dinner." Clarinda's got less affection than I have for our police chief.

"Who's that?" Joe Riddley growled, turning onto our gravel road.

I covered the mouthpiece. "Clarinda. Skell's over at Maynard's insisting that Maynard give back the car. She doesn't want to call the police and have Charlie horning in on the party."

Without a word, Joe Riddley turned the car around and headed back to town. Sometimes it's hard to figure out whether Clarinda works for us or we work for her.

He took the last turn so fast I had to grab the armrest. "That was a come-over-darling turn," I fussed. "We're not in high school anymore, you know."

"Can't come over anyway, with seat belts." He let up on the pedal a tad and peered down the street. "Where'd all these cars come from? There's not a parking place on the dadgummed block." He double-parked by Maynard's green Saturn. "Drive around the block while I go in."

I opened my door. "You drive around while I go in. Look, there's somebody coming out in the next block. You can have the umbrella. It's starting to rain." Before he could object, I jumped out and started up the walk.

He rolled down the window. "Don't you go in there without me."

Heralded by only a few drops, the rain suddenly descended in a deluge. I had to scoot up the walk so fast, how could I pay attention to what he was saying?

I heard Skell shouting as soon as I got to the porch. "Come on, Maynard, I'll practically *give* you any car on the lot. I've got stuff on the line here, man. You gotta deal. You gotta."

Maynard's voice was tight with fury. "I bought the car I want. You tell your other customer *he* can have any other car on the lot. He can't have mine. Now stop spoiling my party."

"If you don't give me that car back, it's gonna spoil a lot more than that. Where is it?"

I rang the bell and pounded on the door, but nobody heard me with all that racket.

"None of your business. It's my car and my house. Now get out."

"Come on, man, deal with me. You don't understand. It was *promised*."

I tried the knob. In the excitement of getting married, Maynard had forgotten his New York training and left his door unlocked. I entered what should have been a vibrant, happy home. Heart-pine floors gleamed beneath white fourteen-foot ceilings. Between them, Maynard had painted the walls a soft coral that would look great with Selena's red hair.

The color didn't do a thing for Maynard and Skell's red faces.

They stood practically nose to nose in the middle of the hall while the wedding party huddled in the dining room, listening to every word. The only member I recognized was our granddaughter Bethany. Most were friends of Maynard's from New York or nursing classmates of Selena's. I sure hated for them to think this was how folks behaved in Hopemore.

Clarinda peered around the swinging door at the back of the hall that led to the kitchen and gave a grunt of relief when she saw me. "Un-hunh. Now you'll have to break it up."

Bethany gave a strangled cry, "Me-mama!" and started

toward me, but I waved her back and marched over to glare up at the men.

"You all running a competition to see who can yell the loudest? Sound the meanest? I'd say right now it's a draw. And you'd better be careful, or your faces will freeze like that, and we'll have to get a couple of paper bags so you don't scare the children. Is this how your mamas raised you to behave?"

They pulled apart, ashamed. Skell adjusted his tweed jacket and Maynard tugged down the sleeves of the navy suede suit he'd dressed up in for the rehearsal. He'd even tied his ponytail with a navy suede ribbon and put a small diamond stud in his ear. "You'd be two mighty handsome young men if you'd rearrange your faces." I gave each of them a little pat.

Their truce lasted as long as it took to draw a deep breath. Then both started talking. "My ears don't work separately," I informed them. "I can't listen to both of you at once."

They took another deep breath and both started in again. This time, Skell reached out and grabbed Maynard's shirt. Maynard had drawn back his fist to hit Skell when Joe Riddley strode across the hall. He hadn't bothered with the umbrella, so he splashed on me as he grabbed a shoulder of each. "Hold on, there." He forced them to step apart. "What's going on here?"

Skell raised a furious face. "Daddy sold Maynard a car this morning that's promised to somebody else. He's coming tomorrow to get it, and I can't afford to lose this customer. I've told Maynard I'll make him a great deal on any other car on the lot." He turned back to Maynard. "Or I'll get you one just like it in a week or so, and lend you my car for your honeymoon."

Now that was an offer. Skell drove a silver Porsche he treated like it was sterling.

"That's a mighty good offer." Joe Riddley looked at Maynard.

Maynard shook his head. "I've got the car I want. He can't promise me that exact car in that color and condition, with so few miles on it. Can you?" He glared, breathing hard.

"Not all those things," Skell admitted, "but as close as I can get. I can't break my word to the other buyer. Daddy had no right to sell it. You gotta help me out of a hole here."

Seemed to me Maynard should feel enough goodwill on the night before his wedding to give in, but I could already tell that his new car meant more to him than sheet metal, bolts, and wheels. I'd seen each of my own boys go through that phase with one particular car. They put their hands on the wheel and the car became part of them. I've never understood what it is about males and cars, but I knew Maynard would no more give up that BMW than he'd give up Selena.

Joe Riddley seemed to realize that, too, because he shook Skell gently while holding Maynard at arm's length. "I think you're going to need to explain to your other customer, son. Tell him that car has gone on its honeymoon."

"He's not going to care." Skell's eyes were big dark holes. "He wants *that* car. He's gonna *kill* me." He glared at Maynard again, chest heaving.

Joe Riddley dropped his hands. "Well, you aren't accomplishing anything here tonight. Maynard has a wedding rehearsal dinner going on, and you're spoiling it. Go on home, or I'm going to have to call the police. You don't want that. Go on home, now."

Skell took a deep breath and held it; then he let it out and glared at Maynard. "I'll go tonight, but this isn't over. Daddy didn't have the right to sell that car. I'm going to tell him he's got to make you give it back." He headed for the door, paused a second when he realized the rain was bucketing down, then hurled himself through it.

Joe Riddley advised the party, "You all have a good time and forget all this. Skell will sleep on it and be fine in the morning. He's afraid he's lost a sale and maybe a customer. He'll be all right in the morning," he repeated. With a wave he headed for the door, grabbing me on his way out and pushing me ahead of him.

"We are soaked," I grumbled when we got back in the car, "but I'm right proud of you."

"I'm not proud of you. I told you to stay outside until I got there. You could have gotten hurt, Little Bit."

"They wouldn't hurt me. I practically raised them both. But why do you reckon Skell is so upset about that particular car?" I jabbed up the heater and hoped my teeth wouldn't chip from chattering before I got warm.

"Maybe he's finally trying to show Skye he can handle the used-car business. When Skye stepped in and sold a car he'd promised to somebody else, it made Skell look real bad. You know, sometimes I'm real glad our boys decided not to come into our business."

I reached out and held on to his arm. "I was thinking the very same thing."

"Great minds run in the same direction," he said with satisfaction.

It's a pity those two great minds could drive all the way home without a single premonition.

When we got home, he paused at the door to the den. "You wanna watch a little TV?"

"Might as well. But let's get out of these wet clothes first." We put on our pajamas, he settled in his recliner, and I snuggled under an afghan to watch a couple of mindless shows.

I hauled myself erect around eleven, but Joe Riddley said, "Wait for the weather."

"Go look at the sky. Your guess is as good as Marilee's."

I have long maintained that when the weather people say "twenty percent chance of rain," it means they've called ten friends and two voted for rain. Seems to me that most meteorologists are accurate about as often as astrologers.

However, because staying was easier and cosier than going, I settled back to see what Marilee read in the cloud-covered stars for tomorrow.

Joe Riddley peered at the screen. "Does she look a little frazzled to you?"

"A bit. Her skirt's crooked and her hair could use some brushing. Of course, it generally looks like she just came out of a wind tunnel, but tonight it seems more haphazard than usual."

"She must have driven back to Augusta too late to allow herself time to get fixed up." He rested his head and prepared to listen to his favorite oracle. He particularly liked the end of her program, when she'd recently started giving friendly little messages.

That night Marilee seemed not only frazzled, but rattled. She may have had one too many margaritas, because she burbled a couple of words and once put up the wrong slide for what she was talking about. Finally, though, she wound up with a summary and concluded, with a charming smile, "Well, I know we're having a bit of stormy weather right now, but it's not going to last much longer. Everything's going to be fine. You have a great day tomorrow, now, you hear me?"

Joe Riddley went upstairs as satisfied as if she'd been talking directly to him.

I slipped into bed to the sound of steady rain on our tin porch roof.

⋽6⋾

Bless Marilee's heart, the sun did come up beaming Saturday for Maynard and Selena's wedding, and at ten-thirty, St. Philip Episcopal was respectably full. Selena's parents had left their old home and retired to Florida, so she'd decided to get married in the church she and Maynard planned to attend the rest of their lives. Folks who'd helped raise Maynard were delighted, of course, and so was the chamber of commerce. The big motel up on I-20 and every bed and breakfast in town were packed with out-of-town guests.

Hubert, Maynard's daddy, had bathed for the occasion, which was an occasion in itself. He was a short, plump little man with a pink face, and he and Joe Riddley had been neighbors literally since they were born. They disagreed about everything from preachers to politics, but we were fond of Hubert and he seemed touched we'd sit with him on the groom's family pew.

Selena was radiant, her hair hidden by a soft tulle net. Her dress, sure enough, looked like something my four-greats grandmother might have worn, but styles are so varied these days that I'll bet most people had no idea she was supposed to look historical. Maynard looked pretty historical himself, in a black suit with tails that Jefferson Davis would have been proud to wear.

As he stepped forward to meet Selena at the blue plush steps, Joe Riddley muttered in my ear, "If he smiles any wider, his jaw's gonna drop off."

The cutest person in the whole wedding party was Ridd's little Cricket, four, who carried the rings with aplomb. The prettiest bridesmaid, of course, was Crick's big sister, Bethany, whose dress showed curves that made her granddaddy frown and brought a lump to my throat.

We missed hearing the vows, though. The second they started saying them, those dratted chimes started playing "Fight the Good Fight" right over our heads, at a volume and tempo that almost inspired the whole congregation to go do battle with whoever forgot to turn them off.

We all went to the country club afterwards. I'd let Maynard use our name to get the ballroom, since cheap old Hubert dropped his membership to Golf Only after his wife died, and I'd consulted with Selena about the menu, flowers, and music, and I'd suggested who ought to bake her cake, but otherwise, I hadn't done a thing.

In the dessert line, I heard a couple of teenagers complaining that they couldn't find Maynard's BMW. As I went to join Martha and Ridd, I said, "Sounds like every boy in town already knows about Maynard's new car, and from what I'm hearing, it's now missing. Skell was hoping to get Maynard to sell it back to him—you reckon he did?"

"Fat chance," Ridd said with a grin. "He came in his old Saturn in case anybody decided to send him away all decorated."

Walker sauntered up, sat down by me with a full plate of cake, and echoed what I'd just said. "Maynard hasn't told a soul where he's hidden that new car."

"You still eat dessert like you've got a football game next week," I observed, wiping sweet gooey frosting from my own lips. "You'd better start slacking off."

"I'm gonna do that." He winked at Martha. "I'll start the

day Mama stops telling me how to eat. You know where the car is?" he asked Ridd between bites.

"Yep." Ridd heaped his own fork like cake was being taken off the approved-eating list in another minute. He made us wait while he chewed and swallowed. "In my garage." Ridd and Martha had a comfortable old bungalow across town with a small detached garage. "I put on a padlock and gave Maynard the key. In fact, Bro, I need a favor. I'll leave the key in the Saturn, and I need you to run it down to the used-car lot later today. I told him I'd do that, but I'd forgotten we had a plane to catch. You don't have to wash it. Skye said they'll do that while they're cleaning it up to sell."

"I might mosey out and have a look at the Saturn then." Walker pulled a bottle of white shoe polish out of his pocket. As he stood, he added, "You can finish my cake, Mama." He'd left all of three crumbs.

"Don't ruin that car," Ridd warned. "I'm thinking of buying it for Bethany."

"Walker will never grow up," I muttered as he swaggered out.

Martha chuckled. "If he does, it will kill you both."

"Speaking of killing, did you all hear what happened at the rehearsal dinner last night?"

Ridd scowled. "Bethany told us. Said you sailed in on your dignity and took care of things."

"The truth is, my knees were knocking, and your daddy was the one who really calmed things down. Those boys were as close as peanut butter and jelly to knocking each other's teeth out. Think what that would have done to Maynard's wedding pictures."

By the time they told me of their skiing plans (they were taking Bethany out of school and would be gone all the next week), we heard a commotion that meant Maynard and Selena were coming. He'd exchanged his tux for a gray suit and a shirt of deep green. She had taken off her wedding gown and put on a brown dress so tacky I knew it had to be the latest style. Selena wasn't as hipped on history as her new husband.

We all hurried outside. The poor Saturn sported enough shoe polish to whiten Selena's nursing shoes for a year. "Know which ones I wrote?" Walker murmured in my ear.

"Sure," I told him. "The ones that make your mama blush." He snorted, but didn't deny it.

Martha shaded her eyes and looked at dark clouds massing in the west. "The wind's rising," she announced, holding her full red skirt. "We'll get more rain by nightfall, but we can use it. Everything's been so dry." She grew up on a farm and knew more about weather than Marilee.

"Don't they look *fine*?" Clarinda breathed at my shoulder. She looked real fine, too, in a dark green dress with satin trim. "I'm glad he saw the light and took back that high-falutin' car."

"He didn't take it back," I enlightened her. "He just hid it in Ridd's garage so it wouldn't get messed up. They're going to get it right now."

She grunted her disappointment.

The newlyweds dashed through a gamut of jests and a hail of birdseed. Maynard helped Selena in, and kissed her thoroughly. As he slammed his door, I wondered how many of the car artists suspected he would only drive it a few blocks—or if they cared.

As they drove away, a silver Porsche pulled out of the parking lot and followed them. "Ridd"—I jiggled his elbow—"that's Skell."

He shaded his eyes to be sure, then nodded. "I'd better go after them, to be sure everything's all right. Tell Martha I'll come back for her, all right?"

"Your car is parked behind three rows of others. Mine's right over here. Come on." I was already fumbling in my pocketbook for my keys and heading to the driver's side before Ridd could offer to drive. He drives like a little old lady.

Skell's Porsche was already a couple of blocks away, waiting at the stop sign for traffic on the highway to pass. "Lead foot Mama," Ridd groaned as I gunned the Nissan and sped after him.

I pulled in behind the Porsche in front of Ridd's bungalow just as Skell jumped out. Ridd's garage door was open, and Maynard was putting suitcases into the BMW.

As Ridd climbed out, I rolled down the window and heard Skell begin his useless refrain. "Come on, man, give me a break." Looked to me like he could come up with a better song.

Maynard ignored Skell and walked back to the Saturn, where Selena was collecting a box of food I'd asked the caterers to put up for them. "We'd better hit the road if we want to reach Orlando tonight." Turning, he added to Ridd, who had just joined them, "You want the Saturn in the garage, or just left here?"

"Leave it. We'll take care of it. Have fun."

Skell grabbed Maynard's elbow. "This is serious, man. Life and death."

Maynard tried to shake him off, but Skell clung like a burr.

"Hold it, Skell." Ridd caught his shoulder the same way Joe Riddley had the night before. It always tickles me when one of the boys acts like one of us, after they spent so much of their growing-up years informing us they would *never* be like their parents.

Skell turned toward him. "Make him listen, Ridd. I'll lend him my car for his honeymoon and sell him another car at cost when he gets back. I can't do fairer than that."

It was the first time I'd seen Skell's face since the night before. He hadn't shaved and I doubted he'd slept much.

His eyes were red, his hair standing on end. He even wore the same clothes he'd had on the day before. Where had he been all night?

Ridd said something too soft for me to hear, then took Skell by the shoulder and steered him toward the Porsche. He held his arm in a firm grip while Maynard and Selena got into the BMW, backed around the Saturn, waved, and roared away. Then Ridd shook Skell. "Go home. This won't look so bad after you've had some sleep."

Skell looked after Maynard and Selena as if his future had driven away with them. "You don't know," he said in a lifeless voice. "You have no idea."

He got in his car and headed down the road in the same direction.

I got home to find Joe Riddley dozing in his recliner. He still tired easily, and between Friday night's fiesta and that morning's wedding, he was worn out. I shook his shoulder. "Come on upstairs. We both need a nap."

I don't know how long we'd been sleeping when the phone rang. I was so groggy and the room was so dim, I thought at first it was early morning and the phone was the alarm. Joe Riddley had to reach over me and carry the receiver to his ear. "Yeah? Yarbroughs'." He, too, sounded half asleep.

I heard the first three words: "This is Isaac James." That's all I heard. Joe Riddley sat up and pressed the phone to his ear. "What? Where?" His voice was sharp. He listened again. "Do they know who?"

I got up on one elbow, feeling a drowsy spurt of resentment. If this was magistrate business, Joe Riddley was no longer the magistrate. Then I recollected that he knew that as well as I did. If the call was for me, he'd have given it to me.

As he listened, he rubbed one hand up and down his

cheek as if trying to massage his brain into working right. Finally he said, "Of course we will. We'll go right now. Thanks."

He handed me the receiver and sat on his side of the bed like he'd been turned to Stone Mountain granite.

I rolled over and touched his arm. "What's the matter, honey?"

He didn't speak at first. When he did, his voice seemed to come from his heels. "Charlie Muggins is on his way to MacDonalds' house, and Ike thinks we ought to get over there and be with Baby Sister and the kids when Charlie gets there. Skye's been killed."

⟮7⟯

"Killed?" The breath left my body with that one word, and I had to fling off my covers and sit up to draw another.

Joe Riddley slumped on his side of the bed, studying his feet. He just nodded.

"He said Skye, not Skell?" He nodded again. "How?" I clutched my head, trying to will it to be less groggy, shocked, and bewildered.

"Hit by a car." He heaved an enormous sigh and stood. "Come on, Little Bit. Baby Sister's gonna need us." He was already by the bedpost, reaching for his pants.

I was trembling so hard, I had to hold on to the door of the closet as I dragged down a khaki skirt. It was half on before I drew a full breath. "Where?" I pulled a green turtleneck over my head and reached for a green-and-blue plaid jacket.

"Out on one of those farm roads just inside the city limits." Joe Riddley's voice was a bit choked, because he was tying his tie. That answered my next question: why it was a matter for the city police. Our county sheriff, Bailey "Buster" Gibbons, is an excellent lawman and a personal friend, while Police Chief Charlie Muggins is one of those people the world could whirl merrily on without. Poor Gwen Ellen, she'd get about as much sympathy from him as a tree gets from a dog.

Joe Riddley spoke from the door as I was freshening my lipstick. "I'm going, with or without you." I didn't take his tone of voice personally. He was mad at whoever killed Skye, not at me.

I fluffed my sleep-flattened hair and hurried after him. "You are sure Ike said Skye, not Skell?" I grabbed my pocketbook. "Skell was driving pretty wild."

Joe Riddley settled his red cap on his head. "Ike said Skye." He lumbered out to his car.

The MacDonalds lived on the other side of town, just inside the city limits, in a big brick Tudor built by some bigwig in cotton back in the 1920s. The house was trimmed in cream stucco and dark brown half-timbering, and all the windows on the front were little diamond casements, like a fairy castle. A belt of virgin forest encircled the property, and thanks to Gwen Ellen, the house now sat on two lovely landscaped acres of trees, shrubs, flowers and Bermuda grass that stayed soft all year.

"You don't have to drive as furiously as Jehu in the Bible"—I clutched my armrest as we sped through town—"and you'd better hope all the police are busy."

"I want to beat the rain." We both knew the rain wasn't on his mind.

Beating the rain would have been a forlorn hope, anyway. No sooner had we turned into the MacDonalds' long drive than we were hit by a frog strangler. Our windshield was so blurred, it was a good thing Joe Riddley knew every curve in the drive. Thick trunks of poplar, sweet gum, oak, and hickory were veiled as we passed through the woods.

Soon the house loomed ahead, surrounded by camellias that glowed like rubies and garnets among shiny emerald leaves.

"Bad word," I exclaimed when we got close to the four-car garage. "Charlie beat us here." His blue and yellow cruiser squatted so close to the door that concealed Gwen

Ellen's powder-blue Thunderbird, it looked like he was keeping her from making a quick getaway.

Everybody in the family except Skell drove a Ford. Even Tansy Billings, Gwen Ellen's maid, drove a green Escort. I was relieved to see it on its pad by the drive. Most folks in town didn't have help on Saturdays, but for nearly twenty years Tansy had taken Tuesdays off while Gwen Ellen volunteered at the hospital. That sure was a blessing now.

I was also glad to see Laura's white Taurus through an open garage door. Since no light showed in the windows above the garage, she must be with her mother. I didn't know if Skell had arrived. The door to his parking space was shut. Skye was always strict about everybody keeping their garage doors closed. Laura had showed how upset she was by leaving hers open.

Joe Riddley pulled in behind the space where Skye always parked his black Crown Victoria. "You'll block him," I fussed without thinking.

"He's not gonna be driving in." Joe Riddley's voice was grim.

That's one trouble with death. It keeps sandbagging you again and again. My eyes filled with scalding tears as Joe Riddley added, "Since Laura's door is up, let's use the kitchen door. No need to bother with the umbrella." Which is why I arrived soaking wet.

As we dashed in and skirted Laura's Taurus, I noticed that Skell's Porsche was not there.

Tansy flung open the door before we knocked. "Oh, Miss MacLaren, we've got trouble here today, for sure."

The maid was the color of coffee, as short as I, and far rounder. Her face was flat with high cheekbones that made me suspect that she, like Joe Riddley, had an Indian ancestor. As always, her grizzled hair was neatly netted and her starched pink uniform rustled as she moved, but tears rolled down her cheeks. As she swabbed them with a paper towel,

Chief Muggins stepped from behind her. "Hello, Judge and Judge."

I do not dislike Chief Muggins because he looks like a cross between a polecat and a chimpanzee, with the least attractive features of each. Many people are ugly and still likeable. I do not dislike Chief Muggins just for the gloating look in his mean little blue-green eyes whenever I get myself in a mess, or the fact that he's a pigheaded bigot whose wife left town after one too many visits to the emergency room. I dislike him primarily because he makes up his mind about a case within five minutes of arriving at a crime scene, then spends the rest of his time shaping facts to fit his conclusions.

For once, he surprised me.

"We got ourselves a real mystery here," he announced. "Skye MacDonald was found around two this afternoon out on a farm road just inside the city limits. He was hit by a car hard enough to kill him, but we don't know which car, or what the dickens he was doin' out there."

Tansy moaned and reached out her hand to clutch mine.

"How long do you think he'd been dead when he was found?" Joe Riddley asked.

"Initial estimates are that he was killed sometime between nine and twelve last night."

"Last night?" I couldn't help remembering that last night Skell drove off saying he was going to talk to his daddy. I couldn't imagine, though, why he and Skye should have gone out there to talk, or why Skye would have gotten out of the car in all that rain.

Unless it became necessary, I flat-out refused to imagine Skell running his daddy down.

"Killed last night, not found until this afternoon," Chief Muggins continued. "Two Mexican kids found the body. They ran back home, but they don't have a phone, so their uncle jumped in his truck and came to town. We got the word around two-thirty."

"Gwen Ellen must have been frantic when he didn't come home." I pushed past Chief Muggins and hurried to the living room.

I always found Gwen Ellen's living room real restful, but Joe Riddley claimed it was like being in the middle of a camellia bush. She'd decorated around a rug she bought in China, painting the walls the soft green of the rug's border and the woodwork to echo its creamy background. She'd covered her chairs and sofa and made her drapes to match the rose, light pink and deep green of the rug's center medallion. The only other color in all that pink and green was a bowl of yellow roses on the coffee table. Gwen Ellen placed yellow roses there every Friday so Skye could enjoy them all weekend. Skye loved yellow roses.

Today the room was not so much restful as frozen. Gwen Ellen huddled on one end of the dark green silk sofa, hugging a rose throw pillow to her chest. Laura stood by one long window with her back to us, clutching a drape. Neither was crying. Laura was staring out into the rain and Gwen Ellen was staring at the end of her world. When I sat beside her, she turned and spoke in a voice so calm it shivered my gizzard. "Skye's dead, MacLaren. He just told me that Skye is dead." Her eyes were bleak and the scent of her perfume seemed out of place, too dressy for the occasion.

"I know, honey. That's why we came." I sat beside her and reached for her hands. They were icy. "Turn up the heat," I ordered Joe Riddley. He loped out to the hall.

Gwen Ellen was beautiful even in grief, her gold twinset a perfect match for her plaid wool skirt. Laura looked blurred around the edges—larger and vaguer than ever in a rump-sprung gray tweed skirt, gray boiled-wool jacket, and a white turtleneck. When she turned to greet us, I saw that her eyes and the end of her nose were pink and the hand

that clutched the drape trembled. When Joe Riddley came
back from the hall, he went to stand behind her. He didn't
touch her, but she stepped a fraction closer to him.

Gwen Ellen shuddered. "Skye's *dead*." This time she
emphasized the last word, as if trying to make herself believe it.

"I know, honey. What happened?"

She took a deep, ragged breath and clutched my hands
harder. Poor darling, she couldn't think fast at the best of
times. Today she was like an actress who couldn't remember her lines. "He . . . I . . . Everything's a muddle. We went
to the new Mexican place for dinner—you saw us." I nodded. "But I had a dreadful headache."

"You looked like death warmed over." I wished I'd chosen another comparison, but she didn't notice a thing.

"I took a sleeping pill when I got home, and went straight
to bed. As I was drifting off, I think I heard the phone ring—
I'm not sure."

Chief Muggins had come to stand in the doorway, a
predator ready to pounce. Always more eager to find a cul-
prit than to console the grieving, he shot his question like a
bullet. "Why aren't you sure? Don't you have a phone by
your bed?"

Gwen Ellen looked at him blankly. "What? Oh, no. I
don't always sleep well, and Skye didn't want me bothered.
But there's one in Skell's old room, next door." She wrinkled her forehead, thinking. "I'm pretty sure I heard it ring.
I heard Skye downstairs shouting at somebody, too, but
maybe that was the television. He talks to it, you know."

Chief Muggins might not know, but Joe Riddley and I
did. Watching a game with Skye was almost like being
there. He jumped to his feet and cheered for good plays,
yelled at the umpires and referees, and encouraged his favorite players at the top of his lungs. Joe Riddley swore
Skye's teams played better if he watched the broadcast.

Gwen Ellen went on in that pale, lost voice. "Sometime later I heard a car on the drive, but I'm not sure when. I'd already been sleeping, I think. I figured it was Laura, coming in, but I didn't look at the clock. . . ." Her voice followed her empty gaze to nowhere. Then her dark eyes flashed at Chief Muggins with indignation. "Why didn't you find him sooner?"

Chief Muggins didn't have a drop of compassion in his veins. "Why didn't you miss him when you woke up this morning?"

"Because I slept so late. My pills always knock me out that way. Tansy was here before I got down." Her hands started to tremble, then her whole body. I slid over and held her so close that the chattering of her teeth seemed like the chattering of my own.

"What did you do then?" I asked softly. Maybe talking would soothe her.

"I went out and worked in the yard. The rain had stopped in the night, and I needed to spread chicken manure on the garden, so it will be ready to plant. But it was so muddy, my shoes got ruined. I don't think I'll ever get them clean."

Charlie took an impatient step forward, wanting to stop talking about manure and mud and get back to her husband's death. I waved him aside. Gwen Ellen needed to move at her own pace in assimilating things. Joe Riddley claimed the reason she was such a good gardener was because she lived at the same pace as plants, slow and steady. Skye hated to see her hot and dirty, but she was never happier than when digging in the dirt.

Charlie was impossible to subdue. "I find it hard to believe, ma'am, that you got up and spent a whole morning in the yard without wondering where he was." From the gloat on his face, Chief Muggins had already decided Gwen Ellen had taken Skye out on that deserted road, persuaded him to stand in front of her car, run over him, then gone home to bed and gotten up to spread chicken manure. In a minute he'd be asking to examine her Thunderbird. I was glad I'd glanced at it when we came in. It was clean and dent free.

I was about to point out that he was talking to a woman who not only loved her husband but was also so tender-hearted, she had Skye take their infants for their shots be-cause she couldn't stand to see them hurt. Then I caught Joe Riddley's glare, and shut my mouth.

"Skye likes—liked—" Again Gwen Ellen struggled for control.

Laura spoke over her shoulder, her voice deep and gruff. "Daddy often leaves—left for work before Mama got up. She'd have no reason to miss him."

"Why didn't you miss him at the office?" Laura had drawn Chief Muggins's fire. I could see the cogs that passed for his brains churning out a case against her instead of her mother.

She fumbled in her pocket for a tissue and dabbed her nose before she answered. As she spoke, she turned toward him, but only slightly. "I was over at Hopemore Nissan all morning, training a new manager. I worked with him until after noon. When I got back to MacDonald's and found Daddy wasn't there, I assumed he'd come home for lunch. He does—did that sometimes, especially on Saturdays. He'd stay here to watch sports on TV; then he'd come back to close up." She bit her lip and turned back to the window.

Gwen Ellen gripped both my hands, and her eyes were tortured. "He had to lie out there all night in the rain. Can you believe that? Wouldn't you think somebody would have found him sooner?" Tears finally streamed down her cheeks, and her shoulders shook. A second later she gasped, snatched her hands from mine, grabbed her abdomen, leaped to her feet, and dashed from the room. The slammed powder-room door muffled but did not cover up the sounds of desperate retching.

"She has a nervous stomach," Laura explained to the police chief.

I heard Tansy hurry from the kitchen and speak worried words through the door.

Chief Muggins wiggled his shoulders and swiveled his hips. "So, young lady, where were you last evening?" His voice was smarmy and insinuating.

As Laura turned to face him, her eyes might have been pink but her voice was perfectly level. "I wasn't killing my daddy, sir. I met my folks for dinner at the Mexican place; then I went back to MacDonald's. We're open until nine on Fridays, and Daddy and I—" She faltered. Without conscious thought, she reached for a strand of her long thick hair and drew it toward her mouth, then noticed what she was doing and flung it away. Gwen Ellen had worked for years to break Laura of the habit of sucking her hair when she was nervous or upset.

Laura swallowed hard. "Daddy and I *used* to take turns closing on Friday. This weekend was my turn." Her voice took on an angry edge. "I had to close out the used-car lot, too, because Skell had disappeared."

"Disappeared?" Charlie pounced on the word.

"Hadn't bothered to come back after supper. He was with us at the restaurant, but he never showed up at his lot after that. With two lots to close, I worked until around eleven. Maybe a little later, even . . ." She narrowed her eyes and nibbled her upper lip like she was trying to remember. I suspected she was deliberately drawing Charlie's attention to herself, away from Skell. She used to do the very same thing when one of her teammates was in a vulnerable position.

Charlie, bless his thick head, fell for it. "You worked alone at night, ma'am? You weren't afraid?" His hand caressed the butt of his gun. I hoped he wouldn't get any ideas about going over late at night to protect her.

Laura gave him an unruffled look. "No, sir. We have a good security system." She also had a gun in her desk. Skye insisted on it. But instead of saying that, she added, "The manager of our service department can vouch for me. He was there the whole time, except when he ran out to Hardee's for a bite to eat. He walked me to my car when I left."

"This mechanic. He always work that late?"

"No, sir, he was finishing up a brake job for somebody who needed his car."

"He get along with your daddy?"

"Yessir." Had Charlie noticed her brief hesitation?

Maybe so, becuse he shot back, "How long would you say he was gone for his supper?"

"About fifteen minutes. He brought back something to eat while he worked. He's conscientious that way." Joe Riddley and I both looked at her in surprise. Her voice was glacial.

Chief Muggins didn't seem to notice. He propped one shoulder against the doorjamb and asked, "So, was your daddy home when you got here?"

She drew her brows together, trying to remember. "I believe his car was gone, but I didn't really notice. He and Mama often went down to Dublin to a movie or something on nights when he didn't have to work." She turned her face quickly to the window, but not before I saw her blink back tears.

Charlie's cell phone rang. He backed into the dining room and we heard him muttering. We heard him finally say, "I'll be out in just a little while. Get the crew on it right away."

He swaggered back in, polecat eyes glittering. "They've

found his car parked over behind the Presbyterian church. It's got a dent in the front—looks like it hit somebody."

Laura gave an involuntary moan, and her knees bent. If Joe Riddley hadn't caught her, she'd have fallen. Her face as pale as fat-free milk, she let him help her into the nearest chair.

The Presbyterian church? That was our church, right downtown on the square, about a mile from the MacDonald house—farther than folks generally walk around here—and a perfect place to leave the car. The lot was secluded behind the big building, and generally deserted on Saturdays. Furthermore, since Skye was forever running over to the church to check on one thing or another, nobody would think a thing about seeing his car there.

Who called to lure him to the church, met him in the parking lot, and got in beside him for that fatal ride? It would have been simple to drive his car back to the parking lot and drive another car away. His might not even have been noticed until Sunday morning, or his body found until the next time a tractor went down the dirt road. I sent up a quick prayer of thanks for two boys who stumbled across his body sooner than the murderer probably expected him to be found.

Chief Muggins wasn't praying. He was rubbing his paws together in satisfaction. "Rain pretty much washed it clean, of course, but if there's anything to find, we'll find it."

Laura trembled, but she didn't cry.

Joe Riddley laid a hand on her shoulder and bent to ask softly, "Where's Skell, honey? You need him here. Does he even know about all this?"

Her voice sounded both angry and forlorn. "Last time I saw him was at the restaurant. I've tried calling his house and his cell phone, but he's not answering." Again she reached for a strand of hair, and this time carried it to her mouth. Only when she caught my eye did she drop it.

Charlie butted into what was clearly a private conversation. "So he *has* disappeared."

I was glad to wipe that gloat off his face. "He was in town this afternoon, over at Maynard's wedding luncheon."

Gwen Ellen came in just in time to hear me. Hope brightened the color in her pale cheeks. "Then he's got to be around town somewhere. I was so afraid he'd gone up to Atlanta. He likes to do that on weekends, especially if he and Skye—" She stopped and pressed a tissue to her nose. "The last time Skell saw his daddy, they were fussing. That's what Skell's gonna always remember." She collapsed on the couch, sobbing.

Chief Muggins stepped forward. "There was a quarrel between your son and his father?"

"A silly disagreement, that's all," Laura corrected him.

"What about?"

She heaved a big sigh that showed how dumb she thought it had been. "Skell was late getting to work yesterday, and somebody called Daddy over to the lot for something. While he was there, Daddy sold a car Skell had promised to somebody else. Skell was upset, but he'll get over it." She muttered to Joe Riddley, "I told Daddy a hundred times that if he meant to let Skell run that lot, he had to let him do it."

Chief Muggins narrowed his eyes and pursed his lips before he spoke. "How upset would you say your brother was with his father?"

"My brother didn't kill my dad."

Her roar didn't surprise me. Laura had inherited Skye's temper, too, but only two things made her lose it: an umpire who made what she considered an unfair call, and attacks on her brother. In grade school she'd beaten up kindergarten bullies who'd called Skell "Bones" or taunted him for preferring music to sports. She had silently endured her mother's disappointment that "Laura just can't seem to be a lady—she keeps getting into fights," without ever telling Gwen Ellen what the fights were about. It was Ridd's wife, Martha, our emergency-room supervisor, who learned the truth when a rough boy broke Skell's arm in fourth grade while Laura was out of town playing soccer. "If Sissy had been here," he'd sobbed angrily, "she'd have beaten that boy silly, like she always does." I had even heard Laura taking up for him down at the motor company not long ago, when Skye came down hard on him.

She certainly surprised Chief Muggins. He took a step back and held up his hands. "I didn't say he did. But we have to investigate all avenues here."

Laura blew her nose and glared up at him. "The only avenues I've heard you investigate so far lead to Mama, my brother, or me. Seems to me like you need a bigger map, sir."

"Laura." Gwen Ellen checked her softly, then turned back to the police chief. "She doesn't mean to be rude, Chief Muggins; she's just upset. But I wish you'd send somebody out looking for Skellton. Laura has tried to reach him a number of times, and he hasn't answered his phone. His people at the lot haven't seen him all day long, and a salesman Laura talked to sounded a little upset—"

"He didn't sound a little upset, Mama; he sounded furious." Laura never had patience with her mother's tendency to soften unpleasantness. "Skell hasn't been there all day. Hasn't even called."

"He must have a good reason," Gwen Ellen insisted. "He may be hurt somewhere—"

Laura gave a deep huff of impatience. "He's just gone off to play, and you know it. He can't make a go of the business if he won't stick around to manage it."

I'd understood her anger when she was defending Skell, but her anger at him surprised me. She must be more worried about him than she let on. I sure hoped she wasn't worried he'd killed their daddy.

She looked at her watch and stood up. "I ought to go down and close up," she told her mother, "out of respect for Daddy. Don't you think?"

Anybody could tell she just added the question out of respect for her mother. Gwen Ellen never made business decisions. She nodded uncertainly. "If you think so, honey."

"I do. I hate to leave you, but I'll just be gone long enough to send everybody home. I'll get back as soon as I can." She picked up her briefcase from behind a chair and strode out. We heard her speak to Tansy in the kitchen, then the swish of her tires in puddles on the drive.

Gwen Ellen shredded a tissue she was holding and dropped the pieces into her lap. I took the bits of tissue from her skirt and stuffed them in my pocket. She dropped her hands and sat with big tears rolling down her cheeks.

Chief Muggins pushed away from the door and hitched up his britches. "I guess I'd better be getting over to see about the car."

"Car?" Gwen Ellen looked up in puzzlement. She'd been gone when his call came.

"Skye's car," Joe Riddley explained. "They found it over behind the church."

"Looks like it's the one that hit him," Charlie added. The man had the sensitivity of a pill bug.

Gwen Ellen fell forward onto her own lap, racked by deep sobs. "I can't stand this. I just can't."

Tansy hurried in and put her plump arms around her. "It's gonna be all right. It's gonna be all right," she crooned, although we all knew it never would, not really.

"I'll be right back," I promised her, and followed Chief Muggins.

"Where exactly was Skye found?" I asked as we reached the kitchen.

"On the third dirt road off Warner Road. Somebody must have driven him out there to rob him. I can't think why he'd be there at that time of night otherwise."

"Rob him of what?"

Tansy's voice made us both jump. She hadn't made any noise coming back. She went to the refrigerator and drew a glass of ice water, then stood as tall as she could, one hand on her nonexistent waist. Her dark eyes snapped. "You told me he was still wearing his Rolex watch. Mr. Skye didn't ever carry a lot of money. What did they rob him *of*? Besides, why would anybody want to rob *him*, when they could have robbed the business—and not got charged with murder?"

I carried the glass of water back to the living room and found Joe Riddley standing over Gwen Ellen while tears ran down her cheeks. He never knows what to do when a woman cries. If God had given him daughters, he'd have spoiled them rotten just to keep their eyes dry.

I handed Gwen Ellen the water and sat down beside her. She took a sip and said in a soggy whisper, "I miss Skye so much. And I am worried about Skell. Where could he be?"

Joe Riddley saw his chance to escape. "He could have come home in the last hour, and not know a thing about all this. Or he may be asleep and not hearing his phone. Why don't I drive over there and see?"

Gwen Ellen's face brightened again with hope. "Would you? There's a key to his place hanging in the pantry. Tansy will get it for you."

In less than a minute his car purred down the drive.

Mama always said if you can't think of a thing to do or say, don't do or say anything. I sat waiting for Gwen Ellen to take the lead. She leaned over so her arm pressed against mine, just as she used to when I read her fairy tales. I wished the whole afternoon were a fairy tale, so I could soon close the book and say, "And they all lived happily ever after." Nobody ever said what happened *after* ever after.

We sat in silence until Tansy brought in a tray holding two cups, a steaming teapot, a sugar bowl, lemon wedges, peanut-butter cookies, and two pretty napkins. "I thought you all might need something hot to drink."

"Go wash your face first," I suggested to Gwen Ellen. "You'll feel so much better."

She climbed the stairs to her room and came back a few minutes later with her makeup repaired and her hair freshly brushed.

"I haven't had a chance to tell you, but I really like your haircut," I greeted her.

Her smile trembled. "Thanks. I thought it was time for a change. . . ."

She stopped and horror filled her eyes. She'd certainly gotten a change.

Neither of us said a word while she poured tea through a little silver strainer, dropped in two lumps of sugar, and passed me the lemon. She sat, stirring her own cup as if the tea were a potion to bring back happiness. Finally, she sighed. "I still can't believe this has happened. I keep expecting Skye to walk in the door and say, 'Honey, what's all this about?' "

"Me, too," I admitted. "He was always so good about taking care of you."

"From the very first day we met." She gave a little laugh. "Remember what Daddy told me when I went to college? 'Honey, go find yourself a loving husband who likes cars.' " Her eyes grew pink again. "I did, too," she whispered.

Bates Skellton had been forty when his only child was born, and he'd never liked selling cars—he just fell into it when his own daddy left him the motor company. Bates wasn't like Skell; he never rebelled, but within five years after Gwen Ellen and Skye got married, he'd turned the business over to them and retired to Vero Beach.

"Skye sure liked cars." I wanted to keep her talking,

thaw the frozen look on her face. "Tell me about those Volkswagen Beetles he started on."

A small smile touched her eyes and lips. "For his twelfth birthday, he asked his daddy for a Beetle he could tear down and rebuild. He saved his allowance and lawn-mowing money to buy parts. When he finally got it running, his daddy had to take it for its test drive, because Skye was too young. But it ran. Skye sold it for a good profit and used his money to buy another, plus parts to fix it. After he'd rebuilt and sold that one, folks with Beetles started bringing theirs by. His mama and daddy got tired of car parts lying all over their lawn—who wouldn't? His father was a dentist, and they lived in a real nice subdivision. So his daddy said he'd have to quit. Instead, Skye begged him to sign the papers to rent a warehouse where he could work. Skye wasn't even fifteen yet. He worked every afternoon and weekend, and by the time he went to college, he'd rebuilt and repaired enough Beetles to pay a lot of his own way."

"Oh!" Gwen Ellen pressed her hand to her mouth. "I must call his folks." She sat forward and looked around like she couldn't remember where she kept the phone.

I pushed her back. "Not right this minute. Pour us each another cup of tea. Tell me again about you and Skye getting together."

She bent to the teapot like she was glad to have something to do. When both our cups were full, she relaxed against the cushions again. "Skye was in my sophomore history class, and from the very first day, I thought he was the handsomest *thing*. We didn't have a man in Hope County who looked that good to me."

I was glad she'd added the last two words. I might have had to correct her, widow or not.

"He kept looking at me, too, and on the third day he offered to buy me a Co-cola after class. We went for a walk and all he talked about was cars, and I told him I practically

grew up in a motor company. I didn't really, of course . . . ,"
she added. She certainly hadn't. I doubted if she was ever
in the business as a child, except to ask her daddy for
money. "Anyway, after that we were always together. We got
pinned in November, engaged in February, and married in
June, after he graduated. I never loved anybody except Skye.
Never." She set her cup on the coffee table and polished her
small engagement diamond with her right forefinger. The
stone was nowhere near as big as Skye could have afforded
later, but I knew how she felt about it. I looked down and
found I was unconsciously polishing my own ring.

"Tomorrow is the thirtieth anniversary of when we got
engaged." Her voice was rough with tears.

Surely that was the cruelest thing of all.

I set down my own tea and gathered her into my arms.
"Oh, honey."

She laid her head on my shoulder with a strangled little
sob. "He's not really dead, is he? Didn't I just imagine it?
Isn't this a bad dream?"

"No, honey. You didn't imagine it."

She drew away from me and covered her face with her
hands. "It's not fair," she whispered. "It's just not fair."
Tears trickled between her fingers.

The best thing I knew to do was sit there and let her cry
her heart out.

Finally she took two deep breaths and leaned against the
fat pillows. Her cheeks were trailed with tears and her lashes
wet. "I loved him, Mac. I gave my whole life to that man."

"Of course you did, honey. And he gave his to you.
That's what marriage is about."

She sat up straight and demanded fiercely, "So why did
he leave me?"

Her anger at poor Skye caught me by surprise. "He didn't
leave you on purpose, even if that's what it feels like." Was
that the right thing to say? I sure wished I'd taken that

course at church on stages of grief. It seemed to me, from what I'd picked up from thumbing through the book, that Gwen Ellen was whipping through several stages at a fantastic rate.

"Where is Skell?" she cried, pressing both temples as if her head would explode. "I want Skell."

A car came up the drive. I hurried to the window, but it was just one of the women from our Sunday school class. Behind her came another. "You've got company," I informed her. "Do you want to see them?"

She joined me at the window, then heaved a sigh. "I'll have to, I guess. I can't be rude." She turned to peer in a mirror over a small table. "I look a mess."

"Go fix your face again and come down when you're ready."

Within half an hour the room was full of people who'd brought potato salad, sliced ham, fried chicken, fruit salads, casseroles, and homemade cakes and pies. None of them cared if Gwen Ellen had a full-time cook. Food in the South is the currency of caring.

I helped Tansy find places for it in the refrigerator and on the countertops while Gwen Ellen talked in a flat, dead voice and told as much as she knew of what was going on.

When the back door opened, I thought it was yet another woman arriving. Instead, Joe Riddley stood there holding a green pet carrier. "What do you feed a ferret?"

Tansy yelped. "Get that filthy thing outta my clean kitchen. I told Skell he couldn't bring it here, and I meant it. Get it out. Now." She flapped both hands in Joe Riddley's direction.

He was so startled, he dropped the carrier. The door flew open and something long and dark flowed over my feet and into the pantry.

"Dang it, that door wasn't latched right." Joe Riddley had the nerve to glare at *me*.

I glared back, wishing I could climb up on top of a counter without looking as silly as Tansy did standing on that kitchen chair. "What was that thing, again?"

"A ferret," Joe Riddley snapped. "And look what you've made me do." He went to the pantry door and peered in. "Does it bite?"

"How should I know?"

"I wasn't asking you, Little Bit. I was asking Tansy. Tansy, does that thing bite?"

"How should I know?" she echoed. "I told Skell when he bought it I wasn't having it in this house, and I meant it. Get it out of here."

"I take it Skell wasn't home." I edged toward one of the chairs and sat down, propping my feet on the seat of another.

"Nope. The place is a mess, and the creature was out of food and water. I couldn't just leave it there." He squatted down and peered toward a far corner of the pantry. "Come here, little feller. Come here." He dragged the carrier to the pantry door and held it open. I watched nervously. Nothing happened.

"Where's the broom?" he demanded over his shoulder.

"In the corner of the pantry." Tansy didn't offer to leave her chair to fetch it. She was even holding up her skirt with one hand, as if the ferret might leap up and cling to it.

Now that she'd mentioned it, my denim skirt was drooping down between the chairs. I tucked it around my knees. I hadn't gotten a good look at the creature, but the little bit I'd seen resembled a cross between a weasel and a rat. Neither are on my favorite-creatures list.

Joe Riddley got the broom and headed into the pantry. "Come here, Little Bit, and guard the door. If he tries to get through, grab him."

"Grab him yourself," I replied. But I warily stood up and went to peer around him. Under a bottom shelf I saw two bright eyes. "I'll prop chairs across the door," I offered. As

I dragged two kitchen chairs and made as good a barrier as I knew how, I couldn't help thinking that Skye MacDonald would never have asked Gwen Ellen to grab a ferret while he chased it with a broom. "Okay, see if you can get him into the carrier."

Joe Riddley swiped with the broom. Like liquid fur, the ferret darted from under the shelf, oozed through my barrier, slithered across my foot again, and headed up the back stairs.

I collapsed in my chair and waited to die.

Did my loving husband give me comfort while I recovered from that near heart attack? No. The guardian of my well-being roared, "You let him get away, dagnabit. You let him get right past you."

"Well whoop-de-do. Did you expect me to grab him with my bare hands?"

He heaved a sigh like he'd never known anybody quite so useless. "We'll have to find him before he tears the place up."

"Them ferrets are real destructive," Tansy contributed from her perch.

"You might climb down from that chair and help us look," I suggested.

She shook her head. "I ain't chasing no ferret. Don't you be sending him back down here, either. I don't want him in my kitchen."

Joe Riddley clomped up the stairs. I followed him, one uneasy step at a time, hoping any second he'd say, "Here he is," and slam the door of the carrier. Instead he said, "You search the master bedroom and I'll check Skell's. At least all the other doors are shut. Maybe he recognized Skell's smell and headed in there."

"Fondly do we hope, fervently do we pray," I muttered as I headed to Gwen Ellen's bedroom. What was I supposed to do if I met the ferret—introduce myself and chat with him until Joe Riddley arrived with the carrier?

I tiptoed to the king-size bed, hiked up my skirt, and took a quick peek underneath. I kept my knees bent, ready to run if I saw eyes. All I saw were Gwen Ellen's slippers.

The closet door was closed, so at least he wasn't in there. I drifted over to the dresser and peered this way and that, but I didn't see anything except a letter Gwen Ellen had left lying open. It was the one from that New Mexico dude ranch. I had had time to read "Dear Mr. and Mrs. MacDonald, We hope you enjoyed your stay with us—" and to feel one twinge of envy when I heard a rustling in the bathroom.

I slammed that bathroom door faster than a cockroach can fly. "I've got him," I yelled.

A woman shrieked.

Then somebody wrenched open the door and demanded, "What are you doing?" A young woman I barely knew glared at me with one eye open and one eye closed. I could tell we wouldn't be getting any of her lawn-and-garden business in the near future.

I backed away. "Did you see a ferret?"

"A what?" Both eyes flew open.

"Ferret. Little black animal—" As she began to cringe, I shook my head. "You'd have known if he was in there. I heard a sound and thought that was him."

"That was me, trying to put my contact back in. I had some mascara in my eye. Now I've dropped the dratted lens, and heaven knows if I can find it on this blue carpet."

Which is why I spent the next ten minutes crawling around on Gwen Ellen's bathroom rug. It's hard enough to search for a blue contact on a blue rug. It's a lot harder when you have to keep one eye cocked to be sure a ferret doesn't sneak in while you're looking for the lens.

When the woman yelled, I jumped at least two feet.

"Here it is. It got caught on my sweater." She picked it off with one long red fingernail and held it up.

I managed not to kill her by remembering something our

newspaper editor likes to say: Half the world is below average, and we can't all be in the upper half.

Mama had never taught me a graceful way to get up from my knees off a bathroom floor and excuse myself to somebody I had scared half to death. I did the best I could, and tiptoed down the hall. "Did you find him?" I called in a soft voice.

Joe Riddley was nowhere to be found. I didn't go into Skell's room, but I called at the door twice. And I knocked on all the other doors before I ran my husband to earth back in the kitchen, drinking coffee with Tansy.

"Where is that blessed ferret?" I demanded.

He waved one hand like the question was unimportant. "In Skell's closet. I shut the door on him, and thought I'd call Cindy."

"Does Cindy know anything about ferrets?"

"You got a better idea?"

I considered. Cindy had known about beagles and parrots, and she'd grown up hunting foxes. Maybe ferrets were like foxes. "No. Call Cindy. But for heaven's sake, go upstairs first and close the bedroom door, too, in case he gets out of the closet. And put a sign on the door so nobody opens it by mistake."

"You close the door and put up the sign. I'll call Cindy."

Tansy condescended to provide paper, tape, and a pen.

I stomped up the stairs with steam coming out my ears and hardened my heart to frantic scratching as I closed the bedroom door and taped up a note:

Loose Ferret. Do Not Open This Door.

Anybody stupid enough to disobey deserved what they got.

⧽ 9 ⧼

As I started back down the stairs I heard a light voice that sounded familiar say, "I came to see how I could help," and heard Laura reply, "That's real nice of you." When I got farther down the stairs, I saw Tansy pulling out a chair at the kitchen table, across from Joe Riddley, for the young receptionist from MacDonald's.

Laura sprawled in a third chair, legs stretched before her and one strand of hair at her lips. I'd seen her slump just like that after a grueling soccer game. I'd also heard her mother beg, "Honey, please sit up like a lady and stop sucking your hair." Today, even Gwen Ellen wouldn't have the heart to correct her. Laura's face was white and drained, and she kept letting out deep, deep breaths. I knew how she felt. Sorrow leaves little lung room for air.

Tansy offered Nicole—that was her name—a cup of coffee, but Nicole refused. Then, as I watched, Tansy poured a cup of coffee, added lots of cream and sugar, and sidled into the pantry to pour in something from a bottle she took from behind the potatoes. I was startled, and a little shocked. Gwen Ellen was a rabid teetotaler. Years ago she'd gone to visit her parents for a week and came back to find Skye had left wine in the refrigerator. She had told me with perfect seriousness, "Mac, he'd drunk nearly half the bottle in a week. If I'd known he was going to stay drunk the whole time, I'd never have gone."

Tansy handed Laura the doctored cup, and she took it with no inkling of what was in it. Her grateful smile was for the coffee. "I tell you true," she told Joe Riddley, "having to listen to folks say how sorry they are is one of the most wearing things I've ever had to do." She took a gulp, gasped, choked, and had to be slapped on the back. Then she gave Tansy a wry grin. Tansy put on an innocent expression and turned to look out at the rain still streaming down.

I came the rest of the way down the stairs and, as Laura took another sip, she glanced up and saw me. "Hey, Mac, you remember Nicole from our front desk?"

Yesterday that young woman had pranced into Skye's office with badly typed letters. Today tousled curls fell in front of her face and her eyes and nose were red and swollen.

"Sure. Hey, Nicole." Her skirt was so abbreviated, I sure hoped she hadn't paid for a whole one. "Did you get everything shut down?" I asked Laura as I took the vacant chair and waved away Tansy's offer of coffee.

"She was great." Nicole held a wadded tissue to her pink nose and gave a big sniff. "People were real upset, but she calmed them down." She threw Laura the kind of look sixth-grade soccer players used to give her after a high-school game.

Laura ignored the look and gulped down the rest of her coffee. "That was good, Tansy." She held out her mug. "Could I have a little more, please?"

Tansy refilled the cup, but only with coffee, milk, and sugar. Laura grimaced and gave her a reproachful frown. Tansy turned again to the window.

"What did Cindy say?" I asked Joe Riddley, who was

busy drawing circles on the blue tablecloth with one fore-finger.

"She's coming over. Said maybe she can entice it with food and water." Seeing Laura's puzzled look, he explained about the ferret.

She shuddered. "I'm glad it's not in my part of the house. Why Skell ever wanted one, I'll never know." She looked from me to Tansy for advice. "Do you think it would be awful of me to go up to my place for a while?"

"I think you deserve it," I told her.

"That's just what you been needin'," Tansy agreed.

Nicole perked up. "Shall I come with you? I could give you a back rub."

Laura's voice was gruff. "Maybe another time. Right now, I'd just like to be alone." As she stood, though, she rested one hand on Nicole's shoulder. "Thanks. I really appreciate your coming over." Laura could always be counted on to think of other people.

Nicole raised a soggy face. "Don't forget what I told you, now. I want to do something with your hair before the—the funeral. You'll be gorgeous if you give me an hour."

Laura's wide mouth twisted into a wry smile. "Some chance. But I won't forget." At the kitchen door, she hesitated, listening.

"Go on." Tansy gave her a little shove. "I'm not leavin' your mama. I'll stay in the spare room a few days, like I did when she had pneumonia a couple of years back."

"You're great." Laura bent to give Tansy a swift hug, then hurried out. She clomped up her own stairs like demons were after her.

"You want some coffee, Miss MacLaren?" Tansy held up the pot. I shook my head.

Nicole sat looking between the back door and the one to the rest of the house. "Do you think there's anything I could do for Mrs. MacDonald? Mr. MacDonald"—her voice wavered over his name—"I can't believe he's gone. He was kind, funny, thoughtful—and I just knew him four months." She ended on a wail. Then she laid her head on the table and just boohooed. "Four months," she repeated through sniffs and sobs. "Four lousy months."

My own heart was like lead, but I'd known Skye thirty years. Nicole's four months at his front desk seemed like a watermelon seed in that patch. So what had turned on her water? Had she carried a torch, hoping Skye might be ready to trade in Gwen Ellen for a younger model?

Across the table, Joe Riddley kept sending me short, jabbing looks to say, "Do something. Make her stop."

Before I could think what to do, Tansy trudged over and patted Nicole's shoulder. "There, there, honey. Mr. Skye wouldn't want any of us carrying on like that. He's in the bosom of the Lord, now. We who are left got to bear our burdens bravely."

Nicole sniffed and wiped her eyes with a napkin. Tansy wiped her own with a corner of her apron and headed back to lean against the counter. I decided I could be as charitable as Tansy. After all, Nicole was very young, and probably hadn't experienced violent death this close before. I touched her arm. "I think the best thing you can do right now is go home. We're going to leave in a few minutes, too. Gwen Ellen—Mrs. MacDonald—will be fine. And somebody will call everybody from work, to let you all know about the funeral and when the business will reopen."

That made her toss back her hair and stick up her chin. Tears had turned her eyelashes into spiky little stars. "It's my job to make those calls. I'm Mr. MacDonald's *secretary.*"

I doubted that Skye ever gave her that title. "The girl out front" was what he most likely called her. And that spurt of pride made me want to jab her balloon with reality. "I think that will be handled by the funeral home or the church."

"It's my job." She jumped to her feet and ran to the door. "Laura? Laura!" When Laura opened her door, she cried, "Don't you let anybody else call everybody from work to tell them when the funeral is. That's my job. Okay?"

Laura paused, as if trying to make sense of what she was hearing. "Okay," she agreed in a heavy voice. "I'll call you when we know. Leave your number with Tansy."

Nicole came back in with purpose in her step and resolution in her eye. "May I have a piece of paper, please?" She scrawled her name and number on the telephone pad Tansy handed her and laid it in the middle of the table. "Don't lose this. Laura is going to call me when they know about the funeral, so I can call everybody from work."

"Fine," I said crossly, "but go on home for now. We all need to clear out and leave the family alone."

Her eyes slewed my way, defiant chips of blue ice. "I—"

"Easy, now," Joe Riddley told her.

She met his gaze, and hers faltered. "Okay, but if there's anything I can do, tell them to call me." She turned to Tansy, anxious. "You will, won't you?"

"Sure I will," Tansy assured her. She'd been comfortable for years making promises she had no intention of keeping.

Nicole buttoned up her raincoat and peered anxiously out the kitchen door. When Joe Riddley offered to walk her to her car under our umbrella, I didn't mind. When you've been married to a man for over forty years, you know how far he'll go. Tenderly putting a pretty young woman in her car was as far as Joe Riddley would go.

However, Nicole had worn me out. "I need that coffee after all, Tansy."

"You want just milk and sugar, or a tad of something extry?"

I was tempted. I wasn't on call to go down to the jail,

and Joe Riddley was driving. But the way I felt, even a nip might put me over the edge. "Just black and hot," I told her, "to warm some of the deep cold places I'm carrying around."

Tansy poured two cups. She handed me one and stood sipping the other. "You and me both, Miss MacLaren. You and me both. My spirit's froze plumb to the bone."

About the time I finished my coffee, Cindy showed up. She got Skell's ferret back in its carrier in a matter of minutes and was well-mannered enough not to ask what it was doing in an upstairs closet in the first place. Neither Joe Riddley nor I felt inclined to explain.

"Have you ever thought about becoming a vet?" I asked as she carried the carrier down.

She laughed like I'd made a joke. "Now when would I have time for that? But I'll keep this little fellow in our garage until you find Skell. Oh, and since Ridd and Martha are out of town, you all come over to our house for dinner when you're done at church. I've already cooked a turkey breast."

I was astonished and touched. Invitations to Walker and Cindy's usually came in cute little handwritten notes a couple of weeks in advance. "We'd love to, honey. What can I bring?"

"A good appetite." With a wave, she left with the ferret.

Before I left, I made Gwen Ellen promise me she'd eat a little something by and by.

"Baby Sister will be all right," Joe Riddley assured me as we drove away.

"Of course she will."

I sure was glad neither of us was connected to a lie detector.

10

It rained all the way home. As soon as we parked, Lulu started reminding us that she was no longer a yard dog and had spent enough time in their company. Joe squawked from the barn, "Hello, Hiram. Hello Hiram," calling his former master.

"Ah, the peace and quiet of the countryside." Joe Riddley handed me the umbrella. "Go get supper started. I'll bring in the animals and feed them."

Having spent years convincing people I don't cook, I take care not to ruin my reputation. "Eggs and bacon enough for you?" I asked.

"If you put toast and applesauce with it. That too much of a stretch?"

"You'll be fortunate if your eggs are cooked," I warned. "They may come flying at you when you come through the kitchen door."

"I'll send in advance troops to check for enemy fire."

I let myself in and set my pocketbook on the counter, hung my damp coat in the utility room, and went to pull out eggs, bacon, and bread. As I cooked, however, I started to sniffle. First I sniffled happily, because it felt good to be able to joke again with Joe Riddley. Then I sniffled sadly, for Skye and Gwen Ellen. Finally I started thinking about the night our neighbor found Joe Riddley shot in the head down our road, and how I could have gotten the same news they brought Gwen Ellen. By the time Joe Riddley ambled through the door with Lulu at his heels and Joe on one shoulder, I was bawlng like a baby.

He hung up his cap. "What's the matter now?"

"You're alive," I said, sobbing. "I'm so glad you're alive."

I think he must have been having the same thoughts outside, because he sent Joe up to the curtain rod and came to hold me. Neither of us cared if supper was a bit cold.

We were eating our last bites of egg and toast when Gwen Ellen called. "I just hate to bother you all, but I don't know who else to call." Her voice was thick with tears.

"Are you by yourself?" Surely either Tansy or Laura was close by at all times.

"Oh, no. Tansy's fixing supper—although I told her I can't eat a bite. I asked everybody else to leave, though. You can only be nice so long." She broke down and sobbed.

Gwen Ellen had always teared up at sunsets and wept buckets in sad movies. She cried at weddings, funerals, even baptisms. If our preacher gave a touching illustration in the sermon, Gwen Ellen would start wiping her eyes. But who wouldn't cry after her husband lay dead for hours while nobody knew he was missing?

It wasn't just Skye that was making her cry this time, though. "Skell still hasn't come home." She was crying so hard I could hardly make out the words. "I'm worried sick."

"Skell's gone away for weekends a lot of times before." That was part of her problem, of course. Disliking Hopemore as he did, Skell was apt to take off in his car for long weekends to hear bands play, watch cars race, do anything that was lively and jammed with people. Since he'd moved into his own place, he didn't always tell his family when or where he was going. Even before Skye died, Gwen Ellen was having a hard time admitting Skell was grown.

"Yes, but this time he didn't go to work or tell them he wouldn't be there."

That was a good point. Skell had never been responsible about getting to work on time or sticking around all day, but he had never failed to show up. I scratched one ear while I thought how best to answer. "Maybe you ought to ask the police again to look for him."

"I tried. Chief Muggins says they can't do anything until he's been gone longer. Tansy and Laura say the same thing you do—stop worrying, he's just off on some trip. But I *can't.* I'm worried sick. MacLaren . . . ?"

She used to say my name just that way when her hair ribbon wouldn't tie, when she couldn't solve an arithmetic problem, or when she wanted me to call her mother and ask for a permission she didn't think she could get herself. When I didn't jump right in to volunteer this time, she added, "Maybe he's just gone down to Dublin." MacDonald Motors raced a car at the NASCAR track. Skell didn't drive it, but he liked to hang out around those who did.

"We're not going down to Dublin at this hour. Besides, I wouldn't know how to go about finding Skell once we got there."

"Could you just drive around town a little bit, then, to see if you can find his car?"

Skell wasn't driving around Hopemore. He'd have run into somebody who'd have told him about his daddy, and he'd have headed home. Only because I felt so sorry for her right that minute did I say, "Okay, we'll go look around. If Skell's in town, we'll find him."

Joe Riddley shook his head, but he laid down his napkin and slid back his chair.

Before we left, I hurried to the downstairs bathroom to wash my face, pat my hair, and put on a little lipstick. Phyllis and I keep my hair the same honey brown it was when Joe Riddley married me, and it still looked nice after her fixing it that morning for the wedding, but I hadn't powdered my nose since I'd had several good cries and two trips through the rain. By the time I felt presentable, Joe Riddley had the dishes soaking in hot soapy water. Over the years I've learned how to gauge that almost to the second.

Cruising up and down the rainy streets of Hopemore doesn't take long, even if you drive slow. What the chamber of commerce euphemistically calls "Greater Hopemore" only has thirteen thousand residents. But I found myself enjoying driving around without talking, listening to the swish of our tires on the wet streets and feeling the warm security of being together.

Joe Riddley looked over at me with a ghost of a smile. "Feels like high school, doesn't it?"

We used to cruise around for hours on weekend nights, trying to postpone the time he'd have to take me home. I reached over and laid my hand on his, glad of its familiar comfort. "Just what I was thinking. Can we go by Skell's once more?" I turned to peer out through the slanting downpour at dim yards and bushes that sparkled under streetlights.

"We've been by twice."

"I know, but—"

I didn't finish, because he was already turning in that direction. "We can swing by there again, but he's not gonna be there."

"Did you remember to give his key back to Tansy?"

He felt for his shirt pocket. "No, I plumb forgot. I'll take it by tomorrow."

I hesitated. Joe Riddley has never been what you might call enthusiastic about my poking around mysterious circumstances. But this might be the only chance we got.

"Why don't we go look at Skell's place and see if we can get any hint of where he might have gone?"

"I was already in there," he reminded me.

"Did you see any signs he planned to leave?"

"The place was such a mess, I don't know how you'd tell."

"Did you look in the closets?"

"He's not hiding in the closet, Little Bit."

"We might be able to see if his suitcase and clothes are missing." When he didn't reply, I added, "Joe Riddley, what worries me about Skell is that whoever killed his daddy might have killed him, too. If I knew a suitcase was gone, I could stop worrying."

"Charlie Muggins is gonna have our hide for this." Nevertheless, he turned back toward Skell's and pulled into a parking place just down from his town house door. I didn't complain that he parked so I had to wade through an inch of water.

He snorted when I covered my hand with the hem of my skirt to turn the doorknob, but I'd been thinking about what he said. "If Charlie Muggins and his deputies ever do get to the point of fingerprinting the place, I don't want them finding mine. You can explain that Gwen Ellen sent you over, but . . ." I didn't finish that sentence. I didn't need to. Charlie had been waiting to arrest me for something ever since we first met.

I left the door cracked behind us for a quick getaway, and stood uneasily in the dark smelling old garbage and dirty clothes. "Turn on a lamp, hon," I instructed. "I'll wait right here. If there's a second ferret in here, and it runs over my feet, I'll join Skye in the bosom of the Lord."

Skell's place looked like he hadn't hung up a single shirt, shelved a single book, or put one piece of junk mail in a wastebasket in the year he'd lived there. Silver CDs lay beside crumpled underwear on the thick black rug. Wadded T-shirts covered an expensive stereo system. A lone sock hung from the lamp shade. Joe Riddley flung that to the floor in disgust. "I'm surprised he hasn't burned the place down. And look at that garbage can spilling all over the floor, when there's a Dumpster just down the way."

"Kids who grow up with a Tansy in the kitchen aren't apt to carry out garbage as often as they should."

Stomping my feet on the carpet to alert loose ferrets, I moved toward the bedroom. It stunk of unwashed sheets. I flipped the light switch with the side of my finger and saw waves of dirty clothes all over the floor. Just as I shuddered at the thought of germs breeding around me, Joe Riddley spoke over my shoulder. "I've seen cleaner slums."

"The funny thing is, Skell always looks so bandbox neat." I went to the closet and again used my hem to cover my hand as I opened the closet door. Skell had enough slacks with razor-sharp creases and well-starched dress shirts to start his own store. I couldn't tell if any were missing.

I jumped when Joe Riddley breathed on the back of my neck. "Find anything?"

We both jumped when we heard a man's voice at the front door. "Skell? Where the dickens have you been? Your sister's worried sick."

Somebody came into the living room and slammed the door.

I voted for hiding and hoping whoever it was would go away. Fear of Chief Muggins makes me a tad unreasonable at times.

Joe Riddley, fortunately, recognized the voice. "Ben? It's us. The Yarbroughs." He turned and loped toward the door. I paddled through the sea of dirty clothes in his wake.

The manager of MacDonald's service department was a long drink of water, six-feet-six and built like spaghetti. In the low light of the living room his brown eyes were dark

as pools of cypress water, and I was surprised how handsome he was. I'd never seen him except in a loose mechanic's jumpsuit and a cap. The green polo shirt he wore
with jeans showed muscles I hadn't suspected he had, and
without his cap, his dark hair was an unruly mass of curls.

"Folks pay good money to get curls like that," I teased to
ease the air.

He ducked his head and scowled. "I'd gladly give 'em
away, if I could."

Joe Riddley swore by Ben when it came to cars, but I
found him a mite morose. I'd never seen him smile, nor
heard him utter more sentences than were absolutely necessary.

He addressed Joe Riddley, his voice urgent. "Listen, have
you seen Skell? Laura asked me to see if he was here, and
when I saw the light—"

"Unfortunately, it's just us, on the same errand. Unfortunately, because he's not here." Joe Riddley turned off the
lamp, leaving us in darkness except for the streetlight in the
parking lot.

"Where the dickens could that kid have gone?" I demanded of the world in general.

Ben had been raised right—he held the door for us older
folks like it came natural—but under his breath, he muttered, "I hope he's sober, driving that silver bullet." The
anger in his voice surprised me, as did the force with which
he pulled the door shut behind him. Was he jealous? Did
Ben yearn to trade in his truck for a Porsche?

The rain still came down like curtains. Joe Riddley put
on his cap, and held our umbrella over me. We huddled
under the roof of Skell's small porch, and I looked around
the parked cars, willing Skell's to appear. "Seems like he'd
have told *somebody* he was leaving," I muttered. At the moment, I couldn't think who Skell's friends were.

"Laura's fit to be tied." Ben slapped his cap against his

leg again and again. "He shouldn't have gone off and left her with all this to deal with on her own."

"He didn't expect his daddy to get killed," I pointed out.

"No, but she had to close for him last night and today both, and if he doesn't get back by the time we reopen, I guess she'll go ahead and run the lot for him, too." He sounded as outraged as if he'd have to do it himself.

"Why don't you come down to Myrtle's and join us for pie?" Joe Riddley suggested.

"I was heading over there for supper," Ben admitted.

"We'll buy you supper while we have pie. Little Bit's feeling real generous tonight."

We ran for our car, and Ben splashed toward his truck. As we drove past Casa Mas Esperanza, I saw that their lot was full again.

Myrtle's, on the other hand, was not. In a town our size, every blip in the economy is felt somewhere. Hopefully it would even out eventually.

As always, Joe Riddley glared at the floodlit sign in Myrtle's parking lot:

Cooking as Good as Mama Used to Do

"She ought to take that down, the way she's cooking these days."

"The food's not as good without a little bacon grease and sugar," Ben agreed, coming up with us at the door, "but I guess your husband needing a heart bypass might tend to make you change your cooking habits."

"My mama cooked with fatback and sugar all her life, and she died at eighty-one," Joe Riddley muttered. "It's genes, not cooking." Mr. Medical Encyclopedia stomped ahead to pick a table.

He had plenty to choose from. The place was nearly empty, and Myrtle's face lower than an earthworm's belly.

When she saw Ben with us, though, she lit up in a smile. "It's good to see you eating with company instead of a book for a change."

"Books are good company," Ben informed her, heading to a table. As soon as we'd settled, Joe Riddley asked Ben where he came from. Up north, folks care about ethnic background. Down here, we want to know where people are *from*. Then we run through a mental list of our own relatives to try to figure out if we are related, and how. If we aren't kin, then we try to figure out who we know in common. That provides security in an uncertain world.

Ben flexed his long fingers and cracked his knuckles. "I grew up over near Sandersville." That was about an hour away. "You all grow up around here?"

"All our lives. What family do you have?"

"Three sisters and a brother. I'm second in line. My older sister is a nurse, the one after me is a high-school gym teacher—she reminds me a bit of Laura, the way they're both crazy about sports—and the third one is in law school. My little sister the lawyer." He gave a little grunt that was either a laugh or a sign of his pride in her. "The baby, my brother, is still in college and can't make up his mind what to do. They've spoiled him rotten, but I guess you always do with the last one." He gave me a quick look, but asked Joe Riddley, "You got just the two boys?"

"Just the two," he agreed. "Your parents still livin'?"

"Yessir. Daddy teaches history in high school, and Mama teaches second grade."

"You always want to be a mechanic?"

He shrugged. "Pretty much fell into it. Comin' up, I liked workin' on cars. I was pretty rebellious back then, too, so I goofed off in school and didn't make the kind of grades that earn scholarships. The year I graduated, my brother had to have a big operation, and it took every cent my folks had. I went to Vo-Tech and got certified as a mechanic, figurin'

I'd earn some money, then go to college when I figured out what I wanted." A little grin flickered across his face. "Turns out this was what I wanted. God's funny, some-times—uses what we thought were detours as shortcuts."

Since he didn't seem to mind talking once he got started (so long as he didn't have to look at me), I asked something I wanted to know. "How do you keep your hands so clean?"

He ducked his head with another flicker of a smile. "Rubber gloves. Sounds sissy, doesn't it?" He spread his big hands out and looked at them. "But Laura says if doc-tors and dentists can wear them, so can we. It took some getting used to, but it makes us more presentable." He flexed his hands and cracked his knuckles again.

Myrtle came by just then to set pint jars of sweet iced tea before us and take our order. After she'd swished her skirts back through the swinging kitchen door, Joe Riddley asked, "What brought you to Hopemore?"

Ben was quiet so long, I figured he hadn't heard the question. With one long forefinger he traced and retraced a circle on the green Formica tabletop. (Myrtle doesn't run to tablecloths and white linen napkins. She just has the best pie in Middle Georgia.) Finally he lifted his head as if it were an act of courage, and his words were so low they sounded like groans. "I was married. We were just coming up on our second anniversary, expecting our first baby, when they both got killed by a drunk driver who ran a stop sign. After that, I needed to go somewhere—it didn't much matter where. I got to talking to Skye down at the car races one day, and he said he could use a good mechanic, so here I am."

"And here's your supper." Myrtle slid that into his sen-tence as neatly as she slid a plate of meatloaf, green beans, and macaroni and cheese in front of him. Anybody who or-dered the special could have dinner on the table in about two minutes flat. But anybody who didn't want Myrtle joining in on their conversation had better find another place to eat. "Chocolate pie coming right up," she promised with a flap of one hand.

"How long you been here?" I asked, to pass the time.

Ben cut a big wedge of meatloaf and chewed while he considered. "I guess it's fixing to be seven years. I've been manager just over four."

"Been here long enough to start looking for a wife," Myrtle informed him, setting pie before Joe Riddley and me.

A flow of dark pink started in Ben's neck and worked its way up to his ears. The way he hunched over his plate, I couldn't see his face, so I didn't know if he was mad or embarrassed. Or maybe he still wasn't over that first wife. Wounds like that can take a while to heal.

Joe Riddley prodded the meringue on his pie, which stood three inches thick with little sugar beads on top. "Someday you gotta tell Little Bit how you do this, Myrtle."

"I'll tell her the day she asks." Myrtle gave me a wink and swept on to the next table. Joe Riddley and I sank our teeth into a little bit of heaven.

I knew to let Ben get something under his belt before I asked any more questions. Only women can eat and talk at the same time. In the distance we heard an ambulance wailing its way to the hospital. The sound gave me shivers.

"I sure wonder where Skell is," I said when we'd all had time for a few bites. "Have you seen him at all this afternoon, Ben?"

"No, but I've been shut in the service department 'til half an hour ago."

Joe Riddley stopped midchew. "I thought Laura closed the place down."

Ben gave a short nod and hunched over his plate. "She did. But we had a shop full of cars, so I told the fellows to pretend to leave, then to come back and finish up what we'd promised. Folks who hadn't heard about Skye were going to expect their cars to be ready. As they came by, we told them what had happened."

Joe Riddley chewed another bite of pie while he absorbed that. "Laura must be grateful."

Ben wolfed down green beans like we were fixing to have a bean shortage and he'd better stock up. He didn't look up as he admitted, "I didn't tell her. She's got enough to worry about right now. When I called to be sure she was okay, after I'd locked up, I didn't say I was going home. I said was going out to run errands and wondered if there was anything I could do for her. That's when she asked if I'd run by Skell's place to see if he'd come back."

Joe Riddley laid down his fork and propped his chin in the palm of one hand. "I got a passel of people working for me, but not one of 'em would keep working if I died. Some would stop out of respect and some, maybe, because they'd be delighted to get a few days off." He waited for Ben's explanation.

"A garage isn't like a nursery." He broke his cornbread and buttered it. "Folks need their wheels. Somebody had to get those cars back on the road."

Joe Riddley bent to his pie, but a muscle twitched in his cheek.

"Were you working on Perez's brakes last night?" I asked. "Is that why you were so late leaving?"

Ben gave me a sharp, surprised look.

"That wall's thin between your office and the ladies' room," I explained, "and I was washing up in there when you and Skye were fighting about whether to fix our car or theirs."

"We weren't fighting, exactly." He kept his eyes on his macaroni and cheese.

"Sounded like it to me. You wanted to fix Perez's car and Skye insisted you fix ours."

"I planned to fix yours," he insisted. "I just wanted to finish theirs first. They don't have any other way to get around."

"I know." I flapped one hand to pacify him. "I thought you were right and Skye wrong. And I think it was grand if you stayed late last night fixing their car."

After that, conversation became an uphill exercise. I was glad when we all finished, shoved back our chairs, and headed home. The courthouse clock chimed nine, and the Episcopal chimes raced through "Be Thou My Vision" a minute later. At that pace, the vision would soon disappear over the horizon.

The rain had stopped at last. As we got in the car, I suggested, "Could we drive over and see where it happened?"

"Won't be much to see." Joe Riddley switched on the engine. "Besides, they'll have the site blocked off."

"I know, but I want to see it for myself. Please?"

"No. Skye was one of my best friends. I don't want you messing around in his life."

He was getting tired, because he'd begun to slur his words, but I was still stung. "I don't want to mess around in his life. I just want to see where he died."

"Not while I'm driving. You listen to me, Little Bit, and listen real good. I don't want you fooling around with this case. You've got enough to do, being a judge and working at the store. Besides, cantankerous though you may be, I don't want to lose you. You stay clear, you hear me?"

I reached out and took his hand. "I hear you, honey."

That didn't mean I planned to pay him one speck of attention. I'd just have to bide my time.

❧ 11 ❧

I was already upstairs undressing when the phone rang. The voice on the other end was breathy and feminine, but my mind couldn't call up a name to match it. "Judge Yarbrough? This is Marilee Muller. I saw you at Skye MacDonald's yesterday."

I stood a little straighter in my petticoat. It's not every night I talk to a television celebrity. "What can I do for you?" It was a good bet she wanted something. The last time I remembered her calling, she was ten and selling Girl Scout cookies. Maybe I'd been chosen to vote on tomorrow's weather. I decided to vote for clear and sunny, to give folks something to hope for.

Marilee's voice was rushed and low, like she didn't want to be overheard. "I didn't know who else to call. Our newsroom got a story tonight saying Skye MacDonald is dead. It's not true, is it?"

She sounded desperate, so I swallowed my disappointment at not being selected to predict the weather. "I'm afraid so, honey. He was hit by a car sometime last evening."

At that point she took the Lord's name in vain, which for some reason has become the primary exclamation in her generation for everything from a panty-hose run to national disaster. Then she apologized (as if it were I, rather than

God, who commanded that the name be respected) and hung up.

I was peeling off my thigh-high stockings when she called back. "I'm sorry. We got cut off." That wasn't true, but I had nothing to gain by calling her a liar. "You were telling me about Skye," she went on. "That's awful. Where was he? What happened?" Her voice was as clogged as if she'd developed a bad cold in the last four minutes.

I figured she was either asking me because she thought a judge would know more than some people, or because her newsroom had asked her to get a quote for their eleven o'clock report. Of course, there was one more possibility. It flitted through my head, leaving a clammy trail. She'd been real chummy with Skye yesterday afternoon, and pretty steamed when he brushed her off last night. Maybe she already knew all about how he died, and wanted to know how much people had figured out. Joe Riddley often says I have a suspicious mind.

I sat down on the side of my bed, trying to decide how much to tell her. On the other end of the line, she muttered "Oh, God, oh, God"—more like a mantra than a prayer.

"I don't know a whole lot," I began. "He was found out on a dirt road just off Warner Road, and he'd been hit with his own car."

"His own car? Do they know who did it?" Was it my imagination, or did the line quiver with her eagerness to know?

"The police are working on that, but they haven't named a suspect yet."

"Will—do you know if the dealership will be open tomorrow? I—uh, I left a scarf in his office Friday, and I'd like to get it back."

"Scarf" my hind foot. I wondered what she'd really left. But I said, sweet enough even to please my Mama, "They're never open on Sunday. In fact, I doubt they'll open again until at least Tuesday or Wednesday, but I'll sure tell Laura to look out for it."

I expected her to hang up after that, but she had one more question. "Do you know when the funeral is? And will there be a—a viewing?" Her voice trembled on the word.

"That hadn't been discussed when we left this afternoon. I would guess they'll have to do an autopsy—"

"Oh, *God*." She paid for two minutes of dead air, then sighed. "Well, thanks. I'm really going to miss him." Her voice had dropped to a whisper.

"We're all going to miss him," I agreed, "particularly his family." I thought we ought to enlarge the picture a tad.

After we hung up, I resumed undressing. I'd gotten down to the bare essentials when the phone rang again. This time it was a male voice I did recognize. "Judge Yarbrough, this is Deputy Adams. Can you come down to the sheriff's detention center for a bond hearing? Entering an auto and auto theft." That last part was the charge against the perpetrators. Deputy Adams always gave that detail, to explain why he was bringing me down there. He was one of the few deputies who remembered that my going to him, instead of his coming to me, was a courtesy.

Maybe this is where I should explain what magistrates do in Georgia. We hold probable-cause hearings to decide if there is sufficient cause for arrest and to take a case to the grand jury. We sign search warrants and arrest warrants for police officers and sheriff's deputies. We hold bond hearings in felony cases to determine whether bail is appropriate, and if it is, we set bail. We adjudicate in issues relating to county regulations dealing with things like evictions and dumping trash. And we hold traffic court in smaller towns. We also process all the bad checks in the county—of which there are far more than you might think. However, except for the chief magistrate, we are part-timers with regular day jobs. We fit judicial work into the nooks and crannies of our days—and nights.

That night, I sure was glad we didn't have vision phones. It wouldn't do my judicial image much good to be caught by young deputies in pink lace undies. "Judge Stebley is taking calls today," I informed him, hoping I sounded as dignified as if I had on my judicial robes.

"Yes, ma'am, he was, but he slipped on a wet sidewalk, fell off a curb, and broke his femur around an hour ago."

What an everlasting day. "That must have been the ambulance we heard over at Myrtle's. I'll be there in a shake," I promised. I pulled on a rust pantsuit and tied a pretty scarf around my neck. A quick dab of powder on my nose, a pat for my hair, and I was hurrying down the stairs. "Gotta go to the jail," I called to Joe Riddley as I caught up my pocketbook.

"Want me to come with you?" I could tell from his voice he already had his shoes off.

I shrugged into my still-damp raincoat. "I'll be fine. Back before you know it."

Right after I got appointed, deputies used to run out to pick me up and take me home every time we had business at the jail at night. I'd finally gotten the word around that I felt comfortable driving myself, even after dark. Hopemore isn't a hotbed of violent crime.

That night, though, as I drove through the rain-slick streets, I was glad it was too wet for pedestrians who might step up to my car at our two stoplights, and I found myself peering at every car that came close to mine. I was relieved to pull into the parking lot dotted with cruisers.

The hearing took longer than I'd predicted. The problem wasn't the three perpetrators, all eighteen and high-school seniors. The problem was one boy's parents. The three perps had been observed driving a car that had been reported stolen an hour before. Possibly influenced by too many movies, they'd decided to outrun the deputy rather than obey his flashing lights. After what sounded like a hair-raising chase on slick roads, they had taken off across what they presumed was an open field. The barbed wire didn't stop them, but the cattle pond came as a real surprise.

Now they stood dripping and shivering beside their lawyers and parents. Two sets of parents were nervous, angry with their sons, and concerned to be sure they learned never to do that sort of thing again. "Throw the book at them," one father urged.

"How could you?" demanded the other boy's mother. Her son didn't meet her eye.

The third set of parents, however, were furious with the deputy and me. "You have no reason to drag these decent boys to jail like common criminals," the father ranted.

I gave him the look that used to chill my sons' souls. "We are now in session. I'll have you put out if you cannot control your outbursts."

"Judges are all the same," he muttered to his wife. "Always trying to pick on kids."

Now I recognized the youth. He had a lengthy juvenile record for auto-related offenses, and was arrested only two months before for what he claimed was "borrowing" a car from a neighbor's yard for an evening's joyride. The neighbor decided not to press charges, so the case was dropped. Seeing his father's face, I wondered if the neighbor had been intimidated.

I set bail for the two first-time offenders—to their parents' obvious relief—and told them when to report to court. I invited the third to enjoy free room and board at the detention center without bond until his case came up. His father got right in my face and shouted, "You can't lock my boy up with criminals."

I pulled myself up as tall as I could get. "He needs to learn his lesson now before he *becomes* a criminal. And I'm fining you for contempt of court." A fine wasn't sufficient. That was one time when I wished I could lock parents up, too.

His mother caught my elbow. "He *can't* stay in jail right *now.* My sister's visiting from Chicago. She's just here for the weekend."

"She can come by and see him before she leaves." That was the most sympathy I could muster.

I added to them all, "I hope you have to pay for that ruined car. It belonged to old Mr. Raddets, and he hasn't a chance of buying another if you don't."

"We'll see what Sky's the Limit's can do," promised one of the fathers, who was taking his son home. "Maybe Skell will let them work weekends to pay for it."

Justice in a county the size of ours can sometimes be down-home and personal.

On my way home, as long as I was out anyway, I took a longer route—one that led down the third dirt road off Warner Road, just inside the city limits. It was, as Joe Riddley had said, designed for tractors, trailers, and trucks—all much higher vehicles than mine. The two ruts were lines of slick Georgia mud interspersed with potholes full of water, and the weeds were so high and so wet that the underside of my car got real clean.

Hoping to goodness I wouldn't skid off the road and embarrass myself by having to call my son Walker to come get me, I bumped between fields and around bends until my lights picked up yellow crime tape strung between two clumps of briers. Come summer, these bushes would be heavy with sweet blackberries. Just now they were razor-sharp ugly briers, just like the pain that shot from my stomach through my chest at the thought of what had happened there the night before.

This murder was different from others I'd been involved with. This was the first time in my life I'd poked around, as

Joe Riddley put it, into the death of a friend. Most murders angered me as an affront to society. This one broke my heart.

To my surprise, as I pulled to a stop I saw a police cruiser at the side of the road. A sudden flashlight nearly blinded me. I put down my window and yelled, "It's Judge Yarbrough. Lower that thing, please." Whoever it was dropped the beam to the ground, and I opened my door. As heavy feet squished my way, I saw why I hadn't picked him up in my headlights. It was Isaac James, his skin as dark as the night, dressed in black jeans, a dark turtleneck sweater, and muddy boots.

"You look like a cat burglar," I greeted him.

He leaned in my open window, smelling of a pleasant aftershave. "You look like somebody who's where she's got no business being. What took you so long? Joe Riddley called half an hour ago saying I'd better get down here, you'd be tromping all over the crime scene in a few minutes."

I opened my mouth for a hot retort, but changed my mind. Admitting one's own weaknesses is, I have always believed, a form of strength. "My hearing took longer than I thought. What is there to see?"

"Not one blessed thing. This is the strangest case I can remember."

"Can I take a look?"

"If you stay this side of the tape." He opened my door and stepped back.

Walking on wet Georgia mud is a challenge. The mud was slick and gluey. Twice it sucked off a shoe and I stepped a bare foot onto the muddy ground, then had to wipe it on wet grass and shove it back in its shoe. Walking in the middle of the road wasn't much better. Dripping grass soaked my shoes and ankles. Briers snagged my pants. Twice I slid back into the mud, adding about an inch to the sole of my left shoe.

I hobbled to the tape as uneven as a cow on a hill. Ike used his flashlight like a tour guide to point out sights of interest. First, a bright blue tarp. "Mr. MacDonald was lying down there in the road, and in spite of that gully-washer last night, the ground under him was dry, so we know he fell before the storm started. The rain may have washed away some of the evidence, but we found footprints and his car tracks going down to where the body was found."

I raised my eyebrows, even if Isaac couldn't see. "Where did it turn around?"

"Backed—pretty crookedly, too. Disturbed the bushes and grass on both sides of the road for nearly a hundred feet to the nearest turnaround, then made a mess of turning. See?" He shone the light behind us, but I couldn't see a thing. Meteorologists may be astrologers in my book, but forensics teams are downright magicians.

"The way he was lying," Ike continued, "it looks like he was coming toward the car when he got hit. He sure wasn't trying to get away."

"How many sets of footprints were there?" I peered at the ground, but couldn't make out a blamed thing in that light.

"We didn't find any except his. Looks like whoever hit him never left the car."

"How cold-blooded." I shivered.

As Isaac dropped his beam back to the ground, I saw a second set of tire treads on the verge up near the body. "Whose are those?" I pointed.

Ike grunted. "Chief Muggins was the first here, and he got too close before he saw Mr. MacDonald. He blurred some of the car tracks and most of the footprints, but fortunately there are still enough to pretty much see what happened."

"So what did happen?"

"Darned if we know. Looks like Mr. MacDonald drove

somebody here, stood in front of the car, and said, 'Here I am, run over me.' Or else somebody had a gun, forced him out of the car, and told him to walk in front of it. He could have turned back toward them, pleading for his life, and they ran him down instead of shooting him."

All of those pictures made my stomach cramp. But I shook my head. "I can't imagine Skye getting into a car with somebody who was a threat to him. And if he did, I can't see him driving his own car this far down a deserted road and meekly getting out so they could kill him." I'd had a dreadful idea. "There's no way he could have done it himself, is there? Rigged the car or something?"

"He'd have to be some rigger to fix a car so it would drive itself over to the church."

"Maybe somebody found the car here, running, and took it back."

"Without calling for help?"

"Maybe they were scared—a poacher or somebody who had no business being here."

"What poacher would risk being caught driving Mac-Donald's car? Everybody knows it."

I scuffed my shoes on wet grass, trying to get rid of some of the mud and adjust to what he was saying. "You all are calling it murder?"

"About have to, don't we?"

"But you have no idea who could have done it?"

Isaac hesitated so long, I knew he had some internal struggle going on. "Chief Muggins is set on Skell," he admitted at last. "We have several witnesses, including me, who say Skell was pretty upset with his daddy for selling Maynard that car. I ticketed him for speeding last night. He told me all about the car, and said he was so mad at Maynard, he hadn't noticed how fast he was going."

"What time was that?"

"Around ten. Not far from here, either. And he was shaking pretty bad. As you might imagine, the chief isn't too pleased with me for letting him drive away with just a ticket."

"How were you to know at the time it could be important? Besides, can you come up with one reason why Skell would kill his daddy? Surely you don't think he'd run him down over the sale of a car?"

"I don't," Ike agreed, "but Chief Muggins is working on it."

"That skunk," I muttered to myself. "You won't let him get away with it, will you?"

He sighed. "I'm doing what I can, Judge, but you know how things stand. Once he's made up his mind about something, it takes an act of God to change it."

I turned back to my car. "Then it looks like God, you, and me had better get to work."

The courthouse clock chimed eleven as I drove past. I tensed up, waiting for the cheerful carillon, but all I heard was silence. Somebody had had the good sense to turn it off at night.

I stumped into the house and propped both hands on my hips as I stood in the den doorway. "You didn't have to call Isaac."

"So you went on over there." Joe Riddley nodded in satisfaction without even looking up from the television. "Figured you would. You want to go on up to bed, or you want to stay down here and catch the weather?"

I figured I might as well stay up to watch Marilee take a guess.

"She looks a little peaky." Joe Riddley leaned forward to get a better view. He was right. Her red dress and bright lipstick made a valiant attempt to hide it, but Marilee's curls had less bounce, her eyes less sparkle, her nose a suspicious pinkness.

Joe Riddley stumped up to bed, complaining, "She didn't even tell us good night."

"Come here, you old bear," I told him. "I'll do better than that."

⇥ 12 ⇤

Sunday after dinner, little Tad took us to the garage to admire the ferret. Cindy had created a ferret Hilton by filling a large dog cage with boxes to climb on and hide under, bowls for food and water, and a soft blanket to lie on.

After that, Cindy suggested that Jessica show me her room. "The decorator just finished. It's a teenager's room now," she added proudly.

I managed to resist pointing out that the child was scarcely eleven, but when I got there, it took every ounce of willpower I possessed not to exclaim, "Who spilled the Pepto Bismol?"

In addition to new furniture, Jessica had soft pink carpet, pink striped wallpaper, and a comforter and pillow shams that looked like a heap of roses on the bed. A battered brown leather pencil holder beside the computer on her desk looked like a crumb of rye bread on a wedding cake. "Do you like pink?" I asked Jessica, not yet able to meet her eye.

She shrugged. "It's all right." The child's mother had dressed her in pastels and ruffles all her life, but her square chin and a certain firmness around her eyes made me wonder whether she liked them or merely endured them.

"What happened to your dollhouse and your other stuff?" Joe Riddley and I had built that dollhouse for her fourth

Christmas, and added to it each year. We'd envisioned it getting handed down to Jessica's own children.

She tiptoed to her walk-in closet and opened the door like she was giving me a peek at a forbidden magazine. The dollhouse, her favorite dolls, and all her stuffed animals were arranged along the baseboard in a small world of their own. I suspected Jessica would enjoy playing in there with the door closed, anyway. She was a very private little girl.

Next she hurried across the room and laid one hand proudly on her desk. "Don't you love this? Mother wanted a vanity to go with the chest, but Daddy said I could have the desk instead. It's got three drawers for all my stuff. And I have my own phone." It was, of course, an extension of the main line. Not even Walker and Cindy were silly enough to give a child her own phone line, particularly in Hopemore. It was also pink, but I was impressed that Jessica had arranged the room to put the phone on her desk instead of beside her bed. It's exactly what I would have done at her age, if I'd had a phone.

I went over closer to admire it. "It's a lovely desk. I like your pencil holder, too."

"Thanks." Her mouth curved up in happiness. "It was Daddy's. He gave it to me." She adjusted it a fraction of an inch. "You can sit down, if you want," she added casually. She sat on the desk chair and twined one thin leg around its dainty curved one. Of course I sat. I couldn't remember sitting down for a solo chat with this granddaughter since she was seven. But just as I settled into the pink-and-white checked armchair near the window, the telephone rang.

She reached over and picked it up with such a professional air, I suspected she'd been practicing. However, she didn't speak, just listened. Walker and Cindy had better be careful what they said on the phone from now on. I couldn't see her face, but Jessica's back stiffened and she listened intently; then she thrust the receiver toward me like it had grown hot. "You take it."

At first I couldn't understand who it was. The words were fast and garbled, hysterical, even. "Slow down," Walker said from downstairs. "I can't understand you."

"They've arrested 'em." Clarinda's voice was an octave higher than usual. "We gotta do somethin'. Maynard and Selena are both in jail down in Orlando."

"How do you know?" I blurted without bothering to announce I was on the line.

"I'm down at your house bringing back the tablecloths and dishes I borried for Friday night's party, and I answered the phone. Maynard only got one call, and you weren't here."

How was I to know I should hurry home from church so friends could call to tell me they'd been put in jail?

"Tell Mama what you just told me." Walker didn't even complain that I'd butted in.

"Police came to their hotel room this morning around eight, poundin' on the door. They weren't even up yet—it was their wedding night, remember? Said they'd gotten a tip about drugs being smuggled, and they'd found 'em up under the fenders of their car."

I untangled pronouns as she went. "Drugs?" I more breathed than said the word. In my five months as a magistrate I'd had to learn to spell the names of drugs I never knew or wanted to know existed. What used to be a trickle was now spreading up from Florida faster than Noah's flood. However—

"Maynard doesn't use drugs," I snapped, then added, "I don't think." Who knew for sure, in these strange days? I had gone cold all over.

"'Co'rse he doesn't. How can you even think such a thing? And Selena a nurse. Somebody planted 'em. I wouldn't have said they had an enemy in the world, but you never can tell where the forces of darkness will strike next. What we gonna do?" Like a diver on a board, her voice rose on the last word, then plunged.

"Do they have a lawyer?" Walker asked.

"Not yet. I told you, Maynard only got one call, and he didn't know who to call except you folks. And then your mama wasn't even here." She paused for the reproach to sink in. "They haven't had a bite to eat, and they won't let him talk to Selena—he's fit to be tied."

Maynard wasn't the only one.

"Let me talk to Walker a minute, then call you right back. Stay there."

"I'm not goin' anywhere."

I hurried downstairs, where Walker was explaining to Joe Riddley and Cindy what was going on. I collapsed onto the sofa beside my husband and took his hand. "We can't tell Hubert," was the first thing he said. "His heart still isn't strong."

"At least now we know why Skell was so upset when Skye sold that car," I muttered. "He'd hidden drugs in it."

"I don't believe Skell is selling drugs," Joe Riddley insisted.

"You think Maynard is?"

He kept shaking his head. "I don't know what to think. Or even how to think." I knew what he meant. I felt so sick right that minute that somebody ought have called me an ambulance—except nobody else in the room looked well enough to make the call.

Joe Riddley's eyes asked a silent question. I nodded and said, "You need to go to Orlando, Walker. We'll pay for your plane ticket and their bail. This is just damnable. And don't everybody look so shocked," I added. "It's exactly the right word for this situation."

"Sure it is," Cindy hurried to agree.

The way Walker's lips were twitching, he wanted to say

something else—probably related to times when he'd used similar words and had his mouth washed out with soap. "How soon can you leave?" I asked, to forestall him.

"As soon as I can pack a few things. But I'll drive. I'll get there sooner than if I have to drive all the way to Atlanta, park, get through security, and catch a flight. And I've got a college buddy who's a lawyer in Jacksonville. I'll give him a call on the way down and see if he knows lawyers in Orlando."

"Pull off to call," I reminded him. I hate it when people drive and talk. "Anything we can do for you while you're gone?"

Walker skewed his eyes toward his wife. "Do you and the kids want to come?"

She opened her mouth, but Joe Riddley spoke first. "This won't be a vacation, son."

"I agree." Cindy went over and put a hand on Walker's arm. "You go down and do what has to be done. We'll be fine here. Mac and Pop will take care of us." She gave us a brave smile. I had never been prouder or happier to have her for my daughter-in-law.

"Where are you going, Daddy?" Jessica stood in the doorway. None of us knew how long she'd been there.

"I have to go down to Orlando for a day or two."

"Without us? You're going to Disney World without us?" Her voice rose in disbelief.

"I'm not going to Disney World, honey. I have to go on business."

"Maynard's in jail down there," I explained. She'd already heard enough to need to know the rest. "Your daddy has to go help him get out."

"What did he do?"

"Nothing. The police just think he did."

Her eyes narrowed. With both hands on her hips, she

turned back to him. "Don't you dare go to Disney World without us. You hear me?"

Walker guffawed. Cindy covered her mouth with one hand and emitted what sounded to me like a snort. Joe Riddley's shoulders shook, he laughed so hard. "Honey," he asked her, "did anybody ever tell you you're the spittin' image of your Me-mama when you're mad?"

Her face grew pink with indignation. "Don't be silly, Pop. Me-mama's old." She turned back to Walker, hands on her hips. "What are you going to do to help Maynard?" She made it more of a demand than a question.

The rest of them were still grinning like dogs who've spotted dinner.

"Don't worry," I told her. "Your daddy will get down there and straighten everything out."

Jessica believed me. I wished I did.

Walker and Cindy went up to pack, and Joe Riddley challenged Jessica to a game of checkers. I slipped into the kitchen where I'd left my pocketbook and called Isaac James on my cell phone. I called his cell phone, too, because if I remembered correctly, Chief Muggins was at the station this afternoon and Ike was home.

When we'd exchanged the prerequisite greetings a Southern phone call requires, I told him the bad news. "That car Maynard bought Friday was picked up in Orlando this morning with drugs under the fenders."

He groaned. "You tryin' to make me feel worse than I do, Judge?"

"Why? I thought you'd like to know."

"What I know is, I gave Skell MacDonald a speeding ticket on Friday night and let him drive off into the night, with his daddy dead. The chief already wants my hide for that. Now you tell me the car Skell was so worked up over was stuffed with drugs, and you wonder why you've ruined my day? Because this is the one thing we've been missing in this case: a good reason for Skell MacDonald to kill his daddy."

"It wasn't Skell," I protested. "He wouldn't—"

Isaac's words sent a chill to the pit of my stomach. "Don't let your feelings override your good sense, Judge. Chances are about a thousand to one that he did."

❧ 13 ❧

By the time Joe Riddley and I headed home, thick gray clouds had moved in again and trees were being whipped to a frenzy by a wind with icy edges. I was so busy hugging my coat around me in the car and waiting for the heater to kick in, I didn't notice at first that Joe Riddley was heading in the wrong direction. "Honey," I asked tactfully when I realized where we were, "where the dickens are you going?"

"Swinging by MacDonald Motors to be sure everything's okay."

Maybe he was clairvoyant, because just as we got there, we saw Laura's Taurus in the lot and Laura herself walking toward the front door. She wore a navy pantsuit with a white turtleneck, and carried her briefcase as if this were any old workday.

Joe Riddley pulled in beside the Taurus and opened his door. "She oughtn't to be working on Sunday. Her daddy wouldn't like it." He started toward the door at a lope. "Laura? Laura."

After my recent conversation with Isaac, I wanted to see Laura about as much as I wanted to see my oral surgeon, but what could I do but follow the ornery old coot?

Laura turned, surprised but with a welcoming smile. "Hey, Mac. Hey, Joe Riddley." The wind gusted around the corner as she fumbled with her keys. I shivered, and Joe Riddley rubbed his hands to warm them.

"What's the matter with you, coming to work on Sunday?" he fussed. "Your daddy would paddle you."

Laura gave him a sad smile as she turned the key in the lock. "He sure would, and I won't make it a habit. But I had to get out of the house for a little while. It's full of people. Besides, I need to count the money in the safe and get it in the night deposit box, because we're closing tomorrow, too." She held the door wide and invited, "Since you're here, won't you stay for a cup of coffee? I was going to make me some." She added to Joe Riddley, "We've got a new can of Danish cookies." Joe Riddley was partial to Danish cookies.

Before I could protest that we'd just eaten, he'd said, "That would be real nice," and followed her. They both headed for a little alcove at the back of the showroom where there was a coffeepot and a sink.

What could I do but follow them?

While she put the coffee on to brew, I asked, "How's your mother?"

She answered while she filled the pot with water. "Better now. Skell finally called around eight last night. Wanted me to go over and feed his ferret."

Relief and fear came out of my mouth as anger. "Where in the Sam Hill is he?"

"I wish I knew. He was on his cell phone, and the call got dropped almost as soon as I answered. I expected him to call back, but he didn't, then all circuits were busy, and finally his phone rang and rang and he didn't answer." Her voice was discouraged.

"Did you tell him about your daddy?"

"I didn't get a chance. When I answered, he said, real fast, 'Hey, Laura, I'm out of town and I forgot about Marvin. Go feed—' That's when we got cut off."

"And he didn't call back? How could he be so thoughtless?"

Laura shrugged as she measured coffee. "The worst part was, Mama got mad with me for not making him tell me where he was."

"I'll go see her a little later."

"Wait until tomorrow." She pulled out the cookies from an upper cabinet. "Like I said before, the house is full of people today. Gran, Grandy, and Uncle Jack and his family arrived this morning, and everybody who wasn't there yesterday has dropped by this afternoon. It's a real zoo." Laura never had liked crowds of people unless they were in the stands and she on a playing field with a fence in between.

When the coffee was done, Laura looked around, puzzled. "Where . . . ? Oh, I know. The mugs are in Daddy's office." Customers got Styrofoam cups, but friends used "Skye blue" mugs with a little white Model T on them. "I'll be right back."

Generally, Laura had the temperament of a cow I raised as a 4-H project back in fourth grade. My daddy used to say if a tornado picked up that cow, she'd go on chewing her cud, waiting to be set down. Laura had that same gift for taking life pretty much as it came, so we were startled to hear her yell. She ran back with eyes big as salad plates, shaking so she could hardly gasp, "We've been robbed."

She turned and stumbled back to the office with Joe Riddley right behind her.

I followed, of course. What else could I do?

There's a reason I keep asking "what else could I do?" About the time I reached Skye's office, it occurred to me I'd better start practicing what I was going to say to Charlie Muggins when he demanded, "And what were you doing on the scene of *this* crime, Judge Yarbrough?"

A closet door in one corner of Skye's office stood open. The door to a safe at the back of the closet also stood open.

Laura went to the safe and pulled out a sheaf of papers and a little white box. "There's not a penny of cash in here."

She sank into her daddy's big chair and burst into tears, holding the papers and that little white box on her lap. Joe Riddley stood there wishing he was anywhere except where a woman was bawling. I hurried over to pat her on the back with one hand while, with the other, I rummaged around in my pocketbook for a tissue. I also took a quick peek around for a scarf, in case Marilee hadn't been lying, but I didn't really expect to see one, and I didn't.

When I handed Laura the tissue, she sniffed, blew, and managed a watery smile. "Thanks. I guess we'd better call the police." With a sigh, she reached for the receiver.

"Don't use that phone," Joe Riddley ordered. "It may have fingerprints."

"Right." Laura hauled herself to her feet, dropped the papers on the desk, pocketed the little white box, and followed him.

I stood there looking at the telephone, wondering why people always say that. How often do burglars make a phone call from the scene of a crime without gloves on? Chances are, most of them have cell phones anyway.

I was running through a scenario in my head—"Hello, Ma? This is Bill. I just rifled the safe down at MacDonald Motors. Need any groceries from the Bi-Lo on my way home?"—when Joe Riddley called, "Little Bit, what are you doing in there?"

He thought I was detecting, and few things make him madder. "Talking to myself," I called back. "We were having a right interesting conversation."

Laura was talking on the phone at Nicole's desk, rubbing a wisp of hair across her bottom lip. Catching my eye, she dropped it.

As soon as she'd finished talking, Joe Riddley jerked his head toward three big "Skye blue" leather chairs set next to the plate-glass windows so customers could admire the merchandise in comfort. "You all go sit down. We might as well drink that coffee. I'll get it."

"I'll get it." Laura turned toward the coffee room, but he waved her back.

"Sit down, woman. Enjoy being waited on whenever you get a chance."

"He is such a treasure," she told me, wiping her eyes with one sleeve.

"Most days," I agreed, rummaging for another tissue.

"Thanks." She blew her nose. "I don't cry very often, but this—this is too much." She collapsed into one chair and let out her frustration in a long breath. "Everything is such a mess. The house is full of people, Mama can't think straight and keeps wanting Skell to come home, the undertaker wants all sorts of decisions made, and now this." She spread her hands, then let them fall to her thighs with a *plop*.

Joe Riddley came from the back with three steaming cups on a tray, the whole can of cookies, a box of sugar packets, and a small carton of half-and-half. "You even remembered stirrers and napkins," I congratulated him.

He handed me a mug. "Been drinking coffee longer than you've been born. I know what goes with it."

"Stop it, you two," Laura said tolerantly. She knows that picking at each other is one way we show affection.

We were so comfortable, sitting in butter-soft chairs drinking coffee, warm and toasty when it was so chill and gray outside, I could have persuaded myself for a few minutes none of the bad stuff had happened if Laura hadn't observed sadly, "All I wanted to do was count the money and drop it in the overnight depository. Was that too much to ask?"

Something had been bothering me. "Why do you all have cash on the premises? I mean, selling cars isn't like selling bags of feed and tomato plants, and even at Yarbrough's we don't take in much cash anymore. Folks use credit or debit cards, or checks."

She took a swig of coffee and nodded. "Car dealers don't get cash as a rule, but we take in some in the service department and down at Sky's the Limit, some people come in and pay cash for a car. Recently we've even started selling a few on a layaway plan. That was my bright idea." Her mouth twisted in a rueful smile. "It's a lot more trouble than it's worth, but we have so many folks in the county who need transportation and don't have credit, so I persuaded Daddy and Skell to let people pick the car they want and pay ten percent down, then come by after payday each week and pay a little more. In most families, several members pitch in to help. When they've paid fifty percent, we let them take it home and keep paying." She finished her coffee and set the mug down by her chair. "Daddy didn't think it would work, but it has so far. Most folks don't want to lose a car they've already got half paid off, and you have to have a car around here."

She was right about that. Public transportation in Hopemore was limited to school buses.

"Most of them pay on Friday or Saturday," she continued, "so Skell goes to the bank Friday for change; then he makes a deposit Friday night and Saturday afternoon. Yesterday, when we closed early, I threw all the money in the safe without counting it. I hadn't even counted out their Friday take, because I was waiting for him to come back and tell me how much he had on hand Friday to start with."

"We ought to see how somebody got in," I suggested.

Joe Riddley waved me back to my chair. "Leave that to the police."

I rummaged around in my head for something else we could be doing instead of sitting around. "You might call

Ben and see if he heard anything here last night," I suggested. "He didn't leave until late."

"That was Friday," Laura corrected me. "We closed yesterday before four."

"I know, honey, but Ben and his men came back."

Her mug stopped halfway to her mouth. "Came back?"

"Yeah. We ate pie with him last night—at least, we had pie, he had supper—and he said he told the mechanics to pretend to leave, then to come back and finish the cars promised for yesterday. He didn't leave here until he called you last night."

Laura sipped coffee and digested that. "Ben's the best thing that's happened to this business in years."

I hated to burst her balloon, but my own mind was on another track. "Can he get into the safe? If he was here alone toward the end, you don't reckon—?"

I hated to even suggest such a thing. Business owners have to trust our managers. If we didn't, we'd all go crazy. Yet every one of us knows that for all the wonderful employees we have, there's the odd bad one.

Laura was a good businesswoman. She should have at least taken time to think it over, but she didn't take a second to make up her mind. "Ben wouldn't. He just wouldn't."

"Could he get into the safe?" Joe Riddley asked again.

She nodded. "Daddy—" Her voice stopped and she had to clear her throat before she could go on. "Daddy gave him the combination when he made Ben manager, so he could put away the money when we were all out of town. We didn't generally leave much in there," she added. "Daddy usually went by and made a night deposit on his way home. But he didn't like me carrying money around town, so the nights I closed, I left it overnight and we made the deposit the next day."

Joe Riddley set his cup down on the floor beside his

chair with a click. "What about Skell? Could he have borrowed the money before he left town?"

Laura took longer to consider her brother than she'd taken to consider Ben, but her conclusion was the same. "I don't think so. Back when he was in college, he took money from the safe once, and Daddy told him if he ever did it again, he was finished here."

I shivered in the warm air. I could think of one set of circumstances under which Skell would have felt safe taking the money: if he knew his daddy was dead. The way Joe Riddley was suddenly fascinated with something outside the window, I knew he was thinking the very same thing—and probably afraid I'd mention it.

In our silence, Laura's eyes filled with tears again. Angrily she swiped them away. I handed her my third and last tissue and realized I'd have to fetch toilet paper if she kept crying. Come to think of it, I needed to go back to the ladies' room anyway.

She sniffed hard and stood up. "I ought to go wash my face before the police arrive."

That answers the question for people who wonder why women always go to the bathroom in pairs. Most of us wait to go until somebody else suggests it.

Washing my hands reminded me of what I'd overheard on Friday. "Did your daddy and Ben fight a lot?" I asked, trying to sound casual.

Laura turned to me in surprise. "Not a lot, no. Daddy spouted off some—you know how he is. But Ben didn't fight. He's—" She seemed to be searching for the word.

"A totem pole?" I suggested.

I was both surprised and delighted when she laughed. "Exactly." She drew herself up, scrunched herself together at the sides, and spoke without moving her lips. "All wood with an expressive face." She relaxed and gave me an impish smile. "It was three months after I got here before he would reply when I said hello. It took a year before he'd speak to me first, and it's just recently that he'll come to me with a question before he's tried everyone else in the place. I've been back from grad school two and a half years, and I don't think we have exchanged more than three sentences about anything except the business. But I'd trust him with my life. He's honest, reliable, loyal, patient with his men—"

"A real Boy Scout."

"Yeah. A Boy Scout totem pole." She splashed water on her face and grabbed a paper towel to dry it.

I nodded toward the mirror. "Friday, when I was in here washing my hands, I heard your daddy and Ben through that wall. It sure sounded to me like a fight. Ben was fixing Perez's brakes and your daddy wanted him to finish Joe Riddley's tune-up first."

"They argued some," she admitted. She unfastened her hair clasp, ran her hands through each side, and dragged the hair back again. "Daddy liked to micromanage. Wanted to run every little thing himself. Ben likes to make his own decisions. I kept telling Daddy to let him run the service department as he sees fit—Ben always gets cars ready for folks close to the time he's promised them, and people are real satisfied with his work. But Daddy couldn't help meddling from time to time, just to show he owned the place." She gave a watery little laugh. "I don't mean to criticize him, or anything—"

"I knew your Daddy before you were born," I reminded her. "You don't have to explain him to me."

As we left, she looked back toward the sink with a thoughtful expression. "We ought to insulate that wall"— she huffed a sad little sigh—"if Skell doesn't decide to sell the place."

"He wouldn't." I stood still, shocked.

"He might. He's never liked selling cars, and Daddy always said he was going to leave the place to Skell." Her voice was gruff and dreary in the dim hall. As we stepped into the showroom, her eyes roamed around all its shiny cars with a look I'd seen in Joe Riddley's when he stood in Yarbrough's. Laura might sleep across town, but this was home.

I couldn't think of a single comforting thing to say.

We'd barely rejoined Joe Riddley in the chairs out front when a siren wailed up the street and a police cruiser skidded into the small no-parking zone right in front of the door, ignoring empty parking places on each side. Chief Muggins himself climbed from the cruiser, settled his hat on his head, stuffed his hands into the pockets of his leather jacket, and swaggered up the walk. His intent, I guess, was to terrify any burglar who might still be lurking around. Heck, he almost terrified me. Laura shuddered. "I'm so glad you all are here. I couldn't have stood talking to him by myself." She moved forward to open the door for him.

He was walking in when the courthouse clock chimed three. As the carillon followed, a half-minute late as usual, I muttered, "That's the perkiest rendition of 'Come, Labor On' I ever heard."

Joe Riddley grunted. "It's a lot more likely to inspire folks to join God's workforce than the usual tempo." I looked at him in surprise. Maybe the speed of those chimes wasn't accidental. Could the church, like Laura, be trying to appeal to a younger customer?

"Didja hear we know who killed Mr. MacDonald?" Chief Muggins greeted us, wiggling his hips a little to show he was the man in charge.

Laura, who had been locking the door behind him, turned white and grew still.

Joe Riddley asked, "Who was it?"

"Garcia fellow—the one who opened that new restaurant."

"No!" I exclaimed.

Charlie ignored me. "We got a tip this morning that he got lit at the end of his opening night, and bragged, 'If that MacDonald lays a hand on my daughter, I will kill him.'"

"No." Laura's face was screwed up in the same disgust I felt. "Daddy wouldn't . . ."

Charlie shrugged. "Probably not, but you know how those people are—hotheaded, always shooting somebody."

"Those people," I said, emphasizing each word just like he had, "are just like everybody else. Some have hot tempers and some don't. And Skye wasn't shot, he was run over."

"You wear blinders, Judge. That's one of your problems. It's him, all right. We've talked to several witnesses who heard him threaten MacDonald. I've got men out right now looking for him. He killed in cold blood, and he'll pay for it—if he hasn't already escaped back to Mexico."

I counted to ten to control my temper, and gave it up as a lost cause. "Do you have any real evidence against Mr. Garcia?"

"Not yet, but we'll get it. When the paper comes out with its annual crime report in two weeks, we won't have an unsolved violent crime in Hope County for these past six months."

So that's what his hurry was.

I wanted to say, "By all means, then, let's arrest somebody—just anybody—to make that report look good," but Laura was looking real queasy, and I didn't want to prolong the conversation.

Joe Riddley asked in a mild voice, "Has Mr. Garcia disappeared?"

"Folks say he's gone down the road to church, for what that's worth."

"He's probably Catholic," I said, a mite tartly. "It's a good thirty miles to the nearest Catholic church. They aren't real thick on the ground around here, you know." Joe Riddley reached over and poked me between my ribs.

"We'll find him," Chief Muggins assured me. He gave what he may have thought was a lordly wave. Looked more like a polecat swatting flies. "So, what's going on down here *now?*"

You'd have thought Laura was creating a crime a day just to annoy him.

With admirable clarity and restraint she explained.

"I see." He strolled into Skye's office. We all followed. "You all stay back, now. Don't contaminate the crime scene." As if he weren't doing that very thing. "What was in the safe?" He peered inside.

"Just those papers and checks on the desk. The cash was gone." Laura didn't mention the little white box. I only thought of it because she touched her pocket as she spoke.

"How much money was stolen?" Chief Muggins was peering into the safe like that empty hole could say anything at all to his naked eye.

Laura explained again about throwing the money in uncounted both Friday night and Saturday. I could tell he didn't believe her. "You got records of sales, haven't you?"

"Sure, but it will take time to compare them with the register receipts, and I'll have to call the bank tomorrow to find out how much Skell withdrew on Friday."

He stuffed his hands into his jacket pockets and stomped around peering at plaques and pictures. "You think maybe the burglar left a photograph of himself on the wall?" I suggested.

Joe Riddley pinched me where the shoulder meets the neck. I glared at him, but he shook his head. I knew what he was saying: "Don't antagonize him."

I pulled away and went over to examine a green convertible. Maybe I ought to get me a convertible. Some sporty sunglasses, too. Maybe I ought to look for a man who wouldn't pinch or poke me, somebody who would respect my opinions and give me credit when I deserved it. Maybe I ought to find a man who would be willing to admit that Charlie Muggins was a—

"Jackass," muttered a voice at my shoulder. "Little Bit, that man doesn't know a crime scene from a hole in the ground. You stay here with Laura. I'm going to talk to Isaac and see if they've really got anything on Mr. Garcia." I hoped he'd remember where he was going long enough to get there.

"Where's he off to?" Charlie demanded, coming to the door of the office.

I shrugged. "You know how men are. They take all sorts of notions and just leave."

"What I don't understand," he said in that smarmy too-friendly voice he uses when he's about to say something nasty, "is what *you* are doing here, Judge. Returning to the scene of the crime?" He threw back his head and emitted the gargle that passes for his laugh.

"I asked her to be with me while I spoke to you," Laura informed him.

"Laura's had a rough weekend and doesn't need to be badgered," I added. He narrowed his eyes, but before he could think of a good reply, I jerked my head toward the chairs. "Is it okay if we sit over there while you call your deputies to come look for fingerprints?"

He stared at me for the several seconds it took him to process that reasonable suggestion, then nodded. "Sure." He pulled out his cell phone and punched in a number, keeping one eye on us the whole time to make sure we didn't attempt a quick getaway.

⊰ 14 ⊱

Before we sat down, I turned our chairs so they faced outside. Scudding clouds and debris hurtling down the street before the wind were a marked improvement over Charlie Muggins's face. As Laura and I watched, a fine hard rain began spitting against the window.

My spirits were as cold and gray as the view. I liked Humberto Garcia. Had he really killed Skye in the middle of hosting his grand opening? And why had he thought Skye would be interested in his daughter? Sure, Skye often hugged women, but he didn't mean anything by it. He was a big teddy bear, a born flirt.

Mr. Garcia might not understand that, of course. And he could have slipped out while people in the restaurant thought he was in the kitchen and vice versa. But I couldn't picture that plump man moving fast enough to dash through his back door, drive to a rendezvous, go with Skye to that deserted place, run over Skye, get the car back to the church, and return before a single soul noticed he was gone.

I was pulled from those useless ruminations by Laura's voice, full of misery and frustration. "Seems like there ought to be something I could be doing."

"I've got one suggestion. Ask Chief Muggins if you ought to call employees who have been in your daddy's office this past week to come here to be fingerprinted. The police will need their prints to compare with any they find, and it's a lot faster to get them all down here today than for them to go individually by the police station. We've been through this once ourselves. That's how I know."

She pulled a hank of hair to her mouth, then thrust it away angrily. "I don't know why I keep doing that. I haven't sucked my hair since I was a kid."

"Losing a parent makes a kid out of all of us, honey. It's normal to revert to childhood patterns."

Her wide mouth curved in a grin. "And now, Dr. Yarbrough, for your next psychological question . . . But seriously, Mac, who would rob us in the middle of all this?"

I shrugged. "Thieves seldom pick a time to rob based on consideration of what else their victims may be going through." I didn't point out that if Skell had killed his daddy, he wouldn't have feared retribution from Skye for taking the money. He might even have considered the money his.

Her thoughts had been roaming in another direction. "You think it's Ben, don't you? But he wouldn't. He's the most honest, loyal, considerate person—" She turned pink and stopped, a puzzled look in her eyes.

"A Scout," I reminded her. "But Scouts can do bad things, you know."

She turned her head and looked up the street. "He didn't do it," she repeated.

"I never said he did," I pointed out mildly. "But speak of the devil . . ."

Ben's truck had just pulled in behind Chief Muggins's cruiser. His long legs swung down; then he stopped to wait for a half-grown golden retriever to climb awkwardly from the cab. Ben hurried to the door with the pup frolicking at his knee. He tested the door, and when it opened, rushed in. "What's going on?" he demanded of Chief Muggins and Laura equally.

Chief Muggins, who still had his cell phone at his ear, waved Ben toward Laura. He headed our way, calling again, "What's going on?"

Laura stood. Her face was flushed, but when she spoke, both her voice and her posture were those of Laura Mac-Donald, competent vice president of MacDonald Motors addressing her manager. "The safe's been robbed. I didn't make a deposit yesterday, and somebody took the cash."

Ben's dog was at that awkward stage when it still thought of itself as small but was, in fact, almost grown. While its master was absorbing the news, it knocked over a waste-basket and brushed brochures off a low table with its tail. Ben bent to retrieve the brochures, muttering, "Sorry about that."

Laura bent to scratch the dog behind the ears. "No harm done. Good boy."

The good boy raised his head and uttered a series of sharp barks. "That's how he says 'hello,'" Ben explained, and now it was his turn to flush. "Hush, Scout."

"Scout?" Laura looked down at me, eyes dancing. "As in Boy Scout?"

I looked out the window so Ben wouldn't see my face.

The pup pranced around, wagged his tail, and toppled a potted dracaena, spilling dirt all over the gray rug. "No, Scout!" Ben said sharply. The pup ran and cowered behind the nearest car. "I'm so sorry." Even more red-faced, Ben began to brush up the dirt with his hands.

Laura squatted and whistled softly. Scout peered around a fender. When she held out her hands, the pup came right to her. She cradled its muzzle between her hands. "You are a pretty boy. Yes, you are. A beautiful fellow. You just aren't ready to work in a grown-ups' place, are you?" She twisted his head gently, in fun. Scout, delighted, lunged to lick her on the nose. She wasn't expecting it, and toppled backwards. Laughing, she rolled over to dodge his caresses, then sat up and roughed his ears with both hands. "You got past the goalie and scored, big dog."

If Ben's face got any redder, we could hang him over Oglethorpe street and save the cost of a new stoplight. He offered her a hand, but she climbed to her feet unaided. Then she said, "Mac here says you worked late again last night. You didn't have to do that." She sounded gruff.

Ben sounded equally gruff. "People needed their cars."

"You didn't see or hear anybody out front here, did you?"

He shook his head. "No, we had a radio on." He looked over at Charlie Muggins again, then checked his watch. "Listen, I've got some paperwork to catch up on, so I'll be in the back a while. Give a holler if you need anything."

"They may want you to come give your fingerprints, since you've been in the front office this past week."

He nodded shortly. "Let me know when." He pivoted on one heel. "Come on, Scout."

She murmured as we watched him go, "He may be carved from oak, but I truly do not know what I would do without Ben. If they could clone him—"

I interrupted. I'd been thinking while she and the pup were fooling around. "What about Nicole? She's was in and out of your daddy's office all the time. She might have picked up the combination to the safe if he left it lying around."

Laura shook her head. "I doubt she'd know how to work a combination. She's not long on mechanical skills." Her voice was indulgent, not critical. But she sighed as she took her seat. "The problem is, I like my folks. I don't want to think any of them would do this to us."

"Why did you hire Nicole?" I'd wondered that since I first saw the young woman prance into Skye's office.

Laura slid down in her chair and stuffed her hands in her pockets with the thumbs sticking out. "I didn't hire her. I went away for a couple of days to a meeting, and when I got back, Daddy had hired her. She'd come in with a real hard-luck story—her mother's terminally ill and she's got a younger brother and sister to support—and Daddy said we'd been needing a secretary around here." Laura gave me her lazy grin. "As you saw, that's not what she's best at, but it turned out she's real good with customers."

"Particularly men?"

"Oddly enough, no. I mean, she flirts with the men, but she's even better with women. She starts talking hair; then they tell her their life's story, and the next thing you know she's sold them rust protection, calmed them down about their car not being serviced yet, and even persuaded them to trade in their old car and lease a new one. She earns her pay." From Laura, that was high praise.

One word puzzled me, though. "Hair?"

"Yeah. She went to cosmetology college before she started here. She says she wants to own her own shop someday. She might even be good at it. I've heard her giving a couple of women advice about their hair that they followed, and they've all looked great. It was Nicole who persuaded Mama to cut her hair. Told her she'd look younger with it short and soft around her face, and she was right, too, wasn't she?"

"She looks beautiful," I agreed.

Laura chewed her lower lip, then blurted, "Nicole wants to cut this mane of mine real short. What do you think?" Her voice was casual, but her eyes were anxious for a second opinion.

I've never been fond of grown women with hair streaming down their backs like little girls or college students. But I've also never been fond of other people telling me what to do with my hair. "I think you only ought to do it if you think you'd like it, but if you try it and don't like it, it will grow back. Hair is like grace. It's real forgiving."

"I'm thinking about it." She tugged on a hank and gave it a dubious look. "I've kept it long because it's so easy to fix, but Nicole says—"

Charlie Muggins finished his telephoning and called over to us without waiting to see if anybody was talking. "I'm goin' outside to wait for the fellows. We'll be back real soon."

"You are going outside to smoke, and two of your fellows are women," I said after he'd pushed his way out the heavy front door. Laura swallowed a snort of laughter.

"You were saying that Nicole wants her own beauty shop," I prompted her. "But if that's true, why is she working here?"

"She told me it's hard to get started as a beautician, and she needs a steady income right now. Does that seem a bit flimsy? I mean, other beauticians start out and make a living at it."

"Honey, just like you, I got out of college and went straight into a family business. I've never had to find a job before I starved."

"In other words, we don't have a clue how the rest of the world lives. That's one of the few things Ben ever said to me before today that wasn't related to work. His dog's cute, isn't it?" She wiggled in her chair to get more comfortable, but I suspected her fidgets were internal. "You know, Mac, Nicole looks ornamental, but there's a woman under all that fluff who knows what she wants and goes after it. Sometimes I envy her."

"Don't be silly. You've already done more with your life than she's likely to ever do with hers. In a year she'll have a husband, in two years she'll have her first baby, and in ten she'll have three kids and a spreading waistline and still probably be working for somebody else."

"Where will I be? Tell me that." Her voice was clogged with unshed tears. "Skell's going to sell this business. I know he will. But I can't buy it. I thought I'd have years to save—"

"Maybe your daddy left it to both of you."

"He wouldn't. Daddy didn't think a 'woman alone' "—her hands sketched the parentheses, but I already knew it was Skye's phrase; I could hear him saying it—"ought to own and run a business. Said next thing we all knew I'd get married, move out of town, and sell the whole shebang." A tear glistened on her lower eyelid and spilled over. She swiped it away, angry. "I don't want to move out of town. I like it here. And Daddy never stopped to consider that Skell might sell the business because he hates it." She ducked her head and glowered at her toes, angry and brokenhearted.

I had no idea how to comfort her. Laura had never even had a beau, that I knew of, so I couldn't assure her in good conscience that she'd meet a man and marry him anytime soon. I couldn't defend her daddy's position, because it made me mad enough to spit. And I sure couldn't say anything against her daddy with him lying across town waiting to be buried. The best thing I knew was to keep quiet while she pretended not to cry.

After a while she heaved an enormous breath, swallowed, and slid up so her back was straight. "So, you think I ought to call anybody who's been in Daddy's office this week, to come get their prints taken?"

"Ask Chief Muggins."

She got to her feet with resolution and strode to the front door. Chief Muggins was sitting in his car with the windows cracked. Wisps of smoke floated regularly through the cracks and rose above the car like little signals. Laura didn't go out into the drizzle, just put her head out and shouted the question. I saw him take two quick puffs, then nod.

"He says yes," Laura called over to me. "I'll need to get the directory from my office—no, Daddy's got one." She hurried into Skye's office, but came out to Nicole's desk to make the calls. "You need anything?" she asked before she began. "More coffee? A Coke?"

"I'll be fine right here." I'd rather have a week on a Greek isle, but a snooze would do.

Charlie's crew arrived before Laura finished. Then her employees straggled in, one by one, dabbed prints on the deputy's cards and left. I watched everything from my chair, proud of Laura. As hard as it was for her, she stood right there and greeted everybody. Most of them—deputies and employees alike—said, "I sure was sorry to hear about this," or "Is there anything I can do?" Like a trooper, Laura accepted their sympathy and told them she'd call if she needed anything.

Nicole pranced in wearing black ski pants that left little to the imagination and a tight blue sweater under a black parka she'd left open. Every man in the place stood up straight and sucked in his stomach while she was there.

"I wish I could stay," she told Laura after she'd had her prints taken, "but I'm in the middle of giving a perm." Given how long she had taken to drive over and back and flirt with the deputy (he took twice as long getting her prints as he spent on anybody else), we'd all recognize whoever was getting that perm.

Laura finally came back and dropped into a chair beside me. "Want me to run you home?"

"I'm kind of stuck," I told her. "I've got the cell phone in my pocketbook, so I can't call Joe Riddley to let him know I'm leaving. I'll just have to wait for him. But I'm fine. Go do what you have to."

"I don't have anything to do." I had never seen her at such a loose end. Again she dragged a hank of hair to her lips.

"The sooner you cut off that hair the better," I told her. "But what will you suck instead?"

As I'd hoped, she grinned. "Heaven only knows. Maybe I'll become a nail biter." She held out her big hands and considered them.

"Don't. You've got lovely nails. I wish mine grew in ovals. Bite your toenails, instead. At least you'll know when you're doing it."

We laughed together, then Laura stopped. "It doesn't seem right to be joking when—"

"When your daddy's dead, your business has been robbed, and your brother's vanished? Honey, that's when you've got to laugh. Now, listen to me a minute. I've been thinking, and I've got some questions I want to ask you."

She lowered her voice so the deputies couldn't hear. "You don't think Mr. Garcia killed Daddy, do you? I don't, either. I can't imagine why he should. Are you going to try to find out who did?"

"Joe Riddley would kill me if he heard I'd said yes to that question, and Ridd would kill me a second time if *he* came home and found out. No woman ought to die twice, so let's just say I hate to see a customer who bought a truckload of plants go to jail before his check has cleared the bank."

She gave me the faintest of smiles, then looked out the plate-glass window where the dark clouds had faded imperceptibly into twilight. As we watched, streetlights flickered, then started to burn a steady yellow glow.

"That's what we need—light on this subject." I leaned closer and murmured, "I hate to pry, but what did you take from the safe? You know better than to remove anything from the scene of a crime."

"Yeah, but—" She fumbled in the pocket of her blazer, brought out the little white box, and held it on her palm. "I think I know what this is, and I don't want them confiscating it for evidence. Today's the thirtieth anniversary of when

Mama and Daddy got engaged, and this is a jeweler's box. Let's see what's inside." From the white box she took a black ring box. When she opened it, we both gasped. A large white solitaire lay on a bed of soft blue velvet. She looked at it for a long time without making a sound. Her eyes reddened, but she didn't cry. "It's the last thing Daddy ever bought her. Do you see any harm in taking it home to her?"

I turned away. "Don't ask me, Laura. I'm an officer of the court. Get rid of that before I look at you again."

"Okay, it's gone." She sighed. "I hope I'll never live through another weekend like this. Where the dickens is Skell when I need him?"

That made me real sorry to have to bring up my next subject. "I know you don't want to hear this, honey, but we have to face the possibility that Skell may have killed your daddy and run. Maybe it was an accident, maybe he's off his rocker, or maybe it's a little of both. At the very least, he seems to have been trafficking in drugs."

"Drugs?" She stared like I'd started speaking some ancient tribal language.

I wriggled in my chair, which felt lumpy with everything I had to tell her. "Maynard and Selena were arrested this morning down in Orlando, because somebody called the police and reported that the car your daddy sold Maynard Friday had drugs under the fenders." Her eyes widened, but I went right on. "The police found them, and Maynard and Selena are both in jail."

"Oh, no." She pressed a hand to her cheek.

"Oh, yes. Walker is on his way to Orlando right now to see about getting them out. Remember how frantic Skell was to get that car back before Maynard drove it away?"

"Skell wouldn't—"

"Honey, since I became magistrate I've seen things that have straightened my perm. You can't say for sure what anybody would or wouldn't do when drugs are involved.

And if Skell is trafficking in drugs, and your daddy found out—"

She shrank back in her chair like she couldn't get far enough away from me. "He wouldn't *kill* Daddy. He *wouldn't*." Her voice rose.

"What's going on?" Ben Bradshaw stood over me before I knew he was coming. His frown was like thunder. Scout stood stiff-legged beside him, fangs bared, looking hopefully at my throat.

"Call off your dog," I said with what voice I could muster.

"Mac thinks . . . Mac thinks Skell may have been dealing drugs"—Laura's voice was equally strangled, but from outrage, not fear—"and that he could have killed Daddy when Daddy found out. And then he robbed the safe—"

She ran out of air and story at the same time, and sat looking up at Ben with a white, stricken face.

"I didn't say he *did* all that," I reminded her. "I said we have to consider the possibility."

Ben glared, his expression no friendlier than Scout's. I hurried to explain. "Drugs were found in the car Skye sold Maynard. I'm just pointing out to Laura that the drugs, coupled with Skell's disappearance and the missing money, raise some questions. That's all."

"That's enough." If I'd thought he would agree with me, I could think again. "Don't bother her. She's had all she can stand." He dropped a big hand on Laura's shoulder, snatched it away like he'd been burned, and shoved the hand in his pocket. "Lock up and go home. You don't need to be down here right now, in the middle of all this."

He glared at me, making it clear that I was a big part of the "this" he had in mind. Scout growled his agreement low in his throat.

Laura looked from Ben to me, then back again. It was clearly not the time to continue our conversation.

⊰ 15 ⊱

I asked one of the deputies to run me home, figuring I could get my car and go find Joe Riddley. Instead, his silver Lincoln shone wet and glistening under our halogen light, next to my Nissan. "Parked me and forgot where he left me," I joked as I wriggled down from the truck.

"Good-bye, Judge." That deputy had called me "Miss Mac" back when he'd had to stretch to put his pennies in our gumball machine, but Joe Riddley had insisted on formal titles with law-enforcement officers, and I maintained the tradition.

"Good-bye, Officer Wilkes. Thanks again."

When I got inside, I discovered I'd forgotten to put my scuffs in the closet when we left that morning. That dratted macaw had tried to make a meal out of one and pooped on the other. I stomped angrily toward the sound of the television in the den, figuring that where I found Joe Riddley, I'd find Joe. Then I'd decide which one to throttle.

My husband was stretched out in his recliner watching Sunday golf, dressed for comfort in a shapeless old gray sweat suit. Joe was prancing along the back of the den sofa. "Where in tarnation have you been?" Joe Riddley demanded without looking away from the screen. "Your car's here, but you weren't. Nearly scared me to death. I was fixing to call the police as soon as this match is over."

I knew at once what had happened: worry had short-circuited his system and erased his memory tapes from that afternoon. A counselor who met with me a few times after Joe Riddley got shot had explained that could happen for a while. She'd suggested that when he had a brief memory lapse, I ought to make a statement repeating his words. That would make him think about what he'd said, and get him back on track. So, instead of saying, "You idiot, you left me at MacDonald's and forgot me," I said, "You couldn't find me here."

Joe Riddley glared like I was the one with the weak brain. "That's what I just *said*. Where were you?"

"Over at MacDonald Motors, waiting for you." I rested one hand on his shoulder. The counselor had also said touch can put a person in touch with reality. She'd never lived with Joe Riddley's reality.

My loving husband smacked away my hand and pointed out in a disgusted voice, "We picked up my car already. And MacDonald's isn't open on Sunday. You can't remember a danged thing lately." He turned his attention back to the champions on the seventeenth hole.

Joe had been sidestepping back and forth along the wide back of the sofa. When I looked his way, he scuttled to the far end and got very busy preening his breast. "You ruined my slippers, bird," I informed him. "I am going to tear you limb from feather."

He bobbed his head and squawked.

"Hush, Little Bit," Joe Riddley growled. "You're bothering me."

That was one more drop than my bucket could hold right then. I climbed the stairs feeling like I'd spent the weekend fighting a bear. I took off my Sunday blue wool suit and pulled on a warm red sweat suit of my own. The only other slippers I owned, which I'd stuck far back in my closet for obvious reasons, were bright green furry ones with big wiggly eyes that Bethany bought for my birthday with her own money when she was ten. I gave a mental shrug as I shoved my feet into them. Who would see me tonight except Mr. Fashion Plate downstairs?

He didn't even notice I'd left and come back, much less that I had changed clothes. I rescued our afghan from under a couch cushion where I'd started hiding it from Joe, slipped off the slippers, lay down, gave Joe a warning look that he'd better not mess up my hair, and covered myself with pure love. Mama crocheted that afghan the last year of her life, choosing bold primary colors in defiance of the grayness that was closing around her.

Joe Riddley's attention was riveted to the green on the screen.

Joe took four sideways steps across the back of the couch, looked at my bright covering, raised one claw, and bobbed his head a couple of times. "You keep your claws off this afghan, you hear me?" I told him. His big white eye glared at me for a long second, but he sidestepped away. I may not have a face that will launch a thousand ships, but I have a glare that will occasionally stop a parrot.

In a few minutes I roused enough to go call Gwen Ellen. We chatted briefly, but she said Skye's relatives would all be there until the next morning, so we both decided I wouldn't go back out in the rain to see her until they had gone. I rested until the golfers were replaced by a commercial. "Did you talk to Ike about Humberto Garcia?" I asked Joe Riddley, adding, "You went to look for him after Charlie Muggins found the safe rifled at MacDonald Motors, which was right after Walker left to get Maynard out of jail in Orlando."

"I know that. But I couldn't find Ike, so I came on back home. You weren't here."

There wasn't any point in going down that road again.

"You want eggs and bacon for supper?" I was so tired I wasn't sure I could cook even that much.

"That's what we had last night," he reminded me.

I got up, put back on my green slippers, and plodded to the kitchen. When I was out of earshot with a closed door between us, I pounded the countertop with both fists. "Lord, how can he remember what he had for supper last night, but can't remember where he left his wife a couple of hours ago?"

I didn't expect God to answer. I just needed to ask the question.

I rummaged in the freezer to see what leftovers Clarinda had frozen in the past couple of weeks. Thank goodness for a cook, a microwave, a daughter-in-law, and quick foods. I thawed and heated two helpings of beef vegetable soup, opened a jar of applesauce Martha had canned back in the fall, and rummaged around for a package of Jiffy cornbread mix I knew we had somewhere. By the time somebody on TV had made ten times our annual income by knocking one small ball into a hole, I was setting supper on the table.

I was fixing to call Joe Riddley to eat when the phone rang. Without wasting breath on unnecessary things like saying who she was, Clarinda demanded, "Walker get to Orlando yet?"

The clock over the refrigerator said 6:30. "He hasn't had time."

"I hope he's driving fast. I hate to think of those babies spending the night in jail. You hear such awful things—"

I'd heard the same awful things, and I didn't like the idea of Maynard and Selena in jail any more than she did, but since she'd said it first, it was my turn to offer comfort. "Walker's driving as fast as he can. He ought to be there around ten or eleven."

"You call me soon as you hear anything, okay? And if he doesn't call you, you call him on his cell phone and find

out what's going on. Then you call me." Having given me
my marching orders, she hung up.

Joe Riddley and I ate in the companionable silence of
two people who are generally fond of each other but don't
have to say so all the time. Afterwards, he did the dishes
while I thumbed through our week's catalogues. He was
washing the soup pot when we heard a car splash down our
drive. I opened the back door so whoever it was could run
right in, but nobody was there. A second later, the front
doorbell rang. Nobody, and I mean nobody, ever comes to
our front door.

I flicked on the porch light. Through the beveled glass
pane in the top of the door, I saw Rosa Garcia. She shivered
in a light trench coat that wasn't half warm enough in that
weather. Her face looked pinched and miserable.

I flung the door wide open. "Miss Garcia. Come in."

She stepped in, hair plastered to her cheeks and coat sop-
ping. Her thick braid hung down her back like a heavy wet
rope. "I look a mess." Her teeth chattered like castanets in
the unheated hall.

I waved one hand down my red sweats and green fuzzy
slippers. "I look like a refugee from Christmas. Come into
the back, where it's warm. Our furnace is on zones, and we
don't heat the front unless—" I was about to say "we have
company," but she was company. "Why didn't you wear a
heavier coat? Or bring an umbrella?"

"I came so quickly—" She stopped, eyes anxious and
shoulders high with tension. "I am embarrassed to have
come at all, but I thought—I hoped—" She stopped.

I hurried down the hall to the bathroom and grabbed a
towel for her hair. As I passed the den, I snatched up
Mama's afghan. "Take off that soaking coat and wrap up in
this. It will warm you up in just a second. Then step into
the bathroom and dry your hair. I'll throw your coat in the
dryer and make us all some cocoa." People always talk best

at our big round oak table with a cup of hot chocolate in front of them.

"Thanks." She handed me the sodden coat and pulled the afghan around her shoulders. It made her plain black dress look very festive. She didn't bother to go into the bathroom, but tugged out the rubber band that held her braid and loosened the plait into a curtain that covered her shoulders. She toweled it vigorously, then started to replait it with deft hands.

"Leave it down to dry," I suggested, taking the damp towel, "and come on into the kitchen."

While I went to the utility room to put her coat in the dryer and the towel in the hamper, Joe Riddley turned from drying his hands. "Why, hello, Miss Garcia."

If she was surprised to see a man in a yellow apron finishing the supper dishes, she didn't mention it. She just said, "Please call me Rosa."

"I'm Joe Riddley, and that's MacLaren over there." He shook hands, then took off his apron and hung it in the closet.

"Hello, hello!" Joe called from his perch on the curtain rod above the sink.

Rosa gasped in delight, and the tense skin around her eyes crinkled into a smile. "He is beautiful. Would he come to me?"

"Hold out your arm. We'll see," Joe Riddley told her. While I busied myself pouring milk into a saucepan, Rosa shoved up the long sleeve of her dress and held out one thin arm. Joe flew down and perched there.

She stroked his back. "I had a parrot when I was a girl." She had a catch in her voice. "Pedro, an African gray who used to turn almost upside down to talk to you. He'd call *Hola! Hola!*—that's Spanish for 'hello'—when anybody came to the house. He was stolen from our backyard when I was twelve, and I cried myself to sleep for a week."

"Not to worry. Not to worry," Joe consoled her, bobbing his head several times.

Her laugh was merry. "You are wonderful."

"Good Joe. Good Joe," he agreed, raising one claw to show he could stand on one foot.

"He knows what I'm saying?"

"Sure he does," Joe Riddley told her. "That's one smart bird."

I stirred powder into the milk, poured steaming cocoa into yellow mugs, and added three marshmallows each. When Miss Garcia got hers, she seemed to be waiting for something. "Do you need something else?" I inquired, wondering if Clarinda had left cookies on Friday. She'd almost stopped making them now that the boys were gone and I was getting what Joe Riddley kindly called "voluptuous."

Embarrassed, Miss Garcia took a quick sip. "No, of course not. It's just that we put cinnamon in chocolate. . . ."

She showed us how to sprinkle it on top, and it tasted real good.

Joe Riddley fetched Joe some peanuts, seeds, dried fruit, and vegetables from his treats jar and put them on the green plastic place mat at what we'd come to call "Joe's place." Joe marched around and around the mat picking up nibbles, then stopped and looked at the rest of us for praise.

As we sat at the table sipping our cocoa, Rosa talked to Joe. "You're a pretty bird, aren't you? Yes, you are. Want a peanut?" She laughed aloud in surprise and delight when he pecked it off her finger. I was glad to see her face losing its pinched gray look.

"Thank you. Thank you." He turned his head halfway around and searched for mites on his rainbow back, as if being fed by beautiful women was his daily routine.

I thought it was time she told us what she'd come for. "What can we do for you?"

She took a deep breath. "I truly am embarrassed. I would never have come, except for this. Even then, you may think I'm silly." She opened her black shoulder bag and pulled out a folded piece of notebook paper. I recognized Jessica's handwriting. Under the title "A Person I Admire," Jessica had written:

> *I admire my grandmother, Judge MacLaren Yarbrough, because she is smart. She is even a detective! When we have mysteries in town the police cannot solve, she finds out the answers and tells them. She even captures murderers, but my daddy does not like for her to do that because he says she will get herself killed, too, one day. I don't think she will. She is too smart. So if you ever have a mystery you need solved, call my grandmother. She will solve it for you faster than the police!*

I read with Joe Riddley peering over my shoulder. "She got that right." He pointed at *she will get herself killed, too, one day.*

I felt proud and embarrassed all at the same time, but I had to tell the truth. "Honey, this is real exaggerated." I handed back the paper. "I mean, I've helped the police with a few cases—"

"—and nearly got herself killed," Joe Riddley added sourly.

"Sic 'em. Sic 'em," Joe advised.

Rosa put the paper back in her purse. "I don't know who else to turn to. When we came back from church this afternoon, the police came to our house and took my father down to the station. They asked him all sorts of questions, and while they let him come home afterwards, he thinks they believe he killed Mr. MacDonald."

Joe Riddley wasn't as good as he used to be at keeping

important confidences. "Chief Muggins mentioned that this afternoon."

Rosa leaned toward me, an urgent look in her dark eyes. "You don't believe that, do you? What reason would he have? He didn't even know the man. Besides, everyone says Mr. MacDonald was killed Friday evening, and *Papi* was at the restaurant until nearly two, cleaning up and closing out the register. Then we went home exhausted and fell into bed. But even if he was out and about for a little while, my father would never kill a man."

I stirred my cocoa and gave her a thoughtful look. "I understand, though, that he was making threats to 'kill that MacDonald if he lays a hand on my little girl.' "

She lowered her gaze to the tabletop. "That was just wild talk. It was all my fault. I should never have told him—"

She paused so long that Joe Riddley got curious. "Told him what?"

A soft pink rose in her cheeks. "*Papi* is very old-fashioned. He doesn't think a man should ask a woman to dinner before he has met her parents."

I was dumbfounded. "Skye asked you to dinner?"

She wrinkled her forehead. "I thought his name was Skeleton." She gave a delicate shudder. "What kind of mother would name her son that?"

Relief would have buckled my knees if I hadn't been already sitting. "You mean Skell? His name is Skellton, with two *l*'s and one *e*, S-k-e-l-l-t-o-n. It was his mother's maiden name."

"Kids tried to call him 'Bones' in school," Joe Riddley acknowledged, "but Laura beat the tar out of them."

"Oh." She sounded thoughtful and more than a little relieved.

To my surprise, Joe Riddley was the one who got us back on track. The way his mind had been working for the past six months, it could have wandered off in four other directions. Instead, he said, "Skell's been asking her to dinner. What about that, Little Bit?"

I knew why he sounded so pleased. The girl Skell had hoped to marry after college had decided she'd rather join the peace corps, and it broke his heart. Folks in Hopemore had shoved every eligible girl we knew his way since then, but he'd never done more than be polite to them at parties.

Rosa hadn't said a word, so I nudged her a tad. "Skell has been asking you out?"

She nodded, looking into her cocoa.

"How did you meet?" She looked like she needed more than a nudge.

"*Mami* asked me to take one of her kitchen crew to Sky's the Limit a couple of weeks ago, to look for a car. Skellton helped us. Inez's English isn't very good, and I went along to translate for her, but to our surprise, he spoke very good Spanish."

"It was his college major," Joe Riddley told her. "He went to Mexico on spring break once, too—helped build a school or something."

"That's what he said. He gave Inez a good deal on a car, and while she was signing papers, we talked a bit. He asked if I'd have dinner with him that night, but I had a meeting at the school, and couldn't." She stopped, and smiled a private little smile into her cup. "Last Thursday, our cars were side by side in the Bi-Lo parking lot. He was getting out of his as I returned to mine, and he gave me a big smile and said in Spanish, '*Hola.* Remember me? I sold you a car. Can you have dinner with me tonight?' I told him I was busy helping my father get ready to open on Friday, and joked that I don't need to go to dinner, because my father owns a restaurant. We laughed, and that was all there was to it." Her lower lip trembled. "But on Friday night, he called me 'Rosita,' as if we were familiar with one another, and *Papi* heard him. After that, *Papi* insisted that I tell how

I knew an Anglo man. He"—she hesitated—"he's determined I will go out only with Mexicans. When he grew up, his family were farmworkers. His little sister was raped by the son of one of his employers, and ever since then he is certain Anglo men have only one thing in mind when they approach Mexican women. Skellton should never have used that familiar name. . . ." Her eyes were huge pools of misery.

"Oh, honey," I told her, "he never meant a thing by that. He probably meant it as a sign he'd met you before."

"Maybe so, but *Papi* will never believe it. Late that night, when just our friends were left in the restaurant, *Papi* told his friend that Skellton MacDonald was making advances toward his daughter. The friend said, 'Oh, the MacDonalds are very rich. Little Rosita is doing very well for herself." She blushed. "I don't want to tell you this, but you need to understand what happened. *Papi* was a bit drunk by then, and he got very grand. He is descended from Santa Ana, and sometimes he thinks that makes him very important. He started swearing that his daughter will only marry the very best Mexican, and yes, he said what they say he did, 'If that MacDonald lays a hand on my little girl, I will kill him.' But he didn't mean it." Her voice ended in a cry of despair. Her big dark eyes swam with tears again, and she covered them with slender fingers.

I didn't think so, either, but I wasn't on the jury. A clever lawyer can do all sorts of things with a statement like that. "Your daddy's best hope is to prove he never left the restaurant," I advised her. "See if you can get people who can swear he was there at—say—fifteen minute intervals."

She took her hands away from her face, but lowered her gaze to the tabletop. "I—I will have to see who is willing to swear he was there." For some reason, the idea seemed to bother her. I wondered if some folks might not want to go to court for reasons connected with their own legal status. As an officer of the law, I wasn't about to ask that question.

Joe Riddley hadn't said much so far. Now he leaned forward, the overhead light making caverns of his dark eyes. "Skell MacDonald's a fine young man."

"Yes." Rosa got up and walked over to the window, looked out into the stormy night, then began to move restlessly about the room. "But he had no right to call me Rosita as if we were friends." She clutched the afghan tight about her. "He is just bored here. I have heard other teachers say that. If I did go out with him, he wouldn't be less bored. What would we talk about? We have nothing at all in common." She came to the table and reached for her cocoa, still standing and tapping one foot.

Poor Skell. She was lovely and exotic. No wonder he was attracted. But his parents might have as much trouble with him dating a Mexican as her father had with her dating a *gringo*—was that the right word? I was a little shaky on the difference between an Anglo and a *gringo*.

I rose and refilled our mugs. Rosa carried hers restlessly about the room, looking at the pictures on our walls and the magnets and cartoons on our refrigerator. It occurred to me that ours might be one of the few homes she'd been inside in Hopemore. But she had heavier things on her mind. She whirled to face me at last. "If we find people who will swear where we were every fifteen minutes that evening, will the police chief be just and fair?"

I couldn't tell her a lie, so I hesitated. Joe Riddley considered, then nodded. "I think a jury will be. If you tell the truth. But tell me something else. How'd your folks decide to settle in Hopemore and open a restaurant?"

This was safe ground. Rosa came back to her chair and sat down. "They've wanted a restaurant for years. They have both worked in restaurants most of their lives—met in one, in fact. My brother and I grew up hearing them say,

'When we have our own restaurant, we will do this or that.'" She waved a graceful hand over the table; then her eyes grew anxious again. "But now, when their dream has come true, I have spoiled it for them." Fat tears rolled down her cheeks, and Joe Riddley glared at me like her crying was all *my* fault.

I fetched the box of tissues I keep on the counter. "How did the dream finally come true?"

She blew her nose and gave me a watery smile. When she began to speak again, I saw why Jessica adored her. Rosa Garcia was a born storyteller, animated and funny, who used her hands to make the story come alive.

"My brother was a terrible student. He couldn't do math or language arts. But he loved skateboarding, surfing—anything that involved taking risks. When he graduated, he became a stuntman in Hollywood. Now they pay him ridiculous amounts of money for doing things *Mami* used to spank him for doing. And he told her, '*Mami*, if you promise not to tell me to stop what I'm doing, I'll give you the money to start your restaurant.' That's how they got to open it."

"Why did they come to Hopemore?" Joe Riddley wanted to know.

"They took a vacation between quitting their jobs and starting the restaurant. They rented a little RV and drove here and there, looking for the perfect spot. One day they saw a sign on the freeway for Hopemore. He told *Mami*, 'Let's go see this place. We have more hope now than we've ever had, so we should visit Hopemore.' They stayed a week last summer, in the campground just outside of town. They met many Mexicans who were settling here. They liked the climate and the size of the town. After southern California, this is so restful. They also learned that the steak house was thinking of closing. They called me and said, 'Rosita, come see this place. Tell us what you

think.' When I came, I learned that Jessica's school needed
a teacher. When I got the job, it seemed a sign from God
that this was where we were supposed to be." She stopped
and her lower lip started to tremble. More tears filled her
eyes. "Now, because of me, everything is in jeopardy."

"Nothing is in jeopardy if your father can prove he never
left the restaurant," I reminded her.

She looked down at the table and said nothing.

Joe Riddley had another question. "You haven't seen
Skell since yesterday, have you?"

She shook her head. "Not since Friday night, when he
ran into me."

"He didn't mean to," I assured her. "He was dashing out
to find a man who'd bought a car. I don't know if he even
saw you until he practically knocked you down." Yet I remembered the way his eyes had roved the restaurant when
he first came in. Had he been looking for Rosa? Or were
we all putting ideas into Skell's absent head? Under our
strong kitchen light, she wasn't as beautiful as she'd looked
in the subdued lighting of her father's restaurant. Sure, her
eyes were dark and lovely, and she had that long black hair
that rippled like a river nearly to her waist. But her mouth
was prim, her nose a trifle long and hooked, her chin a little
too pointed for beauty.

"Oh," she said in obvious relief. A smile lit her face and
her eyes, making her suddenly beautiful. "I thought he'd
decided if he couldn't bowl me over one way, he'd try another."

She might be right. I was sure that Skell—who hated dull
little Hopemore—found her a lot more interesting than our
conventional Southern belles.

"I ought to get home." She stood and unwrapped my old
afghan from around her like it was mink. "Thank you so
much." She folded it and laid it over the back of her chair,
her mouth prim again. "Just talking with you helps me feel

better. I will tell my father we must find people who will swear he didn't leave the restaurant all evening. Thank you so much."

I brought her raincoat, which was dry and warm, and Joe Riddley walked her out under the same umbrella he'd used the day before for Nicole.

While he was gone I realized something. Twice that evening Rosa had said she would look for people who could swear her daddy never left the restaurant. She never said he hadn't.

❧ 16 ❧

I couldn't think of another thing I could do that night for either the Garcias or the MacDonalds, and was debating between watching television with Joe Riddley or going to bed with my electric blanket and a book when the phone rang. A sheriff's deputy needed me down at the jail for a bond hearing on two fellows who'd held up a little mom-and-pop store out on the edge of Hopemore's poorer part of town. "Got away with five hundred and six dollars," the deputy informed me. Sheriff's deputies can set bond themselves for any theft under five hundred. I put back on some decent clothes and headed downstairs. When Joe Riddley asked where I was going, I informed him, "I'm going to ask a dadblamed deputy why he didn't put six dollars back in the till and save me a trip out in this rain."

All the way there and back, the windshield wipers reminded me of eyes blinking back tears. I was blinking back some of my own. I couldn't remember the last time I'd felt that sad.

How was Gwen Ellen going to live without Skye?

And what if Skye had indeed left everything to Skell, and Skell sold the business out from under Laura?

And what if Skell killed his daddy, and that's why he was on the lam?

And what kind of town were we if new people—Mexicans or whoever—got labeled "those people" by folks like Charlie Muggins and automatically got put at the head of any suspect list when a crime was committed?

I didn't get home until Marilee was concluding her eleven o'clock weather report: continuing rain. She looked about as soggy as I felt, and I was surprised and touched when she concluded her report, "I'm very sad tonight because of the death of a special friend. God bless you, Skye, wherever you are."

Walker called right after that, but said little to lighten my personal skies. "I'm in Orlando. I tracked down my college buddy, and he found us a lawyer. He just called five minutes ago and he's over at his beach house. He'll come back tomorrow and meet me here at ten. I don't know how to reach Maynard or Selena this late, so I'll just let them spend one night in jail."

Walker has always been easygoing, but "let them spend one night in jail" was a new high in casual speech.

"You couldn't bond them out?"

"Mama, I don't know how to do all that. They're gonna be fine. You haven't said anything to Hubert, have you?"

"We didn't like to, with his dicey heart."

"Wait until I know something tomorrow. I'll call you as soon as I have anything to report."

Clarinda wasn't any happier with his news than I was. I had to tell her at least four times that Walker was doing the best he could in the circumstances. By then, I almost believed it myself.

I didn't sleep well that night. The rain kept coming in bands: first a downpour, then a patter. We had left our window up a tad for fresh air, so I woke at the thud of each new deluge on our tin porch roof. Then I'd lie in the dark picturing Skye MacDonald lying on his back in the mud while rain slid down his face. I tossed and turned, but couldn't get rid of the picture.

When our alarm went off at seven, rain was still pouring down. I snuggled deeper into my covers, tempted to pull them over my head and sleep all day. Nobody was coming to our Presidents' Day sale in that storm.

Then I remembered the bills I had to pay, the orders I had to place, the call Walker would be making about Maynard and Selena, and the probability that while I was dozing Chief Muggins would be concocting evidence to convict an innocent man of murder. That got me on my feet.

Our office at the back of the store is a good place to be when I'm out of sorts. Over the years Joe Riddley and I have added computers and other modern equipment, but we've kept the oak rolltop desks, filing cabinets, and chairs his grandparents used, and the big wing chair by the window his parents added. Years ago I discarded the yellowed battered shade at the high window and put up blinds and a ruffle, so we'd get more light. That past Christmas, I'd had the wing chair, chair pads, and ruffle redone from red plaid to a print of quail and pheasants on a dark green background. Even with the skies streaming, the office was warm and homey.

Still, nobody had come in overnight and written on the wall what I should do next. I paid bills, chatted with a few customers, signed a couple of warrants, read gardening catalogues, and wished Joe Riddley would come back from the nursery so I'd at least have him to pick at. I was delighted when Walker finally called again.

"Hey, Mama. They're out."

"That's wonderful. What happened?"

"It was real close for a minute. They got a judge who is rabid about drugs, so even after the lawyer explained what happened with the car and Maynard produced the receipt to show he'd just bought it, the judge hemmed and hawed about how this was not a light charge. Finally, bless her heart, Selena got all redheaded indignant and told him she feels exactly the same way about drugs, but was it fair to let whoever put drugs in their car ruin her honeymoon? Then—and this was the clincher—she demanded, 'How would you feel if it was your daughter on her honeymoon caught in this mess?' He blinked a couple of times, and set bond. Turns out that was a lucky shot. His daughter is getting married next month. If I ever get arrested, I want Selena on my side. The BMW is still confiscated, though."

"Well, I'm proud to know you, son. You did good. But poor Maynard. He loves that car."

"Yeah. The lawyer is gonna try to get it back, since they bought it in good faith, but he's not real optimistic. I took them to rent another car, and I'm on my way home. I ought to be back for dinner. I'm leaving Orlando as we speak."

"You aren't talking on that cell phone while you're driving, are you?"

"I love you, too, Mama. Good-bye."

When I called Clarinda with the good news, her "That's wonderful" sounded so much like mine, I wondered if we'd been together too long. She added, "I knew that boy and his sweet bride didn't have anything to do with drugs."

I'd barely hung up the second time when Ike called. "I hate like the dickens to bring this one to you, Judge, but Judge Stebley's still laid up with his broken leg. I need you down at the detention center for a preliminary hearing. The charge is murder, against Humberto Garcia. We found a witness this morning who saw Garcia driving down Warner Road around ten Friday night, when he claims he was at the restaurant. Then Chief Muggins went back out to the crime scene this morning and turned up a book of matches we missed the first time. They're from Garcia's restaurant."

In the face of evidence, judges don't have a lot of discretion. I might feel like refusing to go. I might feel like demanding, "Have you and Chief Muggins gone plumb crazy?"

I couldn't. All I could do was haul myself out to do my duty.

Some storms seem to wash the whole town clean, but that particular rain was dingy and gray, revealing litter in the gutters and splashing mud from sidewalk planters all over the place. As I drove to the jail, Hopemore looked as gray and ugly as I felt.

Mr. Garcia looked gray, too. A face almost as gray as the jeans he wore with a white polo shirt. He turned away in great embarrassment when he saw me. Mrs. Garcia wore jeans and a yellow T-shirt. Her eyes pleaded with me to do something—anything—to make this shame go away.

Unhappiness made Isaac edgy and curt. "Here is the accused, Judge." He handed me the paperwork, and I went around the high semicircular desk that serves as a bench for preliminary hearings held at the jail. When they built it, all the magistrates were tall. I have to climb up on a box.

"I am Judge MacLaren Yarbrough," I informed the accused as I am required by law to do. "Magistrate for Hope County, Georgia. What is your name?"

He replied, bewildered, "Humberto Garcia. You know me."

"Yes, but it is required that I establish your identity for the record. This is a preliminary hearing. You are charged with the willful murder of Fergus MacDonald. Have you read and do you understand the warrant?"

"I did not kill anyone," Mr. Garcia protested. "I was never on that road in my life. I—"

"All that will come up before the superior-court judge," I informed him. "For now, have you read and do you understand the charges against you?"

"Yes." He said it as if he were about to break into another protest, so I spoke quickly.

"Because this is a murder charge, and I am a magistrate, I cannot set bond on this charge. It has to be set by a superior-court justice. I will notify the superior court in Augusta and they will send a judge down to set your bond."

"How long will that take?" Mrs. Garcia asked the question, shaking so hard she had to sit in one of the hard chairs to the side of the desk.

"About a week, normally."

"Madre de dios!" she whispered, and covered her face with her hands.

"A week?" Mr. Garcia turned pale. "My restaurant will die in a week. I can't—I didn't— You say Mr. MacDonald was found on a dirt road off Warner Road. We live on Warner Road, so yes, I must have driven past the road on which he was found. But I never drive on any dirt roads. I don't want to mess up my car. And I did not leave matches near his body. Would I be that foolish? I swear it on my mother's grave."

The words poured out like the torrent pouring just beyond the front door, where the builder had not adequately anchored the gutter, but I could not pay him the least bit of attention.

Isaac said in his bass voice, "We're gonna need to process you now."

Mrs. Garcia started weeping. Her husband turned and spoke to her gently in Spanish, then pulled her to her feet and embraced her.

Isaac sidled closer to the bench and muttered, "You and God had better get to work."

As he was led away, Mr. Garcia turned to ask me in despair, "How can you prove where you have not been?"

Rosa said much the same thing when she called thirty minutes after I got back to my desk. Her mother had called her at school to tell her that her father had been arrested. Rosa called me, crying and praying to every saint in the

Catholic calendar. "What are we going to do?" she finally demanded. "My father never killed anybody."

"He was seen on Warner Road around ten," I reminded her. "He told Chief Muggins he was at the restaurant all evening."

"I know. He was only gone a few minutes. My dress got soaked when Skellton crashed into me and *Mami* was afraid I would catch cold, but she didn't want me to drive so late alone, so *Papi* said he would fetch another dress while I chatted with customers." She ran out of sentence and breath at the same time.

I sighed, wishing I could offer more comfort. "You'll get to say all that in court, and produce your witnesses. Get them lined up, comfort your mother, and pray that the real killer is found. That's the best I can suggest." I hung up, real discouraged.

I know Ben Franklin said, "God helps those who help themselves," but I've found that God offers a lot more help when I can't help myself. I locked my door to keep anybody from walking in and thinking I was crazier than I am, and I spoke out loud. "Okay, God, you know whether Humberto Garcia killed Skye MacDonald, but I don't believe he did. I don't want to think Skell did it, either, but you know I am terrified he may have. I'm not asking for more than I need here, but if there's something I ought to be doing, I need a nudge in the right direction. Please." It wasn't as eloquent as a preacher in the pulpit, but God didn't create me eloquent, just determined.

Feeling better now that I'd shifted the burden to stronger shoulders, I started entering checks we'd written the past week and hadn't yet put on the computer.

God speaks in mysterious ways. Sometimes after I pray, I get a brilliant idea from somebody else who isn't that smart. Occasionally I get a brilliant idea of my own—and I'm not that smart, either. Sometimes a new verse shows up in my Bible right in the middle of a passage I've read a hundred times. Sometimes I get a dream that contains the kernel of truth I need. And sometimes, something or somebody triggers a memory.

That day, I was entering checks from Joe Riddley's checkbook, including the one to help pay for Maynard's car, when I remembered something Laura said Saturday afternoon about how furious Skell's assistant manager was that he hadn't showed up.

That thought kept pestering me like a kitten at my knee. Finally I put down my pen and looked at it from all sides. I could see an employee getting annoyed if the owner didn't come in when she or he was supposed to. But furious enough to complain to another member of the owner's family? Either that employee was an old trusted friend of the family—and I didn't think anybody stuck around Sky's the Limit that long—or this was odd. At the least, it was a loose end.

I picked up the phone and punched in Gwen Ellen's number.

"Hey, Tansy? How're you doin' today? And how's Gwen Ellen?"

"Hey, Miss MacLaren. We're both keepin' on keepin' on, which is 'bout all we *can* do. Seems like the very skies are cryin' for Mr. Skye, don't it?"

"It sure does. Listen, is Laura down there right now, or up in her own place?"

"Sittin' right here eatin' cookies and drinkin' coffee to work up her courage. Here."

"Hey, Mac." Laura's voice came over the line, deep and glum. But she hadn't forgotten her manners, whatever might be the matter. "I sure appreciated your being with me yesterday. We all left in such a hurry, I didn't tell you."

"Glad to be there. What are you working up your courage for?"

She gave an embarrassed little laugh. "Nicole's coming at twelve to cut my hair. Wish me luck. I am terrified."

"I told you, honey, if you don't like it, it will grow. Listen, Saturday you said there was a salesman over at Sky's the Limit who was mad at Skell for not coming in. Do you remember?"

"Sure. Skell's assistant manager, Jimmy Bratson. He was scheduled to work noon till six on Friday and have Saturday off. When he came in at noon, he found Skell had overslept and not gotten there until just before he did; then Skell left to see Daddy and never came back. Jimmy must have called five times between five and six, antsier than a barefoot baby on a hot sidewalk, asking where Skell was and saying he couldn't stay to close, he had important things to do. I had to tell him, of course, that he'd have to stay until Skell came. I couldn't be in two places at once. When I had to call him again Saturday to come in, and had to tell him I still didn't know where Skell was, he was fit to be tied." She sighed. "Between you, me, and the kitchen table, Jimmy Bratson is not one of my favorite employees. He thinks a bit too highly of himself. But he and Skell get along, and that's what counts."

Joe Riddley came in just then, bringing me a cup of coffee. I knew better than to say more about Jimmy Bratson right then. "Laura," I mouthed so Joe Riddley would know who I was talking to, then asked her, "Have you heard from Skell again?"

"Not a word. When I finally get my hands on that brother of mine—"

I heard Tansy remonstrating with her in the background, so asked hastily, "How's your mother doing today?"

"As well as can be expected. She's had so many people to bear up for, she's not had much time to grieve yet."

"You all might want to take some time and get away after this is over."

"I guess we might." Laura didn't sound too enthusiastic.

"My guess is you are itching to do what I'd want to do in your circumstances, honey—go back to your desk and work, work, work. Maybe Skell can take her somewhere, when he gets back."

A common thought seemed to hang between us on the wire—if Skell wasn't in jail awaiting trial. I hurried to change the subject. "Good luck with your haircut. It may make a new woman out of you."

"Or something," Laura agreed, glum again.

"Let me talk to your mother, if she's up to talking."

"Oh, she's up to anything right now. It's lunchtime I'm a bit worried about. Tansy has a doctor's appointment she needs to keep—you know how hard they are to get. I'll be having my hair cut, and all our relatives have left. It will be the first time Mama's been alone in the house since Saturday."

I knew how big and empty a house can seem when its rooms are swelled by grief. "Let me talk to her for a minute." When Gwen Ellen came to the phone, I suggested, "How about if I stop by Myrtle's at twelve, get us both a chicken-salad plate, and bring it over there for lunch?"

"You don't need to bring food. People have been so nice; the kitchen is full. I'll make a pot of tea." She hadn't said I didn't need to come.

ᘒ 17 ᘓ

Gwen Ellen greeted me looking almost as dead as Skye. Crescents beneath her eyes were so dark they looked like bruises. Except for makeup, her face was pale. Her shoulders slumped in a tan wool dress Skye had helped her choose on a trip to New York a year before. "That dress makes you look slender as a teenager," I greeted her, hoping to get a smile.

Instead, she held up her right hand, on which she wore the big diamond Laura had found in the safe. "I've lost weight. Skye bought this just before he died." Her voice quavered. She held the ring toward the kitchen window, but the day was too gray to make rainbows. "It's gorgeous, but look how loose it is." She moved it easily up and down her finger. "I'll need to get it resized."

"Grief can do that to you. I lost a few pounds back in August, when Joe Riddley was so sick." Looking for a cheerier topic, I added, "But that new haircut makes you look thirty-five."

She shook her head. "I feel three *hundred* and thirty-five. Come on into the dining room. Everything's ready."

"The dining room? We're mighty fancy." Generally we ate on their sunporch.

"I cannot bear to look at what all this water is doing to my yard."

Tansy had set the dining-room table with soft yellow place mats, matching napkins, and china I hadn't seen before—white porcelain covered with pastel butterflies. "More dishes? Is this your sixth or seventh set?" I teased. Gwen Ellen liked china better than anybody I knew.

She picked up a cup and examined the pattern listlessly. "We got them last fall when Skye had to go to Germany for some meeting. I went along, and we stopped in France for a few days." Her finger traced a blue and yellow butterfly on her cup. "We went to see the china factories in Limoges, and I got them because they were cheerful." Her voice trailed off into a realm where nothing would ever be cheerful again.

"I brought you something that smells good." I reached into a carrier and brought out a delft pot of blue and white hyacinths.

"Aren't you sweet?" She removed a silk floral arrangement from the middle of the table and set the hyacinths in its place. Their fragrance floated through the room.

As we took our places, she at one end and me beside her, I saw her look at the big armchair at the far end where Skye used to sit. Her eyes teared up, and she pressed her napkin to her lips. "Would you say the blessing, please, MacLaren?"

As soon as I'd finished, I asked about what I knew was on her mind. "Any news from Skell?"

She clenched her left fist beside her plate until her knuckles turned white. "Not a word since he called on his cell phone Saturday night. The call was dropped, and Laura can't get him to answer since—except once when she thought he picked up, but then he hung up immediately. That wasn't Skell, MacLaren. He'd never do that if he saw our number on his screen. I think somebody has him and won't let him come home. I've called the police at least twice each day, but they keep saying they can't even start to look for him until after two today—forty-eight hours since he was last seen." She brushed her hair back from her cheek. "I truly think if I don't hear something soon, I will go stark raving mad."

Lunch didn't get much cheerier than that. We ate thick slices of honey-baked ham, potato salad, squares of cranberry congealed salad with a sour cream topping, and an asparagus and artichoke casserole, but every one of those cooks had wasted her efforts, for all either one of us tasted. They could have brought cardboard and Styrofoam.

All during the meal the rain fell in sheets. While we couldn't see it through the thick sheers at her long windows, we could hear it like a regular drumbeat. So, as we drank our tea in butterfly cups, we talked about what all that wetness was doing to the azalea and dogwood buds, whether we were getting too much or just enough rain for the spring bulbs, and how soon it was likely the ground would be ready to work again. "I hate not getting outside a little bit each day. My garden is going to be so late," she lamented.

"Marilee Muller needs to find us some sunshine," I joked. "It's too bad she can't get some out of the same bottle she uses on her hair."

I'll never know what Gwen Ellen was going to say, because she swallowed a bite of biscuit wrong and choked. By the time I'd pounded her on the back and she'd run to the kitchen for a drink of water, we were both tired of talking weather, so we discussed her new haircut and her new hairdresser—the same one Cindy had recommended to me.

"I hate to admit it," I said, glimpsing my same old hairdo in the mirror over the mahogany buffet, "but I may want to try her myself. You and Cindy both look more like New York than Hopemore."

Gwen Ellen shoved back her hair and gave me a faint smile. "I wonder what Laura's hair is going to look like. That little girl from the office says she has a cosmetology degree, but she doesn't look old enough to be out of high school."

"Isn't it awful how young people are getting? I went to the doctor last week, and they gave me his new assistant, Dr. Jorgensen. She looks younger than Bethany, and it felt real funny taking off my clothes in front of a child."

I'd hoped that would make Gwen Ellen at least smile, and maybe laugh. Instead, she clouded up again. "We never got to Norway. We were planning to go this spring. Oh, MacLaren, I never *imagined* having to live without him. The rest of my life seems so *long*."

I reached for her hand. Its chill made me realize how much effort she was putting into acting halfway normal.

"We loved each other so much," she whispered. "It was so special, while it lasted."

"We who have loved and been loved are very fortunate in this world," I agreed. But the MacDonald house seemed much bigger and chillier without Skye's booming laugh and wide, happy smile. The idea flitted through my mind that I'd like to get into a smaller place before Joe Riddley or I lost the other. I loved our house, but I wouldn't want to live in it without him.

Gwen Ellen put down her fork and stared toward the window sheers as if she had x-ray vision and could see gray dismals outside. "Can I tell you something, MacLaren? I don't think I can get through the viewing. Having to stand beside Skye while people talk about him, looking down and seeing him lying there—" Her voice broke. "And I know my stomach is going to act up. I'll probably vomit all over everybody."

"Viewings are a barbarous custom, sweetheart, but if our mothers got through them, we can, too. You're gonna do fine."

"I doubt it. And to make it worse, his mother insists on an open casket before the service. They've got out-of-town friends who can't come for the viewing and stay overnight, and she wants them to be able to say good-bye." She pressed her napkin to her mouth and spoke through tears. "Oh, MacLaren, I don't want to have to look at Skye in front of everybody, or watch them shut him up and put him in a hole in the ground. I'll scream and wail and make a fool of myself. And if Skell isn't here, I simply won't hold the service. We can't bury his daddy until he gets home."

I could not tell her that Skell would endanger his freedom by coming home, so I said, instead, "You are not going to make a fool of yourself. You just cry and wail all you like—anything you do will be fine, unless you fling yourself on Skye and have a screaming hissie fit, and I cannot imagine you doing such a thing. Dreading it is probably worse than the thing itself will be."

I sure hoped I was right. It seemed to comfort Gwen Ellen, because she took a few deep breaths and went back to talking about her plants and all that rain.

"We've been promised sunshine for tomorrow," I told her. "If we don't get it, we can kill Marilee Muller." Now why did I say that? Was it any way to talk to a woman whose husband just got murdered? Gwen Ellen turned so white I thought she'd faint, and rose to take our plates to the kitchen.

I sat glued to my chair by mortification. "I'm so sorry, honey," I called after her, but that wasn't anywhere near enough.

While she was getting our dessert, I thought of several new topics to discuss. She must have been doing the same thing, because we didn't mention Skye again.

We were finishing slices of pecan pie when we heard feet clomping down the garage stairs. "Mama? Mama. Skell called. He left a message on my cell phone this morning around ten. I just found it when I turned on the phone."

Laura came to a dead stop in the kitchen just out of our range of view.

I was so busy trying to slow down my heartbeat I nearly didn't recognize Nicole's voice.

"Go on," she commanded. "Go show them."

Laura entered the dining room and stood, pink and shy, waiting to see what we would say.

I'm not sure I'd have recognized her if I'd met her on the street. Nicole had cut her hair very short and layered it to fall in shining natural waves to the nape of her neck. Bangs softened her high forehead, and the way the hairline followed her ears, I saw for the first time how lovely they were. Her neck was a surprise, too—it rose long and graceful from her navy turtleneck sweater. She looked downright pretty and even sophisticated. Pounds lighter, too.

"Isn't she gorgeous?" Nicole asked with a grand wave of one hand and a jig that one shouldn't do in mixed company in a skirt that short.

"Gorgeous," I agreed at once.

Gwen Ellen had laid down her fork and pushed back her chair. "What did Skell say?" That was one of few times in her life that I could have gladly shaken her.

The light went out of Laura's face. "He said he's fine, he'll be home tomorrow, and he"—she paused—"he hopes you aren't mad at him."

"But where is he?" Maybe Gwen Ellen didn't mean to accuse Laura of keeping that to herself, but it came out that way.

Laura pinched her lips together. Anybody could tell she was trying to decide what to say.

"Call him back," Gwen Ellen commanded. "All you have to do is push redial."

She didn't mean to insult her, but Laura's generation was the one who taught the rest of us how to use things like cell phones and computers. When Skell went to college, Skye used to grumble, "Nobody should let both their children go away from home at once. Who's going to show us how to make all these gadgets work?" No wonder Laura forgot her manners enough to snap out the truth. "I did that, Mama. He called from a public phone at Disney World. He's not there now."

"Disney World? With his daddy dead?" Gwen Ellen pressed her hand to her mouth and tried to absorb the shock.

Seeing the distress on Laura's face, I reminded Gwen Ellen, "He doesn't know Skye's dead." I pushed back my chair. "Come to the kitchen a minute, Laura." When we got there, I asked quietly, "What exactly did Skell say?"

She kept her voice low, too. "He said he forgot and left his cell phone in the rest stop bathroom Saturday night after our call was dropped—that's the third one he's lost this year—"

"You can deal with that later. What else did he say?"

She heaved a big sigh, fished in her pocket, and held out a phone so small I couldn't find anyplace to speak or listen. She flipped it open and pushed buttons. "Here. Listen for yourself. Then tell me if you think we need to page him to come straight home."

Skell sounded as cocky and irresponsible as ever. "Hi, Sissy. I'm in Orlando. Sorry not to call sooner, but I forgot my cell phone in the men's room at an interstate rest stop." He gave a snort of laughter. "You're gonna have to dock my pay again. But listen, I didn't just hare down here for the fun of it. I had something to take care of, and it was real important. I'll tell you about it when I get home. Since I'm here, I might as well see Disney World. I'd call you at the dealership, but I don't want Daddy to know where I am yet. Is he furious I took the money? I'll explain when I get there. Calm him down for me, okay?"

I handed her the phone to turn off. "That explains who robbed the safe."

"And he doesn't even know Daddy is dead." I saw relief in her eyes, then embarrassment that she'd felt relieved. "You never really thought he killed Daddy, did you?"

She had me between a cocklebur and thistle. I couldn't tell her a lie, and I couldn't tell her the truth. I settled for, "The police have arrested Mr. Garcia, but their case against him doesn't look real strong to me. If they're smart, they're going to be looking for other suspects, as well."

"Then I'd better save Skell's message. Obviously he doesn't even know Daddy's dead."

"Any good prosecutor would point out that if Skell killed his daddy, he's clever enough to make that call to try and muddy the waters."

She frowned. "What should I do?"

"Why don't you let Skell handle his own mess for a change? He's twenty-three years old. You come back in the dining room and let your mother properly admire your hair."

I felt so sick, though, that I could hardly walk behind her to the dining room. Gwen Ellen and even Laura wanted Skell home, but my stomach felt like it does whenever Joe Riddley watches *High Noon* and Gary Cooper starts walking down that seemingly deserted street.

It took all the meager acting skills I possess to tell Gwen Ellen, "Skell ran down to Orlando on business, and because he worked this weekend, he figured he deserved a day at Disney World. Since he's coming home tomorrow anyway, I don't think you need to bother tracking him down. Meanwhile, don't you love Laura's hair?"

Gwen Ellen wasn't finished talking about Skell. "You're sure we don't need to call him? Does he even know about his daddy?"

"No, but what difference does one more day make? The funeral isn't until the end of the week, is it?"

"Saturday." She gave me a wan smile. "He might as well have one more happy day."

Finally she could turn her attention back to where it was badly needed. She considered Laura critically, then nodded. "Your hair is lovely. I really like it."

Laura reached both hands up and clutched her neck just below her ears. "I feel naked."

"You don't look naked; you look beautiful," I told her. "Enjoy it."

Nicole couldn't stand still. "Wait until folks at work see you." She giggled again.

A soft pink rose from Laura's throat to cover her cheeks. "I doubt folks at work will even notice." Her voice was gruff, but I could tell she was pleased.

She turned back to the kitchen. "Can we get ourselves something to eat?"

"Whatever you can find," her mother told her.

We heard them rattling plates and silverware. Nicole was prattling on about clothes now. "You need some bright things. You never wear anything but gray and navy, but you'd be really stunning in red, or kelly green, or peacock blue. I'll bet turquoise would bring out the color of your eyes. Yellow, too—but not pale yellow. The color of egg yolks, daisy centers, and sunshine."

Gwen Ellen gave me a wan smile. "I have said the very same thing to Laura a hundred times, and it hasn't made one speck of difference. She'd just go shopping and come back with another blue blazer or another gray skirt. Maybe this child is going to be good for her."

"I just hope Laura gets full value for her money," I joked. "I've got hems in some of my dresses deeper than Nicole's skirts."

Gwen Ellen looked thoughtful; then she surprised me.

"Laura could wear miniskirts. You might not remember—she never shows them—but Laura's legs are as good as Nicole's."

I was still trying to picture Laura in a wisp of a skirt when she came in with Nicole to raid the biscuit basket. They were both laughing, and Laura looked as carefree as she used to when her house was full of teammates. Had she been lonely since she'd come back home? When I thought about it, I couldn't remember seeing her with any women friends—or with much of anybody except her family—in years. Now, she and Nicole stood tall and golden, with so much energy and youth between them, they made me tired.

Or maybe that was worry about Skell.

The phone rang. Tansy, coming in the back door, bustled to answer it. "Laura? It's for you."

We heard Laura say, "Laura MacDonald . . . Yeah? . . . Sure, she's right here. You want to talk with her? . . . *What?* Oh, no, she didn't. We know . . . No, but . . ." Her voice trailed off.

She came into the dining room and slid into one of the extra chairs. Motioning Nicole to sit, too, she leaned her chair back on two legs and said, "Chief Muggins can be so dumb."

"Now, Laura . . . ," her mother started. "And don't break that chair."

"He wouldn't listen," Laura told her, righting the chair with a thump. "Yesterday I found money missing from our safe while I was down at the dealership, and I called the police. Now he's found a suspect. But we know who took it." Seeing the question in her mother's eyes, she added, "Skell."

"No!" Gwen Ellen protested.

"He borrowed it for his trip—" Laura caught my eye and pressed her lips together. "No, he stole it, Mama, and he's gonna have to deal with me on that. But at least we can call off the police—which I would have told Chief Muggins, if he had let me get a word in edgewise. Instead, he's gonna make a trip over here for nothing."

Nicole stood up and edged toward the door. "I'll be getting home, then. You won't want me here."

"Don't go." Laura reached up and touched her neck. "I may want you to glue my hair back on if I can't get used to this."

"No, I truly do have to go. I forgot, I have an appointment." With a flick of skirt, Nicole slid out of that room faster than a coon caught in the barn.

Chief Muggins strolled in ten minutes later, hands in the pockets of his leather jacket. His face was red and his feet were wet. He came in through the kitchen like he considered himself family by now and—being on an important, official errand—he didn't bother to wipe his feet. Tansy frowned at the trail of gritty prints he left on her clean kitchen floor.

Laura brought him to the dining room. He refused a chair, nodded to me, greeted Gwen Ellen, then looked around. "Where's Nicole Shandy?" He rested his hands on a chair back like it was a podium and he a particularly odious preacher. "I told you to keep her here."

"She went home," Laura told him, "but she didn't take the money."

"Her prints are all over that safe, Miss MacDonald, and over most of the contents, too."

"She was my father's secretary, sir. We didn't generally keep money in that safe, so he often worked with it open and asked her to put documents in it. Besides, we know who took the money. My brother borrowed it to make a business trip to Florida. He called this morning to explain."

"Called? You know how to reach him?"

"No, but he'll be home sometime tomorrow." And if you need to reach me them, I'll be at the delership." Seeing her mother's startled expression, she said firmly, "I'm reopen-ing tomorrow."

I could hardly sit still. Laura thought she was solving a robbery. She probably even thought she was exonerating Skell of any blame for killing their daddy, for she empha-sized that he was scared to death of what his daddy was going to do when he got home.

I was almost scared to death myself. From where I was sitting, I had a clear view of the triumphant gleam in Chief Muggins's eyes.

੩ 18 ੬

I phoned Gwen Ellen again later that afternoon. She said several people had come over after I'd left and worn her out. "I'm just about to go upstairs and take a nap. Sleeping, I forget all this has happened. Sometimes I just want to sleep forever."

"Don't take too many pills," I warned. In addition to a nervous stomach, Gwen Ellen had bad headaches and bouts of sleeplessness. It worried me to hear her talking like that, with the number of sleeping pills and tranquilizers she had around the house. "Where's Laura?"

"She and Nicole have gone shopping. They seem to enjoy each other." With a little laugh, she added something any mother would understand: "Laura listens to Nicole, even if she says the same things I've said for years."

"I'm pleased she's got a new friend. But, honey, you heard me say not to take too many of those sleeping pills, didn't you?"

"Of course, MacLaren. Tansy is here. She's taking good care of me. Call me tomorrow, you hear me?"

"I hear you, sweetie. Have a good nap."

My own sleep that night was again punctuated by rain on the roof, and when I woke up Tuesday, rain was still streaming down.

"Honey?" I poked Joe Riddley in the shoulder until he

opened one eye. "Have you gotten any instructions from the Lord about building an ark?"

He pulled the cover over his ears. "Nary a mutter."

I got up, padded over to the window, raised it, and pressed my ear to the screen. From his warm nest he growled, "What the dickens are you doing?"

I shivered in the chilly breeze. "Listening to see if I hear anybody else hammering."

He heaved himself groggily out of bed. In spite of practicing every day, he's never gotten real good at getting up in the morning.

"What did Marilee say about the weather today?" I lowered the window and padded toward my closet.

He grunted. "Clearing by afternoon, sunny tomorrow."

I scanned the sky. Thick gray clouds as far as I could see in all directions. "She needs to polish her crystal ball. But at least those two corkscrew willows I planted in the side yard ought to be getting enough moisture to suit them."

"You should have planted cypresses. I checked on them yesterday, and they're knee-deep in water." He gave himself a thorough morning scratch and plodded off to his own closet.

We'd barely gotten to work when Joe Riddley got a call. I heard him say, "Yeah, eleven's good." He hung up and reached for his cap. "I'm goin' down to the nursery to check on the shrubs. With all this rain, some of them may be getting pretty waterlogged. And Shyster just called. Wants me to drop in around eleven." Peter Schuster was a member of our church, and he and Joe Riddley served on the missions committee together. Pete was also a lawyer, which made the nickname inevitable.

Joe flew down from the curtain rod and perched on Joe Riddley's shoulder, but Joe Riddley pushed him off. "Stay, Joe." He added to me, "I'm leaving him here. I don't like taking him out in this rain twice in one morning." Not to mention how that parrot had disgraced himself the last time he visited Pete's elegant office.

Joe was not pleased, however, to be left. For two hours the wretch sat on our curtain rod pecking at his feathers and muttering, just too soft for me to catch the words. Given the baleful glances he shot my way and his former owner's vocabulary, I was probably glad I couldn't hear.

I didn't want to hear what Isaac James had to say, either, when he dropped by around ten. First he handed me a warrant to sign so he could arrest a man who had molested his girlfriend's six-year-old daughter.

I read it with my stomach churning, and signed it gladly. "This makes me glad I'm a judge. Yesterday I was ready to take down the sign on my door. You and I both know Mr. Garcia didn't kill Skye MacDonald, but there wasn't a thing I could do."

"Don't get in a stew about that," he told me soberly. "You and I also know I ought not tell you this, but Chief Muggins as much as admitted this morning that he's only holding Mr. Garcia because he hopes that will decoy Skellton MacDonald into thinking it's safe to come home. He's convinced Skell killed his Daddy, and I have to admit all the evidence points that way. Especially—" He stopped. "No, I've already told you more than I ought to."

"More than I wanted to hear," I snapped. "You've ruined a perfectly lousy day."

After he left, I tried to work, but the rain on the parking lot outside my window sounded like a young drummer who couldn't keep his fingers still. The view was so dreary it made me want to cry, and Joe muttered away over my head until I was ready to do that parrot bodily harm. I couldn't help worrying about Skell—where was he? Should we try to warn him not to come home until his daddy's murder was solved? But what if he *had* done it?

I couldn't stand that last thought, so I turned on the

radio—just in time to hear our Yarbrough's ad. Maybe it was the mood I was in, but it sounded tired and stale. Remembering what Laura said about reaching younger customers, I called the station and told them I wanted something more modern, with pep. They said they'd have something for my approval in a day or two, but it would take two weeks to get it on the air.

"Murder can be accomplished in a minute," I told Joe sourly, "but advertising takes two weeks."

"Not to worry," he replied irritably.

"That's easy for you to say," I snapped. "You have an assured food supply."

I couldn't stand my office any longer. I grabbed my pocketbook and umbrella and headed out. As I passed the cash register, I told the clerk on duty, "If Joe Riddley gets back before I do, tell him I've gone to Sky's the Limit to look at a used car for Bethany."

I had learned the hard way not to go places without letting him know where I'd be. Twice already, it had endangered my life. However, there was nothing frightening about Sky's the Limit on a rainy morning. Full of forlorn, abandoned automobiles, it looked about as exciting as a cemetery. Overhead lights reflected beads of water on dripping hoods and bathed the whole lot in a sickly glow. A splash of yellow light inside the little white building that served as a sales office showed where everybody must be.

I pulled as close as I could get to the entrance, wrestled my umbrella up, and splashed to the large glass door. Sky's the Limit wasn't as elegant as MacDonald Motors. The sales office was one medium-size room with three gray metal desks and two gray filing cabinets sitting on a gray vinyl floor. Remnants of pink and blue artificial sweetener packets littered a table containing the coffeepot and the nearby wastebasket overflowed with white Styrofoam cups. The cleaners must have taken Laura literally when she shut down business for a few days. She'd have a fit if she saw the state the place was in.

Three salesmen sat in the sales office drinking coffee and contemplating the dispiriting view: a lot full of unsold cars in a customerless downpour. I suspected they'd also been telling smutty stories, given the shouts of laughter I heard as I pushed open the door and the hush that fell when they saw who was coming in.

I closed my umbrella and shook it out the door, then looked around with my brightest smile. "Hello." Sugar crunched underfoot as I stepped inside.

While I often think I know everybody in Hopemore, I know a lot of them only by sight. Two of these men fell into that category, and the oldest I didn't know at all. None of the three went to our church, belonged to our organizations, had gone to school with our sons, shopped regularly in our store, or had appeared before me since I became a judge. The stringy kid of about nineteen, with a few pimples and greasy yellow hair that needed a trim, might have bagged my groceries at the Bi-Lo a few years back, but he didn't look like he recognized me, so it hadn't been a memorable relationship for either of us.

The two older men exchanged a look; then the one I didn't recognize stood up. He was a tall, bulky fellow with a beaky nose and a few long strands of dark hair combed over the top of his naked scalp. "Good morning, ma'am. Are you looking for a car?"

I considered them. Jimmy Bratson wasn't the pimply youth, so he had to be either this man or the third. I decided to bet on the third. The large man didn't look like anything ever lit his fuse. I bet on the third man, who was watching me even though he pretended he wasn't.

He would be hard to describe once I took my eyes off him: medium height, medium weight, brown eyes, brown hair, no distinguishing features. But he carried his head back on his neck in a way that let the world know he thought highly of himself. And I had seen the other two look toward him before they looked at me.

"Are you Jimmy Bratson?" I addressed him.

"Yes, ma'am. What can I do for you?" He had the manners to stand, and was both casual and efficient. The kind of man who gets the most done with the least expenditure of effort. The bulky man sank back into his chair, quite willing to let somebody else deal with me. The kid earnestly picked dirt from his fingernails like he was being paid for it by the pound.

"I wanted to ask you about a car."

"What kind are you looking for?" Mr. Bratson cast a professional look out the window at my Nissan, probably deciding how little to offer me for it.

I felt a spurt of anger. "I'm not looking for one. I want to know about one you sold Friday to a friend of mine. Blue BMW convertible?"

He narrowed his eyes. "I didn't sell that car." His shoulders were tense; his eyes scarcely moved. "Mr. MacDonald sold it."

"I know, but I can't ask him about it, now, can I? And my friends called. They've had trouble with it down in Florida. They might want to bring it back." I figured that was honest: Maynard *might* want to bring it back, given the trouble it had caused. If he ever *got* it back.

His eyes narrowed. "Florida? That where they are?"

"Yeah. I wondered if the man it was promised to first might still be interested in it. Do you know who he was and how to get in touch with him?"

The tensing of his shoulders was so tiny, I wouldn't have noticed if I hadn't been looking for it. The big man was buffing his nails on the thigh of his pants, no longer paying us a speck of attention. The pimply youth, though, was sitting with his legs far apart, his hands dangling between them, and his gaze fixed on his hands. I saw him give a slight jerk when Jimmy Bratson asked in a flat, curious voice, "Was it promised to somebody?"

"I understood from Laura MacDonald that there was already a customer lined up for it." I turned to the others. "Any of you know anything about that?" Both shook their heads, but while the big man's pleasant smile didn't alter as he shook his head, the pimply youth pressed back against his chair. Walker always did that when he wanted to avoid telling me something. I looked back at Mr. Bratson. "Skell was pretty upset Saturday that it had been sold. He must be the one who promised it. I'll have to ask him about that."

The man didn't so much tense as grow very still. Not even his eyes blinked. My daddy used to say that when a man stops blinking, it's because he's working on a new idea. "You've seen Skell? You know where he is? I sure would like to talk to him. He needs to authorize several hours of overtime for me."

"I'm sure Laura will take care of that. The car came from Florida originally, didn't it?"

He shook his head. "I'm sorry. I don't know."

That was a dumb thing to say. Any assistant manager worth his salt, particularly in a business being run by an inexperienced kid not long out of college, ought to keep track of which cars came from where, in case there were problems with any of them later. But I ordered my lips to smile and said, "Well, thank you." I reached for my umbrella. "Shall I tell my friends you'd be willing for them to return the car?"

He reached for a pad and a pencil. "If you'll tell me where they are, I'll call them and discuss the matter myself." His smile was pleasant, but it is eyes that are windows of the soul. His were blank.

"Sorry," I said helplessly, "I don't know where they are.

They're on their honeymoon. But if they call again, shall I tell them to call you?"

"Please do."

"Okay." I turned, then added, as if it were an after-thought, "Did you all have time to get the green Saturn trade-in washed and on the lot before you closed Saturday? My granddaughter likes it, and it might make a great birth-day present." Both of those were true. The fact that Bethany had just had her birthday was incidental.

The young man raised his head. "Yeah, I cleaned it up. Had a lot of stuff written all over it from a wedding." His snicker wasn't any improvement over the rest of him.

"Could I have a look at it?" I held my breath, hoping they'd send the youngest out into the misery of that awful day.

Mr. Bratson and the pleasant man exchanged the look of men each waiting for the other to volunteer. Mr. Bratson gave the pimply youth a curt nod. "Show it to her, Whit-man."

"It's mighty wet out there for a test drive," the other volunteered.

"I don't need to drive it. I'd just like to take a look at it. Thanks."

Whitman—now I remembered his name on his Bi-Lo badge—came out without raincoat or umbrella, his big shoes squishing in the water underfoot. I offered to let him share my umbrella, but he shook his head. To the Whitmans of the world, umbrellas aren't for real men.

I was delighted to find the Saturn at the far end of the second row of cars, out of sight of the office. "You didn't need to wash it, given all the rain we've had," I joked as we splashed toward it. My pocketbook thumped against my side like a lead weight.

"Yeah," he said lugubriously. I'd never known what "lugubrious" meant until I met Whitman. He certainly wasn't getting any awards from me in the Most Charming, Most Communicative, or Quickest in Thought and Deed contests that morning. Nor for Best Looking, either, with his hair plastered to his forehead and water dripping from his long nose and pointed chin. He hunched his shoulders to keep the downpour from going farther down the collar of his plaid shirt. Poor thing. I felt guilty for dragging him out there to pump him for what he knew. I'd offer to run him home afterwards for dry clothes, to salve my conscience.

Feeling virtuous after that decision, I opened the back-seat door, got in, and slid over. "Come in where it's dry while you tell me about the car." When he hesitated, I repeated, "Come on. You aren't dirty, just wet. The seats will soon dry." I patted the seat beside me. He climbed in, but he left the door cracked for a quick getaway in case I had designs on his scrawny body.

Rain was so loud on the roof, I raised my voice. "You know something about that BMW. I could tell from the way you acted."

"I detailed it," he admitted.

"Detailed it?"

"Washed and polished it, cleaned the wheels, vacuumed it, did the windows and mirrors—you know, took care of all the details before it left the lot."

"You did a great job," I bragged. He relaxed and permitted himself a flickering smile of pride. I shot out the question before he could pull his head back into his shell. "Was it Mr. Bratson who promised it to somebody?"

He pressed himself against the car and nearly shook his head, but I'm not a mother and a judge for nothing. "Was it?" I held his eyes until he nodded.

"Has he promised other cars to the same man?"

"I don't know." His eyes slid toward the window, which answered my question after all.

"Do you know the man's name?" Just then my cell phone

rang. When I answered, "Judge Yarbrough," I saw Whitman's eyes widen. I don't think he'd known until then who I was. It was a deputy telling me he'd need me down at the courthouse in about thirty minutes. I said I'd be there, then hung up, and turned back to Whitman. "Do you know his name?"

I could tell by the way he leaned toward the door that he felt he was in the grip of the law and heading off to life imprisonment at any minute. I didn't say a word to relieve his fears.

"Raymond," he blurted. "That's all I know. Honest. No last name."

"How does he decide which ones to buy?"

He shifted toward the door. Maybe he was weighing what the law might do to him against what Raymond and Jimmy might do. "Comes in and picks them out, I guess."

"Do you have any personal knowledge whatsoever, Whitman, that this Raymond ever reserves a car before it gets here?"

He took his time about answering, scratching one thin thigh with a dirty fingernail. "I don't know if he does all the time, but one time I took a call when the others were at lunch. He told me to tell Jimmy to hold a little white Acura for him that was coming up from Florida the next day." He peered over his shoulder. "They're gonna wonder what we're doing out here."

"I'm asking you about this car. What year is it? What make? How many miles does it have on it? You don't have to answer, but at least you can tell him that I asked an awful lot of questions. Would you know this Raymond if you saw him again?"

He squirmed in his seat. "Look, I could get in a lot of trouble, and I need this job. I'm getting married next month."

Wonders will never cease.

I stopped myself before I said that aloud. "Congratulations. We can go now. Tell Mr. Bratson I'll think about the car and come back on a sunny day to drive it." I had a suspicion I'd need to help Ridd buy the darned car, to square my conscience.

We splashed back toward the office. Whitman tromped inside, and I got into the Nissan, hoping Mr. Bratson hadn't put a bomb under my hood while I was talking in the Saturn. He wasn't somebody I would trust to manage my office. I wondered why Skye or Laura hired him.

I was halfway to the sheriff's detention center when I remembered I'd planned to offer to run Whitman home. Oh, well, maybe he could call his fiancée and she'd bring him a change of clothes. That would put an unexpected pleasure in his dreary day.

My business with the deputy was simple—setting bond for a man who had forged his employer's name to a check to pay his child support. "I ain't got support money," he whined.

If he hadn't been brought before me on a drunk and disorderly two weeks before, I might have gone easier on him. "Stop drinking, and feed those kids," I told him sternly.

Joe Riddley was at his desk when I got back. He wasn't working; he was holding a long white envelope by the edges and staring at it like only he could read the secret writing on the back. When I came in, he looked up, glowering—and if you don't know what a glower looks like, you haven't seen my husband displeased. His eyebrows pull down toward the middle of his nose, his eyes get hard like black marbles, and his mouth purses up like an old-fashioned marble bag. Did I mention he has steam coming out both ears?

Joe squawked and flapped his wings. "Bug off. Bug off."

Even that cold welcome was a lot friendlier than Joe Riddley's. "Where the dickens have you been?"

"The sheriff's detention center for a hearing." I tucked my pocketbook under my desk and slipped my feet out of my soaked shoes. "Before that, down at Sky's the Limit. I left you a message. Didn't you get it? Ridd said Bethany may be interested in Maynard's Saturn."

"Ridd never sent you looking for a car for Bethany." I didn't answer that. After all, it was nothing but the truth. "You were nosing around down there hoping somebody would confess he put drugs in Maynard's new car."

"Sic 'em. Sic 'em," Joe egged him on.

"If I was, I got mightily disappointed." I flopped into my chair. "It's as dead down there as it is here—deader, in fact. At least we've got a few folks wandering around remembering God gave Noah a rainbow and figuring out what they'll plant once the deluge is over. Skell's got three bored salesmen cleaning their nails and picking their pimples."

"Pimples?" I had counted on that diverting him, and it did. He dropped the envelope and turned his chair with a creak to face mine.

"Yeah. One of them looks like he finished middle school a year ago, but he informed me he's getting married next month. He may have to get his parents' written permission."

The diversion had been fleeting. "You're gonna need your parents' written permission to walk out of this office if you don't stop sticking your nose in where it doesn't belong. Leave this to Charlie." Seeing that I was about to say something, he added, "And if you don't trust Charlie, at least leave it to Isaac."

"That's exactly what I plan to do," I informed him with dignity. Seeing that he was about to speak again, I decided a counter-attack was called for. "What did Pete Schuster want to talk about?"

To my surprise, Joe Riddley turned all the way around, so his back was to me and he was looking out the window. Since nothing was happening out there except more rain falling on the almost empty parking lot, it was easy to deduce he was avoiding looking at me. "Skye's estate." He reached up a finger and traced the path of a raindrop on the window. "He left me something." The raindrop kept going toward the ground, but Joe Riddley's voice stopped.

"That was real sweet of him." I reached for a tissue and blew my nose. "What was it?"

He heaved a sigh like the air in his lungs weighed too much for him to carry it. His chair creaked again as he turned back to his desk.

"I wish you'd oil that chair," I told him impatiently. "What did Skye leave you?" I figured it might be his Ford tie tack collection, or even an old Model T he'd kept in a shed out behind his house. He and Joe Riddley spent occasional afternoons out there fiddling with that car.

Joe Riddley picked up the envelope and stared at its blank back. "He made me the beneficiary of a life-insurance policy."

Why, he wasn't avoiding me; he was hurting. I got up and went over to lay both hands on his slumped shoulders and squeezed them. "That was real sweet of him, hon. Did he say why?"

He shoved the envelope into his shirt pocket. "Yeah. He left instructions about what he wants me to do with it." He reached for his cap. "There's a delivery coming in, so I'm gonna mosey back down to the nursery until dinnertime." I backed away, frustrated that he was so curt. He stood up and started out without even saying good-bye. I was too hurt to remind him, as I sometimes did, that men who kiss their wives good-bye live five years longer.

At the door, he turned. "Don't you be goin' off again—you hear me?"

"Of course not. I'll see you at home for dinner."

When he left, I returned to my own desk, puzzled. Seemed to me like he wasn't real jubilant about whatever Skye had asked him to do—which wasn't strange, now that I thought about it. The most likely explanation was that Skye wanted to buy the land for Hands Up Together all by himself, and had left money to do that. Was Joe Riddley disappointed they wouldn't be partners in that, that Skye would get all the privilege—and maybe all the glory? No, my husband had never been one to toot his horn with public giving. If he didn't get to help buy the land, he could contribute to the project some other way. He'd get over his disappointment.

But getting a legacy from Skye must make it very real to Joe Riddley that his friend was really truly gone. I'd cried with and held Gwen Ellen. He'd stomped around as usual, not talking about it much. I didn't know how to best help him.

If our church offered that course on grief again, I was definitely going to take it. The age we were getting to be, chances were we'd be doing a good bit of grieving in the coming years.

Meanwhile, I wanted to call Isaac James. As I reached for the phone, I played over in my mind what I'd tell him: "Listen, I got word that there's a man named Raymond who reserves cars coming up from Florida with Jimmy Bratson, the assistant manager down at Sky's the Limit. One of them was Maynard's car, which got picked up in Orlando full of drugs. I think you ought to check this out."

Then I imagined Isaac asking me Raymond's last name, and how I'd gotten the information, and why I had any reason to believe it was true. Finally, I imagined Isaac saying, "Butt out, Judge. Joe Riddley ought to put a leash on you."

No, he wouldn't say anything that crude. I was getting Isaac mixed up with Charlie. Still, I'd feel a lot better giving Isaac information I'd seen with my own two eyes, not hearsay from a kid who could barely vote. I wouldn't call Ike quite yet. First I'd call Laura. She had said she'd be back at MacDonald Motors this morning.

⤳ 19 ⤴

After Laura and I exchanged greetings, I asked about Skell and Gwen Ellen.

"No further word from Skell, so I told Mama he'll probably get here sometime this afternoon. She had an appointment with the lawyer this morning. Oh—and the funeral home called. The police are going to release Daddy's body this afternoon, so the funeral is definitely set for Saturday. We want Joe Riddley to be a pallbearer."

"I'll tell him. I know he'll be honored." I tried to figure out a graceful bridge between that and what I wanted to ask and couldn't find any, so I let the silence suffice. "Listen, I have one question. Where do you file sales records for Sky's the Limit? Paper files, not computer ones."

"Current records back to six months, we keep down there. The rest are in our file room here. Why?"

"I'd like to go through the records for the past six months. Would that be possible?"

If she'd been asking to go through my records, she'd have had to give me a real good reason, but Laura has always been easy for her friends to get along with. "Sure. You want to tell me why?"

"Not until I see you in person."

"When do you want to go down there? I'm pretty swamped today, but maybe tomorrow morning . . ."

"How about after you all close this evening?"

"What's Joe Riddley gonna say?"

"Joe Riddley has a meeting at the church. The missions committee got postponed because of Presidents' Day."

"Did we have Presidents' Day?" She sounded surprised.

"I'll call you tonight when Joe Riddley leaves," I suggested, "and we can go down then, if that's all right with you."

"No problem. I'll be ready."

She was wrong, unfortunately. There were a number of problems. First, Joe Riddley almost decided to stay home that evening and let the other members run the missions committee. "I hate to leave you," he told me, standing by the kitchen door and regarding me with a frown.

"Go ahead." I waved toward town to encourage him to start moving in that direction. "I'm going to have a quiet evening. Besides, without you they might forget to talk about Hands Up Together. You need to get working on that. We owe it to Skye."

"Yeah, I ought to at least go and talk about that. I went by to look at that land this afternoon after the skies cleared a little, and I think Skye was right—it's what we want. Money coming in for his memorials ought to go a good piece toward buying it."

"Is it on the same road where he died?"

"Right beside it. If I had to guess, I'd say he went out there to have one more look at it, and somebody ran over him. It could have been an accident."

"Don't be silly. He was hit with his own car," I reminded him.

"Yeah. It could have popped out of gear if he left it running."

"And found its way to the church parking lot?"

He scratched his jaw with one long finger. "That's a

problem I haven't quite solved." He took his cap and settled it on his head. "I'll be home early."

"Don't hurry on my account. Lulu and I will be fine." I bent to give her a pat so he couldn't see my face. We *would* be fine; we just wouldn't be fine together.

You'd have thought Joe was reading my thoughts, for he burst into a cackle of laughter on the curtain rod. I frowned up at him. I didn't want him putting ideas in Joe Riddley's head.

Joe Riddley ambled to his car at the speed of a slow snail. I watched his taillights disappear from sight, to be sure he didn't come back for something, then gave him time to get up to the end of our road before I called Laura. "I'm on my way. Is Skell there yet?"

"Not yet. Mama's climbing walls. Shall I pick you up, or meet you there?"

"Meet me there. There's no reason for you to come this far out of your way. I'll put my dishes in the sink and be there in fifteen minutes." I hadn't reckoned on a timber truck that had broken an axle near the railroad. It lay crookedly in my lane, long pine logs hanging off its tail like droopy feathers. Three trucks that had come to help were blocking the rest of the road, so I had to turn and use another route. I didn't have Laura's cell phone number to warn her I'd be late, and when I broke my own rule about not calling while driving to call the operator, I discovered that nobody keeps a record of cell phone numbers. You'd think a society smart enough to develop cell phones in the first place could develop a way to share the numbers, but smart isn't synonymous with intelligent.

By the time I got to Sky's the Limit, Laura must have been waiting a good ten minutes.

She stood leaning against her rear fender taking deep breaths of cool clean air, and acted like I was right on time. "Hey, Big Mac. You doin' all right?"

I was still wearing my work clothes, a taupe pantsuit with a chunky African necklace. Laura had changed into jeans, an oversized kelly green sweater I'd never seen, and loafers. The only odd note was the briefcase at her feet.

"If you aren't careful, people are going to start teasing you about that briefcase like they tease me about my pocketbook," I greeted her. "Our boys have threatened for years to bury me with my pocketbook and Joe Riddley in his cap."

She grinned. "I feel insecure without it."

"Well, you look marvelous. Downright beautiful. That's a great color for you, and your haircut is as chic as the ones your mama and Cindy got at that new place across town." Either the style made her face look thinner or she, like her mother, had lost weight in the past few days. And was that mascara I saw on her lashes? Before I could make sure, she'd turned to unlock the door.

When we got inside, even with the door locked behind us, I felt uneasy. There were no shades on those big plate-glass windows, so anybody driving by could see us and what we were doing. "There's not much privacy in here, is there?"

"We can use Skell's office." She took me through what I'd assumed was a bathroom or closet door, but which led to a narrow hall along one outer wall, with two doors off it and an exit at the end.

Laura unlocked the first door, and we stepped into an office that could have been on a different planet. Soft rust carpet. Elegant walnut desk with leather desk pad and calendar, brass pencil holder, designer lamp. Creamy walls. No windows, but two pieces of signed modern art on the walls in yellow, green, and red-orange. And—what was more useful—two green leather chairs.

"This is beautiful." I looked around in astonishment.

She nodded. "Skell's got good taste. Daddy said he could

have anything he wanted, but he'd have to pay for it. This is what he wanted."

"But it's so clean." *Think before you speak* is a great proverb, if I could remember it in time.

Her deep chuckle filled the office. "You've seen his apartment, I take it."

"Yeah, Saturday evening, looking for him."

She shrugged. "It's his life. Listen"—she motioned me to one chair and took the other—"can we talk a minute before we start going through the files? I've got a couple of things to tell you." Now I knew what was most different about Laura: somebody had plugged in her lights. She positively vibrated with excitement. I hadn't seen her like that since she got the letter saying she'd won a soccer scholarship to college.

Curious, I set my pocketbook beside my chair and crossed my legs. "So talk."

First, though, she pulled a pack of spearmint gum out of her pocket and offered me a stick. When I refused, she unwrapped two. "Ben suggested it. Sure beats chewing my hair." She folded the gum into her mouth and chewed to get it soft. While I waited, I noticed that she was wearing not only mascara, but blusher and the faintest touch of eye shadow.

"Ben suggested the gum?" I was surprised. "You mean he talked about something besides work?"

She blushed, then leaned forward and rested her arms on the desk. "The first thing I wanted to tell you is about Ben," she confided. "He came over yesterday afternoon to see how we were doing, but Mama was taking a nap. At first, he stood in the living room like—what was it you called him? A totem pole? But on impulse, I asked if he'd like to go up to my place for some coffee. I don't know why I suggested it—Ben and I have never been on that kind of terms. But he's been so nice since Daddy died, and I'd wondered

if maybe he could be shy. We used to have a girl on the soccer team who acted stiff because she was desperately shy.
So I took Ben upstairs and fed him coffee and Oreos—remember how they've always been my comfort food? Well,
they are his, too—and Mac, I swear I didn't know that man
could talk so much. It was like somebody took a cork out of
his mouth. We've always gotten along real good down at
work, but we'd never talked about anything except cars.
Yesterday he told me all about his wife—did you know
he'd been married? They were going to have a baby, but
she and the baby were both killed in a car wreck caused by
a drunk driver. Ben told me how that made him lock himself up inside and how he's finally beginning to thaw. Then
he told me about his family, and growing up—did you
know he really was a Boy Scout?" If her smile got any
wider she'd need two-by-fours to prop up her jaws. "He's
even an Eagle Scout. He talked about how he got Scout
from the pound, and what he wants to do with his life—
he'd like to own a car-repair business someday. You'd have
thought he'd been saving words up inside for years. Then I
admitted how scared I was that Skell would sell MacDonald's, and how I had no clue what I'd do if he did, and Ben
said I can come run his business. Suddenly we started
laughing and we couldn't stop. I don't think either one of
us ever talked so much or laughed so hard in our whole
lives."

I had certainly never heard Laura talk that much. Ben
wasn't the only one who'd lost his cork. Only one thing
prevented me from wishing her well and teasing her I'd
dance at her wedding: how timely it was of Ben Bradshaw
to start talking cozy to Laura now that her daddy was dead.
Ben had to know that even if Skye didn't leave the business
to Laura, he'd never leave her destitute.

I was wondering whether to say anything about that
when Laura said, "But that's not all. Guess what?" Without

giving me time to reply, she started pumping air with both fists. "Daddy didn't leave the dealership to Skell; he left it to Mama, and she's giving it to both of us equally!"

"Seriously?" When she nodded, I held out my arms. She surrounded me with hers, and we sat there hugging and giggling like a couple of hyenas until maybe she noticed I was turning purple from lack of air. She let me go and sat back in her chair.

"Daddy hadn't ever gotten around to actually making a will," she explained when we'd calmed down a little, "except one they made years ago leaving everything to each other. But the lawyer told Mama that Daddy called him Friday afternoon and said to draw up a new will leaving the business to Mama for her lifetime, then leaving it equally to Skell and me after she died. He told the lawyer he'd been talking to you and Joe Riddley, and he got to thinking it wasn't fair to leave me out, since I do as much as Skell around the place."

"Twice as much," I corrected her.

She shrugged. "Whatever. I enjoy it, and Skell doesn't. Anyway"—she grew grave—"the lawyer hadn't gotten it drawn up before Daddy died, of course, but Mama told him if that's what Daddy wanted, it's what she wants, too. She told him to draw up papers making us all partners during her lifetime. She'll get income to live on, but the business will be mine and Skell's right away."

"That's the best news I've heard all week." I found myself thinking real fond thoughts about Skye right then. "If Skell's smart, he'll move somewhere else and let you run the place. If he ever gets home, that is. And your mother can travel."

Laura nodded and spoke in her usual common-sense tone. "So, now that you've heard all my good news, let's look at those records. What are we looking for?" The soles of her loafers beat a tattoo on the floor, so I knew she was worrying we were there to find evidence against Skell.

"I came down here this morning and got to talking with your young salesman—Whitman?"

That got another chuckle out of her. "He's not a salesman. He cleans cars when they come in and details them before they leave the lot."

"What a relief. I was sure your business was on the skids. Anyway, he told me, with a little persuasion, that a man named Raymond calls Jimmy Bratson to reserve certain cars coming up from Florida."

"Say what?"

"He calls and tells Jimmy to reserve certain cars that are coming up from Florida."

She sat and digested that for a second. I found myself relieved. Laura wasn't going to lose her business head, no matter how much she talked and laughed with her head mechanic. She frowned. "He said Jimmy? Not Skell?"

"Whitman said Jimmy. That doesn't mean Skell's clean, but one call Whitman took was for Jimmy. I'd be willing to bet Raymond was supposed to get that car Maynard bought."

She sat a while longer, thinking that over.

"How did you come to hire Bratson?" She didn't seem likely to ever speak again if I didn't nudge her a little.

She sprawled her legs out in front of her and slid down in her chair. "I didn't. Skell did, the first month he was here. He was trying to show us he was taking charge of the place. So he announced one morning that he had hired a top-notch car salesman from Savannah who wanted to live in a smaller town. Daddy said it smelled, and I thought so, too, but since Jimmy's résumé looked all right, we agreed to give Skell some rope while he settled in. Used-car salesmen come and go. One more was no big deal." She stopped, then added as if explaining something I didn't know, "Skell needed to succeed real bad right then. He'd lost his girl-friend, and he'd hated his last two years of college; he needed to feel like he was able to do something right. And Jimmy can sell cars—no doubt about that. He's a lot better than the others when it comes to total sales for any given month. When Skell said he wanted to make him assistant manager a couple of months back, Daddy and I had no rea-son to disagree—except we neither one liked the man. But we didn't have to work with him. He and Skell seemed to get along real well. . . ." For the first time that evening, she sounded uncertain.

I spoke briskly. "What I want us to do is look through sales contracts and signatures to see if we can identify cars bought by this Raymond and a pattern to the sales. If we can get even a last name and an address, I think we ought to call Isaac."

She stood up, reluctant but game. "Let's get cracking."

We closed the door between the front office and the back hall, so nobody looking into the building would know we were there, but I begged, "Can we leave Skell's door half open? I never can work in a space without windows with-out feeling I'm underwater in a sub that's about to spring a leak." We left it open just a crack, and got to work.

Laura was faster than I. She knew the forms and what to look for. By the time we'd covered the past three months, she had seven sales forms laid to one side. I had two. The last names weren't the same, and sometimes the name was Raymond, sometimes Ramón, and once Richard, but the scrawl on the bottom was written by the same hand.

She looked at me with frightened eyes. "This is bigger than I imagined. I thought maybe once or twice. But this—" She waved her big hand over the desk. "Every car came up from Miami, every one was expensive, every one was paid for in full with cash. I didn't know Skell was taking in that much cash—he did his own books; that was part of what Daddy wanted. But this could close us down."

I mustered a lot more cheerfulness than I felt. "Not necessarily, if you didn't know anything about it."

"But Skell—Skell . . ." She couldn't say it. She pressed her lips together and looked away. "How could he?" she demanded. "Daddy worked his whole life to build up this business. How could he jeopardize it like that? It's not like he was short of money—we pay him well."

"Porsche money? Enough to fix up his office like this?"

She shook her head. "We both inherited money from our grandparents, in a trust fund. We got the accumulated interest on it when we turned twenty-one, and control when we turned twenty-five. Skell used his interest for the Porsche and office furniture." Her mouth twisted in a sad grin. "He wanted to look prosperous." She'd always understood Skell better than the rest of us.

"What did you buy with yours?" I couldn't remember a thing she'd ever bought except a few clothes. She didn't even go anywhere except business trips and family vacations.

She smiled, but her eyes were wistful. "I was saving to buy Daddy out. I thought if I could get together enough for a down payment, he'd know I was serious." She sat up again and her eyes were now worried. "If Skell goes to jail, won't they confiscate the business?"

I heaved a heavy sigh. "I have no idea, honey. It would depend on how involved the business is in criminal activities. I think it would just be Sky's the Limit, in any case."

"This is going to kill Mama. It will be the absolute last—"

"What are you doing here?"

Jimmy Bratson must have come in with deliberate stealth. Neither of us had heard a sound until he spoke from the open office door. He looked from me to Laura and back again, a tic jumping in one cheek. When he saw the sales records, his eyes narrowed.

"Hey, Jimmy." Laura swept the records into a pile, covering the ones she'd separated, and her voice was normal and friendly. "I needed some sales figures and asked Judge Yarbrough here to come down with me so I wouldn't be alone."

"What figures did you need? I'd have gotten them for you."

"I know, but I wanted them this evening. With everything I have to do since Daddy died and Skell left town, I'm having to work evenings for a while. I knew you'd worked a lot of overtime already this past week, so I didn't like to bother you."

She was as cool and calm as a June magnolia. I was so proud of her I wanted to burst.

It was time to contribute my bit. "Are we done, honey? I told Joe Riddley I'd be back by—" I checked my watch and didn't have to fake my alarm. "Heavens, we've been here longer than I thought." I reached for my pocketbook.

"Who is it?"

That was another voice, deep and rough. Jimmy Bratson stepped into the office so the other man could fill the door—and fill it he did. He was big in every sense—a big head with thick dark brown hair, big shoulders, and legs like tree trunks, encased in a brown suit classier than we generally saw around Hopemore. The gold buckle to his belt was almost hidden by a paunch that indicated he'd enjoyed more big meals than were good for him in what I guessed to be about forty years of living. As he held open the door, I saw the gleam of a watch that looked a lot like Skye's Rolex. As his eyes moved from Laura to me, it took all the willpower I possessed not to shudder. Those bulbous brown eyes were the deadest I'd ever seen. If there was still a soul behind them, God alone could see it.

Laura stood and held out her hand. "I'm Laura MacDonald, one of the owners. And you are—?"

The other man looked at her without saying a word. Jimmy answered quickly. "A customer. I told him I'd meet him here when he got off work." He gave a little laugh. "Anything for a sale these days, you know."

Laura gave the big man her wide, friendly smile. "You're in good hands. I hope you find the car you want. And if you decide you'd rather have a new car, come on up to Mac-Donald Motors. We'll see to it that Jimmy doesn't lose his commission. Good night." She'd been gathering the records into a pile and stuffing them into her briefcase. Now she turned off Skell's desk lamp, so that the only light came from the hall behind the big man. Still smiling, she started toward the door as if it were the most normal thing in the world to leave these two thugs in her brother's office. But I'd seen that smile on Laura's face before. It was the smile she wore when she planned to lead her team to slaughter their opponents.

"Lady, we're going to need to see what you've got in that bag." The big man hadn't moved from the door. Now he put out his hand like a father asking for a smutty magazine.

"Sorry, these are confidential files." Laura continued walking toward the door. "If you all will excuse us—" Jimmy Bratson shifted nearer to me, and I felt trapped in a very small space with too many people. My corner didn't hold as much air as I was going to need in the next few minutes. I reached for my pocketbook, wondering if we could bluff our way out of this. That man in the doorway was the most unpleasant customer I'd seen in a long time.

"Give me the briefcase." He reached out a hand the size of a salad plate to take it. Laura swung it behind her, turned like a discus thrower, and delivered a knee to his groin.

"Pocketbook!" she shouted. As he doubled over in pain, she threw her shoulder at him. Off balance, he toppled. I heard him crash to the floor, but I didn't stop to look. I was busy.

I swung my pocketbook hard. It hit Jimmy Bratson's most vulnerable parts with a most satisfying *thwack*. Jimmy fell to the floor, yelping and clutching himself. I circled him and hared after Laura faster than I knew I could run.

❧ 20 ❧

We dashed out the front door into the glare of the parking lot halogen lights—straight into Isaac James, who had his arms raised and his gun drawn. He jerked us away from the glass door and thrust us roughly aside. "What you doin' in there?"

I was panting too hard to talk. Laura caught her breath and explained.

"There's two men in Skell's office writhing on the floor, wishing they'd been born female. I got one with my knee and Mac took out the other with her pocketbook. We think those lowlifes have been using this place to pass drugs."

I noticed she didn't mention her brother.

Ike put a heavy hand on my shoulder and another at Laura's shoulder. "That's why we're here." He shoved, not real gently. "Go. We can talk later."

I looked around and saw several officers peering from behind cars.

"There's a back door," I warned as Ike hustled us toward our cars.

"We got it covered," he promised. "You all go home."

When Isaac growled in that tone of voice, people obeyed.

Laura and I headed for our respective vehicles. She looked as pale and wrung-out as a bleached dishrag. My knees were so wobbly, I could hardly walk. "Honey, we both need a stiff drink after all that," I told her. "Come out to our place for a cup of coffee."

She hesitated. "I'd like to go see if Skell's home. Come to our place, instead."

"Just for a few minutes."

On the way, I pulled over and tried to call Joe Riddley, but he wasn't there. No point in leaving a message—he never checked the answering machine.

When I parked in front of the MacDonalds' big garage, Laura came to meet me. "Skell's car's not here, and Mama and Tansy are in the den—probably watching TV. I don't know about you, but I'm too shaky to go in there. Come up to my place. Okay?"

I agreed. We didn't want Gwen Ellen asking what had us as white and trembling as dogwoods in a gale. Besides, I was curious about Laura's apartment. You can tell a lot about a woman from how she fixes up her home.

While we climbed the stairs, I heard the boom of a deep-voiced clock chiming nine. Laura looked back with a worried frown. "I still think I ought to be over at the used-car lot. I don't like not being around when something's going on."

"Ike will call you if he needs to," I reassured her. "He knows where to find you."

She gave a short, not-funny laugh. "He sure does. After I blurted out to Chief Muggins yesterday that Skell was coming home today, every police car in town's been watching us. They've had a cruiser at the end of our drive all day, another outside the dealership, and one over at Skell's place. Nobody's here just now, but when they're done down at the car lot, they'll be back." She unlocked her door and held it wide. "I wish I'd invited you up here before. This isn't the happiest of times, but welcome."

I stepped in to the scents of lemon polish and potpourri, and spoke without remembering to be tactful. "Why, honey, this is lovely." I dropped my pocketbook on the nearest chair and stood there staring and smelling like a kid at the circus.

She wore a smile as she turned on lamps. "Did you think I'd just thrown together a place to sleep in?"

That was exactly what I had thought, but Mama used to say there are times in a woman's life when the truth just won't do. "Of course not," I said with all the indignation I could muster. "But some folks don't fix up a place if they are mostly there to sleep." Her brother's stinking, cluttered apartment came to mind. "This is wonderful."

She'd painted the walls taupe and the woodwork white, and put in oak floors that were bare except for two striking Oriental rugs in a pattern of greens and blues. Valances in the MacDonald green-and-navy tartan hung over oak miniblinds at the two windows in the front wall, and oak bookshelves lined the back wall. Her grandmother Skellton's grandfather clock sat in one corner. That's what I'd heard coming up the stairs. Three big square chairs—one green, one blue, and one in the MacDonald tartan—sat diagonally in the corners of one rug, and each had an ottoman in front of it and a small table beside it with a good light for reading and a place to set a mug. "You make me want to sit down and read for hours."

"I do," she admitted, setting her briefcase on a small bench by the door. "When I walk through that door, I drop my work right here and forget all about it." She moved with her long, graceful gait to the other side of the long room, where a round oak table with four chairs sat on the companion rug and a compact kitchen lurked behind louvered doors. "Coffee or tea?" She pulled down thick white mugs.

"Coffee—leaded. After what we've been through, I need all the lead I can get."

"Would you like to wash your hands while it brews?"

"I feel like a shower after meeting those two charmers, but I'll settle for a good wash."

She led me into a small bedroom with pale green walls, white muslin curtains, bare floors except for two small rugs beside the bed, and a tailored spread of—what else?—the clan tartan.

I looked around admiringly. "This is real restful. You've created a beautiful home."

"Thanks." Her cheeks grew so pink with pleasure, I figured she hadn't gotten many chances to show it off. "Bathroom's through that door in the corner."

The bathroom was as simple as the bedroom, but it smelled like Irish Spring soap and was full of thick towels and one real good pencil drawing that not only soothed my spirits, but made me want to go home and do something to spruce up my own bathroom a bit.

I was just stepping back into the main room to the tempting smell of fresh coffee when we heard feet on the stairs and a soft tatoo on the door. It opened a crack. "You here, Sissy? You got Marvin?"

Skell peered around the door. He wore white jeans with a sharp crease and a freshly ironed shirt. He also had that pink look of a man who has just stepped out of the shower. His dark curls were still damp.

His face brightened as he saw Laura. "Hey, you cut your hair! It looks great. And Mac. Hey! How're you doin'?"

Laura and I both knew Skell was being charming to disarm. She flew across the room, grabbed him by the shoulders, and shook him furiously. "Where the dickens have you been? You—"

"Don't loosen his fillings," I chided, hurrying over to give Skell a hug. "We've been missing you, boy." I almost reached up to push back a curl that fell over his forehead before I recalled that he was grown now, not the little boy who used to come stay with us for long weekends.

"Yeah, we missed you all right." It distressed me to see how much Laura's frown mirrored Skye's when he was displeased with his son. "You sure picked the wrong time to skip town, Bro."

I reached for my pocketbook. "I'll go. You all have got a lot of talking to do."

"Don't leave." She caught my arm. "Stay and keep me from killing him."

He looked from one of us to the other, puzzled. "Hey, I'll pay back the money. Is Daddy furious? I'm going to see him in a minute, but I thought I'd better come up here first to test the waters."

Laura and I both froze. I wondered how she'd break the news. She did it with two silver bullets: "Daddy's dead."

"Dead?" Skell took two steps backwards.

He'd forgotten he still stood in the doorway. He would have fallen downstairs and possibly broken his neck if she hadn't grabbed his arm. She hauled him back and headed him toward the big green chair. "He was killed Friday night. They found him Saturday afternoon."

"Killed? How? By who?" Without waiting for an answer, he muttered, "No way," and sank into the chair. He stared up at us and we stared down at him. Pain was thick around us, and the only sound in the room was the ticking of the grandfather clock.

At last, Skell spoke in a choked voice, "What happened? Have you already buried him?" His face had lost so much color that his eyes looked black—and bleak.

Laura leaned against a bookshelf, started at the end of his questions, and worked her way back. "The funeral's Saturday. They had to do an autopsy. He was run over by a car out on a dirt road off Warner Road, but they don't know yet who was driving."

"No way," he repeated, shaking his head. Then he buried

his face in his hands and crumpled forward. "Oh, God. I wish I'd known."

Laura glared down at him. "I wish you had, too. We could have used you around here. Why didn't you call? If you had called the dealership, you'd have heard the message about why we were closed."

"I"—he started out firmly enough, but tapered off—"didn't want to talk to Daddy." His breath came in quick little puffs. "And they don't know who killed him?"

Somebody had to tell him. Laura didn't, so I was elected. "They think you did. They've arrested Mr. Garcia from the restaurant—"

"Rosita's daddy? No way!"

"Yes way," I said, using our grandson Cricket's favorite comeback to that, "but they don't have a lot of solid evidence against him. And Chief Muggins has mentioned several times how funny it looks that you disappeared just before the body was found."

"They've been watching the house, the business, and your place, waiting for you to come home," Laura added.

"I wouldn't kill Daddy!" He pressed his temples and shook his head. "I can't believe this. After all I've been through—"

"All *you've* been through?" Laura's eyes were blue fire, and she pitched words at him like boulders. "We've got a business to run here. People to take care of. Cars to sell and service. You can't just go off and party any time you feel like it without telling a soul where you are."

Skell's anger rose, equally hot. "You think I was partying? You don't have any more faith in me than that?" His face was as pink as hers, his mouth equally tight. "I was trying to save your—"

I held up one hand. "Stop it, both of you. Skell, the police are busy right now, but they'll be back. Bring your car into the garage."

"No, put it down in the woods behind the garage." Laura reached down and hauled him up by one arm. "We don't want Mama knowing you are here yet. But hurry! And take off your shoes. We don't want her recognizing the sound of your big feet." I knew for a fact that he wore an eight, she an eleven.

He slipped off his running shoes and padded downstairs carrying them. Laura sank into the blue chair, kicked off her loafers, and drew her long legs up to hug her knees. She used to sit like that as a little girl when one of childhood's tragedies had gotten to be more than she could handle. Resting her chin on her knees, she said, "Sit down and take the load off your feet, Mac. I'll get the coffee in a minute."

"Let me get it, honey. It will give me something to do besides look at your unhappy face."

I poured milk into the pitcher she'd already put out and was setting a steaming mug beside each chair when Skell came back as quietly as he'd left. As soon as he came in the door, I started talking, hoping to calm the air a little. "We mothers are amazing, when you think about it. We recognize our children by all sorts of little things—your footsteps, the sound of your sneezes and coughs. I even read somewhere that no matter how many children a woman has, she can tell you which one took off a T-shirt by the smell."

Skell grinned as he closed the door behind him. "Mama sure could if she got a whiff of the one I took off tonight. I'd had it on two days. I didn't want to buy more than one outfit on the trip, but I figured everybody would appreciate it if I stopped by my place and cleaned up before—"

Death has a way of sneaking up on you again and again. I saw the exact second when Skell realized his daddy wasn't going to appreciate anything he did, ever again. He came to a full halt and his eyes got pink. "Where is Marvin?" he asked hastily, blinking rapidly as he peered around.

"Over at Cindy and Walker's," Laura told him shortly. Anybody could tell her mind wasn't on ferrets.

Skell, though, looked like he needed a bit more time to pull himself together, so I added, "Cindy's feeding him, and the kids are spoiling him rot—"

"That ferret is the least of our worries."

Laura would never have interrupted me if she wasn't so upset.

❧ 21 ❧

I took the plaid chair, propped my feet on the ottoman since they didn't reach the floor, and picked up my coffee. "Sit down and drink your coffee, Skell. Then tell us where you've been and what you've been up to."

He dropped into the chair, laid his head against the chair back, and closed his eyes. When he spoke, his voice sounded two hundred years old. "You all have no idea what's going on."

"Try us." When Laura started to speak, I waved for her to be quiet. "Go on. Tell us."

We waited while he collected his thoughts. Normally I enjoy sitting in silence in a room full of the smell of hot coffee while a clock gently ticks. That night we were all too jumpy to enjoy anything. Skell's right leg was jiggling so much it jingled the change in his pockets. Laura kept reaching for a hank of hair that wasn't there. When the ice maker dumped ice, I jumped like somebody had shot me. Even my coffee tasted bitter.

Skell finally began. "When I got to work Friday—and yes"—he opened his eyes and looked at Laura—"I was late. Very late. I'd been out the night before, and my alarm didn't go off."

She started to speak, but again I flapped a hand at her.

"Hush. You've got the rest of your life to fuss at him. Let him tell his story."

He sipped his coffee, then cupped the mug in both hands like he needed the warmth. "When I got to work, Bratson was in my office, talking to somebody on my private line. He knew not to use my office when I wasn't there—I'd told him a hundred times. I walked in on him, thinking I'd really raise sand this time. As soon as he saw me, he muttered, 'I'll call you back,' and hung up. But before I could light in on him, he started in on me. Said I'd really blown it this time, that Daddy had come down when I wasn't there and sold a car that he—Bratson—had promised to his best customer, and if I didn't get the car back, the guy would take his business elsewhere. Now, I'm not the best car dealer in the world, but I know a fishy story when I hear one, and all the time he was talking, a muscle was jumping in his cheek like something was trying to get out. I played along at first—told him we'd find an equally good car for his customer. But he kept getting more upset until I said, 'Why don't you tell me what's really going on?' "

Skell stopped to take an enormous breath. Laura's chair creaked slightly as she shifted. "So Bratson said, 'There's thousands of dollars' worth of merchandise in that car—you understand me? Expensive merchandise. And the person who put it there is not going to be happy when his man comes to pick up the car and it's not here. You'd better get it and get it fast.' Then he moved around so he was between me and the door—" Skell stopped and shivered.

Laura's eyes met mine. "We know how you felt, honey," I told him. "We had a little run-in with Mr. Bratson tonight. He's a scary person."

"You know?" He whirled toward Laura. He read the answer in her eyes. "How long have you known?"

"Only since tonight. And I can see how you'd be scared of him and that goon he's partners with, but—"

"I never saw his partner."

"Count yourself fortunate," I said at exactly the same time Laura asked, "Why didn't you just go tell Daddy the truth?"

"Are you kidding? I hired Bratson practically over Daddy's dead body." Horror dawned in his eyes. "They killed him, didn't they? They thought he knew, but he didn't. They killed him!"

He looked so wretched, I wanted to hold him on my lap and promise everything was going to be all right. Instead, I sighed. "It's certainly a good possibility." Such a good possibility, in fact, it was what had sent me to look at their used-car-lot records that very night.

"You should have told Daddy." Laura's whisper was raw with anguish. Again she drew up her knees and wrapped her arms around them. This time she laid her face on them as well.

"Look," Skell appealed to the top of her head, "I wasn't doing a good job of running the lot. We both know that. But I didn't need him flinging it in my face that I'd hired a drug dealer to help me run the place."

Skell's whimper was the signal for Laura to come over to his side. She'd always done it before. She clasped her arms tighter around her legs, and I sensed the battle she was fighting within. I held my breath. Would she comfort her little brother one more time and assure him she would make everything all right? Or would she let him face the fact that this time the consequences of his irresponsibility were bigger than she could—or even wanted to—fix?

She raised a face pink with tears and shot me a look of pure pain; then she said sadly, "You really messed up. You hired that scum, and you didn't watch him."

Her unexpected reproach stung him. "I couldn't know

every dang thing that went on at that lot. I couldn't be thinking about it every minute. I have a life, you know." She didn't say a word, just looked at him. "Besides," he ploughed on, "I thought at first I could fix it pretty easy. I headed over to MacDonald's to tell Daddy to call the person he'd sold the car to and get it back. But Daddy wouldn't even try. He said Maynard bought that car for his honeymoon and wasn't likely to return it. I told him he had no business working our lot just because Bratson and I weren't there, that I've got other salesmen, and this was real important. Then he started yelling, like he always did. He yelled that I was supposed to be at the lot, but if I wasn't, he'd sell cars to whoever he da—" Skell shot me a look and amended that to "whoever he pleased. Finally he told me if I wanted that car back, I had to tell Maynard myself." Skell had gotten all fired up with indignation, but he suddenly stopped. Regret spread over his face like a cloud. His voice dropped to a husky whisper. "I only saw him twice that day, and both times we yelled at each other." He blinked back new tears.

We could have plied him with platitudes about how his Daddy knew he didn't mean it, but the truth is, sometimes we *feel* guilty because we *are*. Fighting with his daddy that last day and never making it up was something Skell would have to make his own peace with.

"Why didn't you explain to him what was really going on?" Laura repeated.

"Can you imagine what he'd have said if I'd come right out with, 'Look, Daddy, I need you to get me out of a scrape here. Jimmy Bratson is using Sky's the Limit to pass drugs from Florida to the north, and that car you sold Maynard is full of them'? He would have kicked my butt from MacDonald Motors to kingdom come."

"Maybe so," she said soberly, "but he might have been

able to help. And no matter how loud he yelled, Daddy really did want you to make a go of it."

Skell angrily brushed away a tear. "Daddy wanted me to be him. I'm not him. I never was and I never will be. But I did want to make him proud of me. I thought if I could handle this—if I could make this one thing come out halfway right—maybe just once he'd be proud of me." He dropped his face to his hands, and his shoulders heaved with sobs. "I never did a thing in my life that made Daddy proud."

"Mama's proud of you," Laura said gruffly. "You've always had that." Her own eyes were full of tears. "And Daddy loved you. He loved you the most." Her voice was a harsh whisper.

"Stop it," I snapped. Sure, I wished I could reach out and hold that whole hurting family in my own short arms, but we needed some facts before we smothered in sentiment. "Your parents both loved each of you, but they weren't perfect. They had some dreams for you that you didn't dream, and sometimes they didn't understand the ones you did dream. That's how earthly parents are. Fortunately, you have—"

"—three parents," Laura finished for me. She hiccupped and sniffed. "And all we have to worry about is making our heavenly parent proud. He's a lot easier to please, anyway." She gave me a watery smile. "I'll bet you thought I wasn't listening to all those Sunday school lessons back in seventh grade."

"I thought your mind was one hundred percent on soccer," I admitted. "And that little redheaded boy with the freckles—what was his name?" I got my feet down off the ottoman and headed for a box of tissues.

Her voice followed me. "Barry Wilson. He could swing a mean bat. But I was listening, Mac. I just didn't absorb what you said until later."

I rested a hand on her shoulder as I thrust the tissue box under her nose. "Here, you both need these."

I refilled our mugs while they wiped their eyes and blew their noses; then I sat back down and informed Skell, "So far you haven't told us much we don't know. We know what happened Friday—you looked for Maynard and finally found him, but couldn't get him to trade cars. Then you tried again after the wedding, but he still wouldn't. What happened after that? For starters, where were you Friday night?"

He sniffed a few times and took a fortifying gulp of hot black coffee. "You don't know jack. Sure, I looked for Maynard all Friday afternoon, but I wasn't trying real hard. Mostly I was mad at Daddy and avoiding going back to work and good old Bratson. I figured I'd find Maynard eventually, and when I did, I'd take that Beamer straight to Isaac James and tell him the whole story. But then, around five, Bratson called on my cell phone, and it was like he was reading my mind. He said he hoped I wasn't getting any funny ideas about going to the police with the car, because if I did, he'd tell Chief Muggins— who plays poker with him every week—that Daddy and I both knew everything that was going on. He said he had somebody who would back him up in court. They'd plea-bargain and get off for testifying against us, and we'd both go to jail. Then he laughed—he actually laughed— and he said, 'Bye, bye MacDonald Motors.'" Skell shook his head in disbelief. "He was going to take down the whole company, Sissy. I couldn't let that happen if I could help it." You'd have thought Skell had been MacDonald Motor's greatest champion since birth. "That's when I really started looking seriously for Maynard—and you," he nodded toward me—"told me where he was. I offered to practically give him any other car on the lot. I even offered to loan him my car for his honeymoon, but he wouldn't deal."

Laura blinked in surprise. "You offered him the Porsche?"

"I had to. I was desperate." Skell massaged his temples with both hands in memory of that headache. "I was afraid to go home—afraid Bratson would send some goons to rough me up. And I was afraid if I came over here, they'd follow me and—I didn't know what they might do."

He stopped and stared into the futility of that evening. "I never thought they'd hurt Daddy."

"We don't know that they did," I reminded him.

"Who else would? Everybody loved him. He was great—"

"Finish your story, honey. Just finish your story."

"I spent Friday night parked in one of Ridd's cornfields down by your place, figuring nobody would look there. I drove up the road to Spence's place early Saturday, but Maynard's car wasn't there, so I decided he must be staying over at his new place. I didn't want to ruin the wedding, so I lay low until it was over; then I tackled him again before they left. You were there, Mac. You know."

I nodded.

"By then, I'd had time to think, and I was scared something might happen to Maynard and Selena if Bratson's folks caught them driving the Beamer. For all I knew, his pals were watching all roads out of town. When Maynard wouldn't take the Porsche, I decided I'd have to follow them and try to keep them safe."

"Just like that," I said. "You'd go down to Orlando, find two honeymooners out of the entire city, and guard them for a week. Did you plan to share their room?"

"I didn't plan anything, I just knew I didn't want them getting hurt. We sold them that car, and MacDonald's takes care of its customers."

Laura's eyes met mine, equally astonished at the thoroughness of Skell's conversion.

He was too deep in his story to notice us. "I followed them far enough to see that nobody seemed to be tracking them, and that they were heading toward I-95. Then I doubled back to the dealership. I was going to ask you for cash, Sissy—my credit cards are all maxed out, and I didn't have enough money for the trip. But you weren't there—I didn't see a soul, in fact. So I went into Daddy's office and took what I needed."

"Not bothering to write a note," she pointed out, not crediting him with sainthood yet.

"I couldn't find a pen in his desk, and I was in a hurry to catch Maynard before Bratson's men got on his tail."

"It didn't occur to you to call afterwards to say you were leaving town and taking the money?"

"I tried calling, but you weren't at the dealership—the salesman who answered said you'd gone home for something. I sure wasn't going to call there and risk getting Daddy."

"You couldn't," she reminded him. "I'd gone home because Isaac James called and told me to go home to be with Mama—they'd just found Daddy's body."

Skell pounded the chair arm in frustration. "Don't!"

She sighed. "Okay, but I wish you'd been here. It's been rough on Mama. Having you here would have made it a little easier. And you didn't *call.*"

"You've played that theme already. I'll try to make it up to Mama. I really will. Right then, all I could think of was catching Maynard and Selena. I drove like a wild man, but he's fast, too. I didn't catch them until well past Brunswick. By then I'd thought about poor Marvin, and how I'd forgotten to feed him Friday morning. My phone was in my jacket, which was in the backseat, so I couldn't reach it until they stopped for dinner. By then we were in the middle of God only knows where, and the call got dropped. I needed to grab something to eat and get back

to the parking lot before they came out, so I hurried to the
john, then grabbed a table near the door and ordered
something I could eat fast. I figured I'd call you again
when I got back on the road. That's when I realized I'd
left the phone on the counter in the john after I washed
my hands."

"That's three in one year, Skell. You've got to—"

I held up a hand to stop her. "Let him finish, honey. You
didn't think Maynard and Selena would be all right once
they got out of town, Skell?" I felt very old and stodgy listening to his adventures. I'd have been ready to turn around
after I saw them safe as far as Brunswick, and come home
to bed.

"I didn't know what to think." His voice rose in despera-
tion. "But that car had come up from Miami through a lot
in Orlando. I was afraid whoever put those drugs in the car
was still down there, and might recognize it."

"Somebody did," I affirmed. "The police got a tip-off
about the drugs the very next morning." I was about to add
"and arrested Maynard and Selena," but Skell was already
talking. "That was me." He dismissed that incident with the
wave of one who has done something clever but refuses to
be praised. "I'd had a hell of a night. I don't know how de-
tectives do stakeouts, because hotel security booted me out
less than thirty minutes after I started lurking in Maynard's
hall. So I parked my car near theirs and tried every trick in
the book to stay awake watching it, but I kept falling
asleep. I hadn't slept much the night before," he added defensively.

"About five I woke and saw two guys lounging over at
the edge of the lot, eying the Beamer. They could have just
been interested, or they could have been regular thieves,
but I was afraid they could be Bratson's people. I was so
scared, I nearly wet my pants. I realized I could never keep
watch all week. I'd have to sleep sometime. And even if I

caught Bratson's men near the car, what could I do then? I'm no television hero. I couldn't think of a single way to keep Maynard safe until I realized if the police had the car, Bratson would have no reason to go after him. So I went to a pay phone in the hotel and tipped them off about drugs in the car."

I choked on my coffee. Laura asked in a disbelieving voice, "You put Maynard and Selena in jail to keep them safe?"

"I didn't think the police would *arrest* them," he said hotly. "I figured Maynard would tell them he'd just bought the car Friday, produce the sales papers that were probably still in it, and the police would take away the car and call MacDonald's. I knew at that point Daddy would have to know what was going on, but I figured he'd know what to do."

"Bratson had already threatened to swear in court your Daddy knew about the drugs," I reminded him.

He sighed in utter weariness. "Look, I didn't think of everything, okay? I was going on sleep deprivation at that point. I'd done what I could, and was ready to let Daddy take it from there. All I could think of was how to get rid of that car so Bratson's folks would write it off as lost and lose interest in Maynard and Selena."

"That logic may be hard for you to explain to Maynard and Selena," I warned. "They're out on bail—Walker went down and took care of that—but you'd better plan on going back with them to testify in their defense."

"Of course."

Had I ever been that young? I'd certainly never gotten through life on money, good looks and charm, as Skell had. He could be about to find out the limits of how far they could take him.

Laura rose to refill our cups. From the slump of her shoulders, I saw she was still, to some measure, carrying her little brother's burdens. But she was also upset enough with him to turn and demand, "So you got Maynard and Selena safely tucked away in jail on what—Sunday morning? Why didn't you come back home then? Or at least call?"

He shrugged. "Look, I didn't know there was anything wrong here, and I was dead tired. I'd saved Maynard and Selena, hadn't I? All I could think about was crashing. I slept twenty-four hours. Then I went out and bought some clean clothes, and as long as I was in Orlando, I figured I deserved some R and R. It had been a while since I saw Mickey Mouse, so I went to renew our acquaintance." He gave her his old saucy grin, then saw that Laura wasn't thrilled with his explanation. He added defensively, "And I did call almost as soon as I woke up—I left a message on your phone." When she still didn't answer, he muttered, "I wanted you to square things with Daddy."

"Which I couldn't," she replied with a fierceness that surprised him and me both, "because all the time you were fighting with Maynard, hiding in Mac's cornfield, and driving around the country, Daddy was dead. Do you hear me, Skell? He's dead. And now that you're home, you're in a heck of a mess. Not about the money—although Daddy would have skinned you alive and nailed your hide to the barn if he'd found out about that, and I may still do it—but because Chief Muggins honestly believes you killed him. Do you realize that? You are in deep doo-doo, Bro, and there's not a thing either one of us can do about it." Her voice choked. She rested her palms on her countertop and her strong body shook with sobs.

I just couldn't stand to see her like that. I went to put my arms around her waist. "Shush," I said softly. "You've both been through a horrible week, and you're tired. Don't say things you will regret. I'll call Ike when I get home and see what we can do."

I was offering comfort where I probably shouldn't, but

we'd all had as much as we could stand right then. I caught the time from the corner of my eye and exclaimed thankfully, "Is it past ten already? I missed a chime in there somewhere. I'd better hurry. Once the news comes on, Joe Riddley will start noticing I'm gone. Skell, stay here with your mother and don't show your face around town until you hear from me. I don't know how we'll work this out, but we will. Laura, go to bed. You look too tired to move."

I grabbed my pocketbook and headed for the door. "After tonight, I don't think it will be too hard to suggest to Isaac that Jimmy Bratson may have run over your daddy."

"On Friday night?" Skell's head had fallen to the back of Laura's chair and lay like it might never rise again. He shook it without raising it. "It wasn't Bratson. He was at the lot until nine and went straight home. I know, because I swung by the lot after I left Maynard's, and followed him. I wanted to be sure he wasn't out around town following me. I even swung by his place twice after that, to make sure his car was there, and I called six or seven times. When he answered, I hung up. But he was definitely there."

"He may have been as scared as you," Laura pointed out. "Maybe he figured he'd let you get killed while he stayed home." Her eyes met mine, and hers were bleak. "If it was one of the others, we may never know."

On that cheerful note, I left.

The streets were deserted, so I broke my own rule about driving and talking to call the station on my way home. I caught Ike finishing up his paperwork. "Thought I ought to tell you why Laura and I were over at Sky's the Limit tonight, and what we found." I explained about talking with Whitman and what he'd said about Raymond. I also explained what Laura's records showed about sales of cars to a person who used several names but seemed to be the same man.

"Great. That, with what we've already got from jail

ought to put them away awhile. Of course, they'll probably just start running their business from jail." He sounded both bitter and discouraged. "You and I both know, Judge, how much this 'war on drugs' amounts to. Heck, drug dealers go to jail and run huge networks inside, aided by crooked guards with small salaries and big dreams. And no drug dealer ever gets the same sentence for years of successfully planning and dealing desolation that a person gets for one botched murder. If I had my way, the whole issue of capital punishment would center not on whether to use it, but on who to use it against. I'd start with drug lords and pedophiles."

"If you'll add corporate executives who walk off with fortunes and leave behind ruined businesses with depleted pension funds, you might get my vote. But listen, you need to know something. Laura and I learned tonight that Bratson plans to say that Skye and Skell were both in this up to their necks—that they knew all about the drugs." If Ike thought we'd learned it from Bratson himself, he'd drawn his own conclusion. I never said it.

He surprised and pleased me. "That bird won't fly. Skye suspected something funny was going on a couple of months ago and asked us to put somebody in there undercover, to keep an eye open. It was our man's report that sent us out there tonight."

Poor Skell. Thinking he was saving his daddy while his daddy was busy saving him. If only he had told his Daddy the truth about Maynard's car . . . Then I had a most embarrassing thought. "Not Whitman?" Surely our police force wasn't that desperate for undercover agents?

Isaac's laugh rumbled through the receiver. "Heavens no. Fellow named Bumby. We brought him in from out of state, so nobody would recognize him. Big guy, looks real soft and easygoing. . . ."

I sighed in relief. "I saw him. Glad you got your men.

Even their mothers would have trouble loving that pair. But that's not all I wanted to talk to you about. We've heard from Skell."

Before Ike could growl more than "Where is—?" I hurried on. "He says he didn't kill his daddy, and I believe him, but he thinks it's possible the big man you arrested tonight may have. He also says Jimmy Bratson was home Friday evening—they were in pretty close phone contact while Skell was trying to find Maynard's car."

"So Skell was involved in this." Ike sounded both convinced and discouraged.

"I don't think so. He says he learned about the drugs Friday afternoon, which is why he was so frantic to get that car back from Maynard. He even followed them to Orlando, in case Bratson's men closed in on Maynard and Selena."

"What the heck did Skell think he could do? You may not remember, but I coached that kid in T-ball, years ago. His confidence always has been bigger than his ability. But heck—who could hit a ball with his daddy sitting there yelling at his every mistake?"

I sighed. "He's made some whopping mistakes this past week without his daddy yelling at him. I have advised him not to show his face in town until all this is cleared up, but meanwhile, could you check on the whereabouts of Mr. Bratson's friend Friday evening?"

"I'll do that, Judge. But you leave the detecting to us. You hear me? This is the big leagues, not T-ball."

❧ 22 ❧

Wednesday's weekly *Hopemore Statesman* carried a fine article on Skye and his many services to the community, and said the funeral would be Saturday morning at ten. Friends could visit with the family at the funeral home on Friday evening.

Thursday morning, the world started going downhill in a go-cart with faulty brakes.

Around eight-thirty Isaac called. "You seen this week's paper yet?"

"Got it right here. I was reading about Skye's funeral."

His voice was sour. "You see the picture on page one?"

I couldn't miss it. The entire front page was devoted to how our police arrested Jimmy Bratson, former assistant manager of Sky's the Limit, and Richard Smith, alias Raymond Smythe, alias Ramón Suarez, on charges of conspiring to ship drugs between Florida and northern destinations. The article was accompanied by a three-column picture of the two men limping out the Sky's the Limit door in obvious pain.

"That picture's gonna give us trouble in court," Ike grumbled. "They're sure to allege police brutality. The only way we can prove we didn't beat up on them is to call you and Laura to testify that you immobilized the suspects before we even got there. When the jury learns you hit Bratson with your pocketbook, we're gonna get laughed out of court."

"Maybe you ought to make pocketbooks standard police equipment," I suggested.

"I'll tell the chief. Meanwhile, let me give you the worse news. Jimmy Bratson's friend has an airtight alibi for Friday night. He was at a political fund-raising dinner in Miami, at the head table, until nearly eleven, and went out for drinks with the candidate and some other people until well after midnight. It all checks out. As far as Chief Muggins's suspect list is concerned, Skell now occupies second place after Mr. Garcia—"

"—and Mr. Garcia only gets first place because he's Mexican," I finished sourly.

"You said that; I didn't. But you don't hear me contradicting you."

I hung up feeling awful. It took me nearly an hour to realize it wasn't just because Skell looked like the only real suspect for killing his daddy. My throat was scratchy and beginning to feel like somebody was pouring boiling oil down it, real slow.

At noon, Rosa Garcia came by my office upset and angry because I couldn't "do something" to get her daddy out of jail. She and her mother were holding the restaurant together, she said, but barely. I told her I wished I could do something, but I really couldn't.

By the time she left, I felt dreadful. My head was fuzzy and my nose streaming. I finally admitted I was afflicted with more than failure and poor self-esteem, and headed home. I have never admired thoughtless people who stagger on with a cold, dispensing germs to everybody in range. Seems to me that the considerate thing to do when you get sick is admit you aren't indispensable, endure the inconvenience of a day or two in bed with a book and your favorite music, and let your germs die a natural and isolated death.

I told Clarinda to make up a bed in a spare room for Joe Riddley so he wouldn't catch whatever I had; then I put on flannel jammies and turned on my electric blanket. In a few minutes she brought up a hot lemonade well laced with her secret ingredient—which is a lot like Tansy's. I climbed into bed figuring the world could manage to revolve for a little while without my personal oversight. If it couldn't, I didn't care.

I did call Gwen Ellen to tell her I was coming down with something and to suggest she gargle with Listerine, in case I'd shared a few germs. I also told her I was real sorry I couldn't get by the funeral home the next evening, but whatever I had felt like it had come to stay awhile. I promised I'd be at the funeral—on the back pew. I had the perfect excuse to sit where I could watch everybody who showed up, to see if anybody looked guilty.

Joe Riddley woke me up when he came home just before six, banging around in the closet taking off his work clothes and putting on some old khaki pants and a shirt he could putter around in. I've told him a hundred times I am less likely to wake up from the closet light than I am from the racket he makes without it, but he has never believed me.

When he came out, I saw that he was walking like a man who was carrying not just the world but the whole universe on his shoulders. I roused myself enough to ask, "What's the matter?" My mouth tasted like I'd been sucking on Joe's perch, and I felt like I'd gained twenty pounds since noon, all of it in my head. My shoulder muscles flat-out refused to lift that load from the pillow, so I lay back and prepared to hear that we had black spot on our entire new delivery of roses down at the nursery or that mealybug had infested our entire stock of houseplants.

"Nothing." He dragged himself to the mirror and smoothed his hair.

"You look mighty down in the mouth."

"Yeah, I reckon I am. It's this infernal rain."

That got me up on one elbow. "Joe Riddley Yarbrough, you know rain never made you this downhearted. It's Skye, isn't it? You are mourning. Why don't you admit it—to yourself and the rest of us? You are grieving like a rooster in quarantine."

He sat on his side of the bed with his back to me. "I'm grieving all right, but it's not just that he's dead. It's—" He sighed. "I can't tell you, Little Bit. He asked me not to. And I wouldn't if I could. You wouldn't like it."

"You don't like it either, honey. Tell me."

His next sigh nearly carried him through the floor. "I told you, I can't." He hung his head and began shuffling one toe on the rug, which he knows good and well drives me crazy.

I prodded him with my foot to get him to stop shuffling and start talking again. "It's about that legacy, isn't it—the life-insurance policy?"

He nodded.

"I've been thinking about that. It's odd he didn't leave it to Gwen Ellen instead of you."

"He left a letter with it. He wanted me to do him a favor."

This was like pulling teeth with tweezers. "What was the favor?"

He stood and went to the window. Rain was still streaming down like it had heard Middle Georgia is a great place to retire.

When my husband turned from the window, the room was so dim that all I could see was his outline. His face was a shadow and his voice a rasp of pain. "I've told you, I can't say. Skye asked me not to. Now stop bugging me and get back to sleep. If you don't start looking better soon, I'm going to take you down to the mortuary to see if they can pretty you up a little." Satisfied he'd done what he could to comfort the sick, he clomped down the stairs.

*   *   *

Friday passed in a fog. Clarinda trotted upstairs with soup and more hot lemonade, and I slept for hours. I didn't really wake until Joe Riddley came upstairs to go to bed.

"You go to the visitation?" I called drowsily.

He came and stood in the doorway. "I went." He tugged off his shirt and threw it in a ball on the chair.

"Were there lots of people there?"

"I wasn't counting." He pulled off his pants and added them to the chair. He'd never have gotten away with that if I'd been well enough to remind him that I unlock our clothes hamper each evening between eleven and twelve for his personal convenience. The old coot was being irritating on purpose, seeing if I was too sick to notice.

I wasn't too sick to notice, just too sick to care. "What does Marilee say about tomorrow's weather?" I muttered.

Taking that as a sign I was wide-awake, he turned on the overhead light. "Marilee didn't do the weather. They had a new boy who didn't look any older than Bethany. You could tell he was reading the monitor, and he got the slides all mixed up. I laughed so hard, my sides ache."

"What'd he say tomorrow will be like?"

"Fair and sunny, but I doubt he knows a thing about it."

He surprised us. We woke up to sunshine.

"Maybe they ought to give that kid the weather job," I said as we ate breakfast. I wasn't feeling good, just halfway human. "He's better at it than Marilee."

Joe Riddley chewed his cereal and considered the matter. "He's not as pretty."

Joe gave a ribald laugh from his perch above the sink.

Not until we were getting into the car did Joe Riddley remember to ask, "You feelin' any better?"

My first thought was that Skye always remembered when Gwen Ellen was sick and sent a yellow rose each day until she was well. My next thought was to be grateful for what I had: a living husband.

"I feel lousy. I don't have any fever left, just the nose-running, eye-streaming, throat-scratching nasties." I rubbed my face, willing my sinuses to stop aching. "I took a pill that will stop my runny nose, but do I look like Mrs. Balloonhead, or just feel that way?"

He peered from beneath his bush eyebrows. "Mrs. Balloonhead with a red nose."

"I ought not even be going, but I shouldn't infect anybody on the back pew. I don't think the funeral will fill the sanctuary. Do you?"

"If it does, you can go into the narthex and listen on the ushers' speakers. Sorry you have to sit by yourself." As a pallbearer, he would sit on the front row across the aisle from the family.

"Cindy called to ask if they can sit with me. I told her about my cold, but she said Walker never gets sick and she's been exposed to every germ in the universe at the kids' school. She also said she depends on me to show her what to do." Cindy was raised Episcopalian. Walker had gone to our church every Sunday until he left for college, but since they'd gotten married, they spent Sunday mornings lazing around reading the paper and drinking coffee or playing a round of golf.

That bothered Joe Riddley and me so much, I expected him to say something, but he just rolled down his window and took a deep breath. "Smell that air. It's spring, almost. And you'd think somebody ordered this day just for Baby Sister, wouldn't you? Not a cloud in the sky, fruit trees and dogwoods fixin' to come out, and look—there's a deer." A white flag disappeared into the forest across from Hubert's pond. Joe Riddley had probably forgotten the streaming, nippy weather we'd been having. Short-term memory loss has some advantages.

Soaking up sunshine, we didn't need to talk. I didn't feel good enough to talk, anyway.

It wasn't quite ten-thirty when we got to the church. The music hadn't started, but a gray steel casket was already up front, the top half open, the other covered with a blanket of yellow roses. I didn't want to go down there, but Joe Riddley insisted. "Come on, Little Bit. Pay your respects."

"I've god this awful code," I reminded him, making it sound even worse than it was.

"You aren't going to give Skye anything. Come on."

I trudged behind him down that interminable aisle and stood looking at the friendly, lovable face of one of my dearest friends. Tears stung my eyes and a sob ripped my poor sore throat. As Joe Riddley put his arm around me to escort me back to my distant pew, I saw Gwen Ellen, Laura, Skell, and Skye's parents through a blur of tears. They were gathered in the little session room off the sanctuary, with the door half closed. I wanted to go tell Skell to sit in the balcony out of sight, but my legs didn't have the strength. Besides, Chief Muggins couldn't arrest Skell without first letting Mr. Garcia go—even if he was low-down enough to arrest somebody at his daddy's funeral.

I sank gratefully into my pew's soft red cushion, and Joe Riddley went to sit by the aisle on the left front pew where the pallbearers would be. Our funeral director always lined pallbearers up alphabetically, so Joe Riddley always sat by the aisle. He looked handsome and distinguished in his black suit.

I grabbed a wad of tissues and tucked my pocketbook under my pew out of the way; then I cried awhile. It must have been the medicine, because I'm not much of a crier in public. That morning, I cried for the good things Skye had been to all of us, and I cried for all the things he had not been for Skell and Laura. Finally I remembered a prayer we used back when we still had a preacher who believed in confessing your sins: *Forgive us those things we have done which we ought not to have done and those things we've left undone which we ought to have done.* I prayed that for Skye and me both, until I began to feel better.

Chief Muggins made me feel worse again when he sauntered in and sprawled on the back pew across the aisle. He gave me a little nod, but otherwise ignored me. Because he was wearing a brown suit instead of his uniform, I figured at first he was sitting back there because he wasn't comfortable in church but wanted to pay his respects to the dead. From the way he was looking around the congregation, though, I began to get real nervous about Skell coming out and sitting up front.

The organist started playing a series of familiar old hymns. That music reached down inside me and dredged up sadness like a golden, aching cord. Knowing it was still partly the medicine and fearing I was about to get maudlin, I concentrated on watching people line up in the center aisle to look in the casket. A good many had sent flowers, even though the family had requested donations to Hands Up Together. Seeing that notice at the bottom of the program, I remembered how Skye and Joe Riddley were talking about the project on the very day Skye died. I'd have started sniffling again if Ben Bradshaw hadn't walked by on my outside aisle right then, stiff as walnut. Such self-control was inspiring.

He took a seat right on the edge of a pew not far from my own. I was astonished at how good Ben cleaned up when he made an effort. In a charcoal-gray suit and a white shirt, he looked real prosperous. He might as well give up trying to slick down those curls, though—several had already worked their way out of whatever spray or gel he was using to confine them.

He didn't go up front to pay his respects, and he didn't slide across his pew to sit nearer a couple who were over by the center aisle. Instead, he propped his arms on the pew in front of him and lay down his head. He looked like he was praying, but he could have been resting or even crying. I was embarrassed to look too closely, because our denomination takes Jesus's instruction to pray privately so much to heart, we'd almost rather somebody caught us naked than praying.

Walker and Cindy also came down the side aisle, and they slid into the pew beside me. I thought he looked real handsome in a dark blue suit, but I'd never say that out loud. Walker looks so much like me, I've never known if he's good-looking or if I'm prejudiced.

Cindy, now, anybody would have voted her "exquisite" in that suit of fine black wool with a gray silk shell. A chunky necklace and earrings of jet, granite, and amber saved her from looking like the chief mourner, but just sitting beside her made my navy suit and white blouse—which had looked both respectable and smart in my dresser mirror—curl at the hem and retire from the best-dressed list. Even Cindy's shoes were gorgeous—sleek black pumps that probably cost about what I paid for my whole outfit. If we kept getting chummy, I might ask where she shopped and whether I could go with her sometime. My wardrobe could use some sprucing up.

"You look awful," Walker greeted me. "You want to go down front?"

"I've been."

Cindy declined, as well, so he climbed over us both and strolled down the aisle. I wondered if he was remembering, as I was, how he used to process down it with the choir every Sunday. I was feeling real sad again until Cindy took my hand and gave it a squeeze. Then she held it. I was surprised how much comfort that gave me.

I turned around at a rustle in the narthex, and saw the crowd parting for Marilee Muller. Marilee looked as chic as

Cindy, but she wore a white silk suit. It seemed a little dressy for a funeral, but who was I to criticize somebody else's clothes?

I sure could describe her face, though. The word ravaged immediately came to mind. She didn't look thin, she looked gaunt, with red eyes and a very pink nose. Yet she held her head high and her chin up as she marched down the aisle. Her hair had that fluffy look that proclaimed she'd just left the beauty parlor, and she wore such high heels that she stumbled as she walked. If Walker, on his way back, hadn't caught her elbow, she might have fallen on her face.

When she reached the casket, she stood looking down at Skye for such a long time that the woman behind her touched her elbow. People were backing up behind her.

Marilee shrugged her off and bent forward. Was she touching him? I couldn't see. When she turned away, she was trembling so hard she weaved her way back up the aisle. But she wasn't crying. As she came back toward us, I saw that her eyes were stormy and she was pinching her lips together so hard, all you could see was a narrow rim of lipstick where her mouth was. I don't think I'd ever seen anybody look that angry at a funeral.

Marilee was heading for the back pew across from mine until she noticed Charlie. She stopped short and turned in a few rows ahead. She sank into the red cushion and froze. The only time she moved until the service started was to raise one knuckle to her lips and put it all the way into her mouth. Walker leaned across Cindy and nodded toward Marilee. "She used to do that in school when she got mad or upset," he whispered. "Sometimes she'd bite herself so hard she'd bleed."

Having shared that tidbit about our local celebrity, he reached for a hymnbook and perused it while the organ continued to play. I watched wistfully, remembering what a good voice he had and how much our choir needed bari-

tones. Not to mention how much Walker and Cindy needed
God in their lives. I sure wished they'd get themselves and
their children into a church.

Afraid he'd read all that in my face, I watched Marilee
some more. She merited watching. What had Skye Mac-
Donald done to make her stare at his casket with so much
fury? They'd been friendly enough Friday afternoon. Seemed
to me she'd been clutching his arm like she thought she had
a claim to it, but in the restaurant later she'd been annoyed.
Now, she leaned forward in her pew as if an invisible rubber band drew her toward that gray box up front, gnawing
her knuckle. Would anybody get that mad about losing a
good car deal? Maybe she was just being overly-dramatic.
She was, after all, a television personality.

Charlie Muggins watched her with slitted eyes. But he
was also watching Ben. And me.

My attention jumped to the front of the church when
Gwen Ellen, Laura, and Skell came in with Skye's parents
and his brother, Jack, Jack's wife, and their children. I held
my breath, but Charlie Muggins didn't move. Just watched
Skell with the unblinking eyes of a lizard.

Marilee continued to bite her knuckle while the family
walked with dignity to the casket and grouped themselves
around it. Like me, none of them wore black. Those who
knew and loved Skye best had dressed not for the end of his
life, but to celebrate his graduation from one stage to another. The men all wore dark suits. Skye's mother wore a
soft gray-blue dress with a large white collar. His sister-in-
law had on a brown suit, and her little girl wore a pink
dress. Gwen Ellen had chosen to wear a dark green jacket
dress that was one of Skye's favorites. Laura had on a suit
of peacock blue that had to be new. With her new haircut,
she was stunning. I noticed several people staring and turning to whisper to one another.

One by one the women placed something in the casket.

At the last minute, Gwen Ellen reached back in before she turned away. I saw her shove her hand in her jacket pocket as she took her place on the end of the family pew.

I was real proud of her. She walked in quiet dignity, her eyes and mouth composed. She might scream and throw things in private, but she would not disgrace Skye now.

Ben was also watching the family, but since I couldn't see his face, I had no clue to what he was thinking. I wished somebody would comfort Laura. Her shoulders shook, and she kept lifting a wad of tissues to dab her eyes and nose. Several times I saw her hand creep to the side of her neck, and knew she was reaching for a strand of hair that was no longer there. Gwen Ellen didn't seem to notice, but her grandfather put his arm around her and held her close.

At five minutes past ten, after the ushers had already closed the swinging narthex doors and just as the funeral director was moving in from the side to close the casket, Nicole opened the sanctuary door.

She was dressed in a short black dress and black stockings, but she paused at the door like a bride. A woman in a black skirt and sweater stood behind her, half a head shorter than Nicole and twenty years older, with her slight plumpness distributed in all the right places. Her strawberry-blond hair was as curly as Nicole's. I'd have been willing to bet neither had ever needed a perm in their lives. Nicole's lashes were thick with mascara that had run from crying, but the older woman wore nothing but powder over a sprinkling of freckles that gave her the look of an impish child. She had a friendly mouth, a pert little nose, and grave blue eyes, more worried than sad.

Nicole seemed unconscious that hundreds of people were watching as she took the woman's arm and led her down the aisle straight toward the casket. The funeral director hovered, uncertain whether to shoo them back or let them come. Neither woman noticed him. Nicole's attention was all on Skye, the woman's on her. The director dithered and darted a couple of steps forward, a couple back. Miserable, he looked toward the family pew, but only Skye's father noticed his dilemma. Mr. MacDonald turned to see what he was looking at, then waved for him to let the women alone.

They walked to the front of the church and stood looking down at Skye, as so many had before them. Then, instead of turning to walk away, Nicole burst into tears. She didn't weep quietly, she boohooed. Loud heartbroken wails rose over the soft organ music. Her shoulders shook. At last she clutched her stomach, bent over, and sobbed like Gwen Ellen had been afraid *she* would do.

The older woman tugged her arm to draw her away. Nicole jerked free angrily. The woman spoke and pulled again. Nicole stood like she was a permanent part of the church decor, bawling.

Laura would have gotten up, but her grandfather restrained her. Gwen Ellen's face was desperate and pale as she looked toward the funeral director, begging him to do something. He looked toward the preacher, begging him to do something. The preacher looked down at Joe Riddley on the pallbearers' pew up front. Joe Riddley got up, took Nicole by the shoulders, and turned her around. From his expression, everybody knew he'd rather be anywhere than escorting a weeping woman up that long aisle. But between his arm around Nicole's shoulders and the woman's firm hand on her arm on the other side, they began to make headway.

Nicole continued to wail. Her blue eyes were wild, her mouth twisted in grief. She boohooed so loudly that the organist started playing "Amazing Grace" at the rousing volume and with the fervor usually reserved for "The Battle Hymn of the Republic." Pretty soon we'd be keeping up with the Episcopalians.

Joe Riddley marched up that aisle with sturdy determination, but when they reached my pew, he grabbed my arm so hard it hurt. Short of making a scene, I had no choice but to go with them.

As our awkward little recessional reached the narthex doors, Nicole turned and gave the casket a pitiful look. Then she uttered a piercing wail. "Oh, Daddy. Daddy!"

ঽ 23 ঽ

I shoved Nicole through the swinging doors. As the others followed, I turned to make sure the doors closed. That's why I bumped smack into Chief Muggins, coming out with us.

The older woman gathered Nicole in her arms. "Hush," she said in shocked tones. "Calm down, honey. This won't do. It won't do at all."

When Nicole continued to sob, the woman shook her, hard. Nicole sniffed, hiccuped, and blinked several times. "I'm sorry, Mama. I just can't stand to go off and leave him in there." She opened her mouth to wail again.

Her mother covered her mouth with a freckled hand with short slim fingers. "Hush." She apologized to Joe Riddley, Chief Muggins, and me over her shoulder. "I knew we shouldn't have come, but Nicole insisted."

Chief Muggins stepped up and flashed his badge. "I couldn't help overhearing what the little lady said as she came out just now. Is she claiming that Mr. MacDonald was her father?"

"He is." Nicole lifted her chin, and her wet eyes flashed. "And I just knew him four months. Four months out of my whole life."

"Hush," said her mother again. She turned a faint pink under her freckles. "You are embarrassin' me to death."

"I need to get back in there," Joe Riddley told me in a soft, urgent voice.

"Go on. You aren't any use here. Can you take Chief Muggins with you?" It sounded more like "Cad ju take Jeef . . ." because my nose was so stuffy, but I'm not going to translate the rest. I hung back, clutching my wad of tissues and keeping my germs to myself—although for one wild minute I thought about grabbing Chief Muggins and breathing all over him.

Joe Riddley bent and spoke in the police chief's ear. "Why don't you wait and talk to her later, when she's not so upset?"

Chief Muggins shrugged him away. "I want to make it real clear that we won't tolerate folks slandering a good man in this town."

Joe Riddley looked at me. I nodded toward the sanctuary door. With relief, he made his escape.

Chief Muggins pulled a notebook out of his pocket. "Your names, please?"

The woman's voice was soft, but clear. "I'm Maisie Shandy. This is my daughter, Nicole. I'm sorry we caused a disturbance." She held her head with dignity I had to respect.

Chief Muggins ignored her apology. "Residence?"

She gave an address in Augusta.

"And what is your relationship to the deceased?"

Maisie lifted her chin. "None, at the present. He was my daughter's father."

"Do you claim that you and Mr. MacDonald were ever married?"

Her voice was calm and firm. "No, we weren't."

He swung to Nicole. "How long have you been in Hopemore, and what was your reason for being here?"

"Four months. I worked for him," Nicole said. She sniffed, and added proudly, "I was his secretary."

"He know who you were?"

"Of course not," her mother answered for her. "She told me she wanted to get to know him, so I told her she could take the job but not to tell him who she was."

Chief Muggins shut his notebook and put it back in his pocket. "I don't know who you all are, but I know your type. Find out that a rich man has died, then show up claiming to be his fancy family. You think if you make a lot of trouble, the real family will buy you off." Ms. Shandy opened her mouth to protest, but Chief Muggins rolled on like a bulldozer. "We won't stand for that around here. Go back where you came from, and don't let me see either one of you again or there'll be trouble. You understand me?" Without waiting for an answer, he turned and marched back into the sanctuary, a general who had mopped up one particular battlefield.

"Don't mind him. He's an old windbag," I told Ms. Shandy.

I could have used some wind myself. The stuffing had been knocked plumb out of me. Skye? And this woman? But now that I knew to look, I saw that Nicole had Skye's coloring and the big nose that had been the bane of Laura's childhood. She could, of course, be just another large-nosed tall blonde, but she also had Laura's high forehead and "Skye blue" eyes.

Poor Gwen Ellen. Poor all of us.

I was feeling a little light-headed about then, and my knees were getting wobbly. Maybe that was my cold, but maybe it was because it had occurred to me that Nicole could easily have killed Skye. She could have called him after Gwen Ellen was in bed, arranged to meet him, and ridden with him out to the deserted road—a private place to talk. Whether she could have driven over him in cold blood I did not know. Maybe I could find out.

I pointed to short pews at the back of the narthex where

old folks and small children usually waited for their families to finish talking after church. Nicole's mama helped her toward one, and she collapsed onto the red cushion, sobbing and gasping for breath. Skye's younger daughter had certainly inherited his sense of drama.

I tottered after them and took a pew across the narrow aisle. "I'm MacLaren Yarbrough," I told the woman. "A friend of the MacDonalds."

"I'm Maisie Shandy," she said again. "Pleased to meet you, but I wish it was under better circumstances."

She put out her hand for me to shake, but I shook my head. "I've got a terrible cold, so I don't want to touch you."

"You know Nicole?" She patted her daughter on the back. Nicole didn't lift her head.

"Oh, yes. Last time I saw her, she had just cut Laura MacDonald's hair."

"Nicole's real good with hair," her mother bragged. "When she finished her trainin', she had offers from several places in Augusta—but she wanted to come on down here."

"I wanted to get to know Daddy." Nicole lifted her tear-drenched face and looked at me through flower eyes with blue centers and spiky lashes for petals.

Maisie had the grace to look embarrassed. "I wish I hadn't ever told her who he was. But she kept beggin' and beggin', until she plumb wore me down." She sighed. "At least you never told him who you were." She added, anxiously, "Did you, honey?"

Nicole stood. "I need to go to the bathroom. Do you know where it is, Judge Yarbrough?"

"Down those stairs, then turn to the right."

"Judge?" Her mother had noticed the word, so I explained about being a magistrate while Nicole clomped down the wooden stairs.

After that, her mother sighed. "I know you're wonderin'

who the dickens I am, and"—she lifted both slim freckled hands, then let them drop in her lap—"everything."

"I don't need to know a thing. It's none of my business," I said—because Mama had raised me to be polite. The truth was, I was dying to know who the dickens she was and "everything."

She looked toward the swinging doors. "Nicole has made it the whole town's business. Somebody ought to know what really happened, in case wild stories start. And we can prove it, if that sheriff tries to make trouble."

"He's not the sheriff, he's the police chief," I corrected her, "and making trouble is what he does best. But I'll do what I can to put a lid on it."

Her beginning was unexpected. "Skye and I never meant a thing to each other, and that's the truth. If his wife needs to hear it, I hope you'll tell her. I used to work for a car dealer up in Augusta, and I'd see Skye when he came up on business. He was always real friendly and everything, so we'd laugh and talk, but that's all there was until one night it was closin' time when he got ready to go. He asked if I'd like to get a bite to eat before he drove home." She bit her lip and looked at her hands. "I knew he was married, and I was going steady, but my boyfriend was a sailor and he'd been away on sea duty five months. I figured, 'What the heck? It's just dinner.' Skye took me to a real nice place, and while we were eatin', he talked about his wife—how much he loved her, and how pretty she was. Then he started goin' on about how she was real sick right then and had to stay in bed all the time. Now you and I both know that was a line, but I was nineteen and hadn't learned all the lessons life still had to teach me. One thing led to another, and after that he started comin' up around one night a week. But we were both just lonely. We weren't in love."

She looked at me and waited for me to show I understood—maybe, even, condoned. I didn't. Nineteen is old enough to have common sense and morals, and loneliness is seldom a fatal condition. I nodded just to move the story along.

"I wasn't careful enough, obviously. When I knew Nicole was on the way, I was frantic. Skye was great, though. He said we needed to stop seeing each other, but for me to open a bank account and send him the deposit slips, and he'd put in enough to cover my hospital expenses, then he'd send a check every month until the child was eighteen. He did, too, even after I wrote him I was married and didn't need his checks anymore." She hesitated, then added, "I didn't marry the sailor. I married Jack Shandy when Nicole was eighteen months old. He adopted her, and he's always been her daddy. He's never made a speck of difference between her and our other two."

"Have you been ill? Nicole told Skye she needed a job because her mother was ill and she had to help support her family."

Maisie gave me a rueful smile. "Nicole is always makin' up stories. The truth is, she was just dyin' to meet her daddy. I never meant to tell her about him, but when she turned fourteen, she pestered the livin' daylights out of me to at least know who he was. She said I might die or somethin' and she'd have no idea how to get her father's medical history in case she developed a rare disease. Oh, she's a smart one. So one night when Skye was doin' a car commercial on television and it was just me and her in the house, I pointed and said, 'There he is. That's your daddy.' I unleashed a monster. Have you ever said anything you'd give your right arm to take back?"

"Several times," I conceded. I couldn't help liking this woman, and could see why Skye had, too. I squelched that disloyal thought and concentrated on the rest of Maisie's story.

"That's how I felt about tellin' Nicole about Skye. Especially since she kept pesterin' me after that to know more and more. At last, I told her almost everythin'. I never dreamed she'd come down here to find him, though, as soon as she finished cosmetology school. She was gone all day, but I figured she was lookin' for work. When she came home and said she'd come here and gotten herself a job in his dealership, I was sick with worry."

"You didn't need to worry. He liked me. He liked me a lot."

We hadn't heard Nicole coming back. She'd taken off her thick-soled sandals and come up in stocking feet. I hoped she was being considerate of the funeral, and not a sneak. She stood glaring down at us. "You were wrong about what I told him, too. I told him right off who I was, and I said I didn't want anything from him or his family. I just wanted to get to know him, to see what I'd missed. It was him who thought up that story about me working to support my sick mother and her children. He thought that was funny, and said he'd have to have somethin' to tell Laura, her bein' in charge of hirin' and firin' people. He also said he'd always wanted three children, but his wife couldn't have any more. I think after a while he'd have told his family who I was, when the time was right."

I couldn't imagine Skye working up that kind of courage, but Nicole stood with lifted chin, a golden tower of faith in Skye's integrity and good intentions.

I felt sicker than I had all week.

In the sanctuary, the organ started playing "For All the Saints, Who From Their Labors Rest." "The service is almost over," I warned.

"We're goin'." Maisie grabbed Nicole's arm and stood.

Nicole pulled away. "I want to go to the cemetery."

"You are goin' to your place to pack your bags," her mother told her, "and you are comin' home with me. Skye's family doesn't need you right now."

"Laura likes me," Nicole insisted.

"That was before you made that scene in there. Now, come on. We're goin' home."

It was too late. Skye's casket was already being wheeled through the door. Nicole sank beside her mother and sobbed. Her mother held her as best she could. I sat miserably on the adjacent pew and watched as the pallbearers and family marched behind it. Neither Laura nor Skye's family noticed me, but Gwen Ellen threw me such a look of sad reproach, you'd have thought I was personally responsible for Nicole's existence.

⌁ 24 ⌁

Walker and Cindy weren't going to the cemetery, so they offered to run me home. Since I'd left my pocketbook under the pew, I waited until the crowd all came out, left Walker and Cindy talking to friends, and hurried back into the sanctuary. The music had stopped, and the air was settling back to the thick holiness that fills all empty churches on a weekday. Everybody was gone except Marilee Muller, who was staring at the front as if Skye were still there.

Embarrassed, I crept into the back pew and bent to retrieve my pocketbook, but somebody had kicked it way under. I had to get on my knees to grab it.

I jumped when I heard her speak. "I am not sorry." Her voice was soft but urgent. "I am not sorry for one little thing. I have nothing to be sorry for."

I grabbed my pocketbook strap and peered over the pew in front, thinking she was talking to me. She was still looking at the front, talking to air.

Her voice grew louder. "And I'm not going out there to watch her play Queen Bee. That's all she's got left. Let her have it." She sprang to her feet and whirled into the aisle. When she saw me, her eyes widened and she froze.

"I had to get my pocketbook." I dangled it from one hand and felt like an utter fool. "I forgot it." I climbed to my feet and hoped she didn't hear my knees pop.

"Oh, Judge Yarbrough." She gushed as if I were one of her dearest friends, and sank to the cushion of the pew in front of mine like a graceful panther. "May I speak with you for a minute? I just have to talk to somebody, and you are such a sympathetic person."

Where on earth did she get that idea?

"Besides"—she tucked her long legs underneath her and turned sideways, resting her arm over the back so she could face me—"I need some advice."

I am a sucker for people asking my advice. It happens so seldom. So I sat down, wiggled to get comfortable, and prepared to help in any way I could. She had, by far, the more uncomfortable position, but managed to look glamorous even at that angle.

When she began, "I don't want you to get the wrong idea or anything but . . ."all my flags went up. She must know good and well I wasn't going to like what she had to say. "Skye MacDonald and I were in love." She gave a breathless little laugh.

She'd been right. If she expected me to say something, she'd be waiting a long time. She had plumb shut off my water—which was already running at a trickle after Nicole's little drama.

She rested her left hand over her right on the back of the pew. I was looking at the poor knuckle encircled by even teeth prints until Marilee wiggled the bare third finger of her left hand. I'd never noticed before how strong her hands were, with long, thick fingers and dark red nails filed to talons. A predator's hands that reached for what they wanted and seized it.

She must have interpreted my silence as astonishment, because she added with the smile that charmed thousands every night, "Really. We were." She started nodding. So help me, I nodded back. Nods can be like yawns that way. "We never meant it to happen," she added with boring predictability—as if other couples went out on Wednesday mornings and said, "Well, let's fall in love."

She continued in a confidential tone that implied I was one of the girlfriends she shared secrets with. "We had to work on that old committee for the college, you know, and being together so much—well, we realized we were absolute soul mates. I didn't know love could be so wonderful. I used to send him little messages at the end of every broadcast, and nobody ever knew. That was our little secret." She gave me another dazzling smile. I wondered where she had learned that. College? Acting school? Back in high school her smile had been more like a shadow, here one second and gone the next.

"When you saw us Friday, I'd told Skye I wanted him to give me a definite time when he'd inform his wife he wanted a divorce. I mean, there wasn't any sense in putting it off, was there? As unpleasant as it was going to be, it had to be done. We were going to get married, and needed to make plans." She heaved what could have been a heartrending sigh if I'd felt like having my heart rended right then. "I'd even bought this suit for the wedding." She stroked one of the white silk sleeves.

I considered mentioning that Skye already had a wife, and that telling her he was leaving would have been a lot more unpleasant for Gwen Ellen—and for Skye—than for Marilee, but I bit my tongue. After all, I was such a sympathetic person. Besides, here on a platter was another motive for murder. For once, Skye must have found himself in a real bind. Marilee wasn't like Maisie. Barracudas don't swim off just because you get tired of playing with them.

"Did he call you Friday afternoon?" I asked, adding, "I remember you asked him to."

"Oh, yes. He said he wouldn't tell her until after Sunday. They had some little anniversary that day, and he didn't want to spoil it for her. I got real mad at the time, but now . . .

well, that was just like him, wasn't it? He was the sweetest, most considerate man in the world."

He wasn't winning my vote at the moment. Fortunately, she wasn't looking for a reply. All she really needed from me was an ear. If I could have detached it, the rest of me would have gone back home to bed.

She dabbed her eyes with a wisp of lacy white handkerchief. "I don't think I can live without Skye. I honestly don't think I can."

She was utterly besotted. Also selfish. And dumb.

"I knew we couldn't get married for a few months, of course," she admitted. "People can act real funny, you know?"

I knew some people who would have acted funny if Skye had paraded a glamorous young wife around Hopemore with Gwen Ellen still alive and kicking. Me, for one.

Marilee went rippling on. "This is what I wanted your advice about, though. With Skye gone, I don't know how I ought to go about telling folks. I mean, I don't want to hurt his wife, but in fairness to Skye, I think people ought to know he loved me. What do you think?"

That's the point at which I started praying. What I said was, "Help! How the heck did I get myself in this mess?" I didn't have a clue how to answer Marilee. What I wanted to do was shake her and Skye both until their teeth rattled.

I took a deep breath to make my voice as calm and wise as I could. I even leaned forward and placed one hand on her elegant arm. The silk was soft and expensive under my fingers. "I think you ought to let whatever you and Skye had stay between the two of you, honey. There's nothing to be gained by telling people now. You'd ruin his reputation and your own. A lot of folks wouldn't believe you, either, since Skye's not here to back you up. You don't want to be branded a liar, do you?"

"I'm not!" But the veneer of glamour she'd acquired

slipped a little. All of us, deep down, have ugly, uncertain places. Marilee had been called enough names growing up in Hopemore not to relish the idea now. She began twisting her big hands back and forth, kneading her sordid little story into something she could admire and hold on to. "We were in love. We were going to get married."

"I'm only telling you what people will say. Nobody's going to believe you. You'll just be causing yourself a lot of grief around here."

In an instant, her face changed from unhappiness to a child's naked fury. "We had everything. Then it all got ruined." She jumped up and ran out the door.

I stayed a minute after she left, suspecting I'd given her more germs than sympathy. I doubted if I'd said any of the right things. I also wondered exactly when things got ruined. I remembered Marilee at Casa Mas Esperanza, trying to beckon Skye to her side. I also remembered how he'd dismissed her with a little wave and gone on his way. Silly me, I had thought he had disappointed her about the price of a car. Had he disappointed her even more cruelly? Had she gotten her revenge?

On our way home, I didn't want to talk about the funeral, Nicole, or Marilee, so I admired Cindy's suit and shoes. "I get almost everything at Phipp's Plaza in Atlanta," she told me. "Next time I go for a weekend, would you like to come? We could see the historical society gardens, too." She sounded like she meant it.

"I'd love to," I said, and I meant it, too. Don't ask why it took us fourteen years to get to that place. Maybe, I had to admit, because I'd expected Cindy to be like Martha, with whom I canned fruits and vegetables and went out in Hopemore late at night to eat chocolate pie. For fourteen years, I hadn't appreciated Cindy for the beautiful person she was. But at least now I was getting there.

When I saw how happy that made Walker look, I could have kicked myself for not trying to get there a whole lot sooner.

I'd left Clarinda a note to say we'd need dinner as usual. Joe Riddley wouldn't be going to the buffet over at Gwen Ellen's after the graveside service, but would come home to eat and change clothes before going to work. When I staggered in, she was by the stove.

"You want a tray up in your room?" she asked over her shoulder.

"No, I'll just rest in the den until we eat."

She turned, obviously relieved. Clarinda isn't much younger than I am, and doesn't need to carry any more trays upstairs than she has to. But instead of a simple "Thank you," she said, "The way you look, you oughtta go to bed for a week."

"Thanks. That makes me feel a whole lot better. We got any cold Co-colas?"

She frowned. I only call Cokes that when I'm too tired to remember it's the twenty-first century.

She fetched one and popped the top for me before she went back to her stove. I tottered toward the recliner, hoping I'd live long enough to get there.

Clarinda set stuffed pork chops, baked sweet potatoes, and green beans in front of Joe Riddley, and a bowl of homemade chicken soup in front of me. As soon as she'd gone to claim the recliner for herself, I asked him, "What did the MacDonald women put in the casket?"

"I don't know." He held out a little piece of roll to Joe, who pecked it off his finger.

"What do you mean, you don't know? You were right there on the end of the front pew."

He picked up his pork chop and began to worry big bites off it. He was raised, like the rest of us, to use a fork on pork chops, but always claims they taste better gnawed off the bone. When I kept looking at him, waiting for an answer, he added, "I wasn't watching."

"You were, too. I saw you."

He frowned. I couldn't tell if he'd forgotten or was just using his occasional memory lapses as an excuse to be cantankerous. Finally, though, he said, "Yellow roses. Everybody put in a yellow rose except Laura. She put in a little blue car." He finished his first pork chop and dropped the bone on the floor for Lulu, who had sat there grudging him every bite.

"Honestly, Joe Riddley, you'd think we lived in a barn. What did Marilee do when *she* reached into the casket?"

"I didn't see." He could tell from my expression I didn't believe him, because he fumed, "I wasn't watching the whole time, you know. Seeing Skye like that gave me the creeps. Don't you dare have an open casket when I die." He fed Joe a bite of sweet potato.

"Tell that to your next wife," I advised, sipping my soup. "I have every intention of going before you."

Joe ducked his head several times. "Not to worry. Not to worry."

I knew Joe Riddley wasn't telling the truth. He hadn't watched the casket the whole time, but he'd had his eyes glued on Marilee—like every other man in the church. But our strongest tractor wouldn't pull that admission out of him. I recognized that tone of voice.

I sipped more soup, then asked, "You want to know what Nicole and her mother said after you left?"

"Not particularly." He added a dollop of butter to the rest of his sweet potato and mashed it together. Joe watched greedily. I might as well tell Clarinda to start setting that bird a plate.

I waited until Joe Riddley had his potato mashed to his satisfaction, then said, trying to sound casual, "She's Skye's secret, the one you're supposed to keep, isn't she?"

He pointed toward the den, to remind me to keep my voice down. "I don't remember. My memory's not what it used to be, you know."

I pulled myself up as high as I could in my chair and gave him what our boys used to call "Mama's Killer Glare." "Don't you give me that. Your memory is almost well by now. You just can't remember sometimes what you ate for breakfast."

"Did we have breakfast? You're right. I can't remember."

I leaned toward him and said in a soft but menacing voice, "If you don't admit to me that you already knew Nicole Shandy was Skye MacDonald's illegitimate daughter, you won't live long enough to eat supper."

He cupped one hand to his ears. "What's that you say? Eh? I thought you had every intention of dying before me."

"That was before I remembered how ornery you can be." I heaved a real big sigh to show how disgusted I was. "Come on, honey. It's not private any longer." My voice wobbled. "And I thought he *loved* Gwen Ellen."

Joe Riddley pushed back his chair. "Clarinda forgot to put salt on the table." He didn't need salt. He just didn't want to have that conversation. But when he sat back down and found me sitting there with my lips trembling, he reached over and cupped my head in one large hand. "Skye did love Gwen Ellen. Loved her, respected her, thought she hung the moon. But—"

"But?"

"Yeah, but. The fool never learned you can't have your cake and eat it, too. He thought he could please everybody all the time, including himself."

"Tell me what he said in the letter he wrote you."

First, to justify having gotten up, he shook salt all over everything on his plate. Finally he admitted sourly, "I guess it's okay, with Nicole shouting it all over the place. Skye

wrote the letter twenty years ago. He started out by reminding me that Gwen Ellen had just been real sick. Remember?
He said he'd gotten involved with a young woman over in
Augusta. He was real ashamed of it, but she was going to
have his baby, and he wanted to make sure the child was
decently cared for. He said he was opening a bank account
and would deposit money for the baby as long as he lived,
but he was taking out this policy in case anything happened
to him. In that case he asked me to send a check each
month until the child turned eighteen—"

"—which happened at least a year ago."

"Yeah. And he said if he didn't die until after that, he
wanted me to deposit the policy benefit into the account for
her to use as she saw fit. He begged me not to tell anybody
what that policy was for—to make out that it was for a secret charity, if anybody found out about it." Joe Riddley
looked at me with eyes full of unhappiness. "I didn't like
not telling you, Little Bit, but what could I do?"

"And what would have happened if you'd died before
Skye. He was a lot younger than you."

Now he looked unhappier than ever. "The letter would
have gone to Ridd."

"Ridd? He'd have made Ridd carry that secret around all
his life?"

Joe Riddley nodded and picked up his second pork chop.

I sat there furious with Skye, who thought he could pass
his own burdens off to our family as easily as he passed us
a good car deal—which, come to think of it, weren't always
any better than we could have gotten somewhere else. But
seeing the pain in my husband's eyes, I reached out and
squeezed his arm. "I am so proud to know you, honey. Who
else could anybody trust with that delicate a thing and believe they'd never mention it to anybody?"

Joe Riddley's face lost some of its troubled look, and he

started shoveling in sweet potato and green beans like he'd just come in from a day's work in the fields.

I picked up his left hand and kissed his big gnarled fingers. "I do love you, Joe Riddley Yarbrough. And it may make you feel a little better to know that Nicole's mama said Skye did send a check every month, and she bears him no grudge. She says they made a mistake, but she doesn't regret having Nicole."

He chewed thoughtfully. "I wonder if Skye had any inkling Nicole was his little girl."

"Nicole claims he did, since four months ago. She came to town and told him. I think that's why he hired her. She says he said he'd always wanted three kids, and Gwen Ellen couldn't have but two. But she thought he'd take her home one day and introduce her around. I can't see him ever doing that, can you?"

Joe Riddley gave a sound I can only describe as a moan. "I can't say what Skye might or might not have done, now. I'd never have suspected him of tomcatting around. And I'm glad it's the good Lord and not me who has to weigh the good and harm he did." He held out a bean to Joe, who took it and greedily waited for more.

"Me, too. And speaking of weighing, if you keep feeding that parrot half your food, you'll be skin and bones and he's gonna be a little tub."

"Back off," Joe advised me. He squawked, flapping his wings. "Back off."

I wasn't finished with what I had to say, though. "Honey, if I ever find out you've been tomcatting around, as you so elegantly put it, you'd better take a deep, deep breath, because it will be your last."

He nodded. "I know, Little Bit. That's what's kept me on the straight and narrow all my life."

Suddenly his face creased into its craggy smile. He held out his arms, and we both leaned over to hold each other close. It was good to sit there warm and safe in each other's arms.

Inside, though, I felt sick with far more than a cold. I wanted to crawl into a corner somewhere and stay until the world became a cleaner, healthier, saner place.

⊰ 25 ⊱

After Joe Riddley left, I hauled myself up to bed, wondering what Chief Muggins would do with the information that Skye MacDonald had an extra child. I soon found out.

The phone rang about four. I was dozing, but woke at once when I heard the voice on the other end. Laura sounded like she was trapped on the tracks in the glare of an oncoming train. "I know you're sick—Clarinda told me. But we need you. Could you possibly come over here?"

I took a second to collect what few wits I had left. "What's going on?"

"Chief Muggins has been here worrying Mama to death. He says Nicole claims to be Daddy's daughter, and he insinuated that Mama found out and killed Daddy. Skell got so offensive I sent him to his own place. Now Mama's having a conniption, and I can't do a thing with her. I'm even scared to go to the bathroom, for fear she might hurt herself."

"Where's everybody else—your grandparents, your uncle, folks from the church?"

"They left right after they ate. Uncle Jack had to get back to Auburn, and Granddaddy has a four-hour drive and doesn't like to drive after dark."

"Isn't Tansy there?"

"No, she stayed to clean up, but she's been over here all

week, and Mama told her to go on home until Monday. I know you don't feel good, Mac, but if you could come for even a little while, I sure would appreciate it." Laura's voice was taut. "I think Mama's going crazy."

It was so rare for Laura to ask a favor that I already had my legs over the side of the bed. "I'll be right there. Meanwhile, call her doctor. He might suggest she take something to calm her down."

I won't repeat the things I said in the privacy of my car as I drove over, but most of them were addressed to Charlie Muggins and dealt with what I thought of a man who would threaten Nicole and her mother as if they were lying, and then almost immediately threaten Gwen Ellen that Nicole was telling the truth.

I arrived to find Gwen Ellen huddled on the green silk couch with Laura, still in her funeral suit, hovering over her like a large peacock minus the tail. "I offered her a couple of aspirin, but she wouldn't take them. I didn't know what else to give her, and I can't get the doctor." Laura's eyes were terrified. She could manage a motor company without getting in a flap, but coping with a hysterical mother was beyond her.

Gwen Ellen raised a haggard face to mine and said in a shaking voice, "I don't need pills. I need a gun, so I can shoot Chief Muggins. You wouldn't believe the lies he came over here telling, MacLaren. He claims Nicole, down at the motor company, is Skye's daughter. Can you imagine? Doesn't he realize I would have known if Skye was—" She cast a quick look at Laura and stopped without completing that sentence. "Of course I would have. Any wife would."

"Don't say that, Mama," Laura cried. "Chief Muggins thinks you *did* know. That's why he came. He thinks you found out who Nicole was and killed Daddy."

"If he's dumb enough to believe I'd kill your daddy over

something that happened twenty years ago, he's dumb enough to believe anything. I certainly wouldn't—if it happened at all, which I refuse to believe. What kind of fool does Chief Muggins think I am?" She began waving her arms like an orchestra conductor gone wild. Startled, I wondered if she'd taken a pep pill or something. I'd never seen her so animated. "Would I give up all my happiness, all my love, because some little tart came prancing in here claiming your daddy was also hers? You notice she didn't make that claim when Skye was alive. He'd have sent her packing, I can tell you that. He'd have sent her back to wherever she came from so fast her head would have spun completely off its scrawny neck. Your daddy was a decent man. Don't you ever let anybody tell you different, honey. Your daddy was a decent man."

She sat on the couch like a lump of reasonable self-righteousness. To me, she looked about one inch this side of crazy. I could see why Laura was scared. I was a little scared, too.

I'd never seen Laura so upset, either. "I know he was, Mama. I know he was." She was crying and shaking. She collapsed into the green chair closest to the sofa and buried her face in her hands. I moved over and stroked the exposed nape of her neck, which looked vulnerable and very white.

Gwen Ellen looked over at me and said in a perfectly level voice, "I am going to kill Chief Muggins, MacLaren. I'm going to shoot him five hundred times. You wouldn't believe what he's been saying to me, with my daughter standing right there." She spoke as if shooting Charlie was the reasonable solution to all her problems.

I sat down beside her. She smelled strongly of peppermint, which I knew she hated. That's when I suspected what the matter was. Giving her a hug—from which she tried to turn her face away—was enough to confirm it. She had found Tansy's secret ingredient. Gwen Ellen MacDonald was drunk. Not stagger-and-fall-down drunk, but drunk enough to lose the gentle inhibitions that governed her life. I saw now why liquor is called Dutch courage. I didn't know about the Dutch part, but Gwen Ellen sure had courage she hadn't had before.

Knowing what the matter was, I knew how to handle her. "Calm down, honey. Calm down. You know Charlie loves to get people upset. Don't give him the satisfaction."

She sat up straighter and held her head high. "I won't." She turned to Laura. "He's just looking for a reason to arrest me. He's always hated your daddy, and he'd do anything to bring down our family. That is one vicious, mean policeman."

Laura gave me a frightened, startled look. I held up one hand and patted the air, hoping she knew I meant things weren't as bad as she'd imagined. Laura frowned, but at least some of her terror subsided, so she could sit up and lean toward her poor inebriated parent. "You aren't going to shoot anybody, Mama, but you don't to have to pay him any attention. I've called our lawyer. He said to call him back if Chief Muggins returns."

Gwen Ellen looked at me, solemn as a cat. "I won't have that tacky policeman spreading lies about Skye. I saw you talking with that girl today. What did she and her mother tell you? We need to know so our lawyer will know how to fight them."

I could not lie, but wished I'd decided beforehand what to say. I also wondered how much Gwen Ellen could absorb in her condition, and how much Laura ought to hear. I tried to stall. "We'll discuss it later, honey." But Gwen Ellen pressed me until Laura signaled me to answer. I took a deep breath and admitted, "They both say Nicole is Skye's child."

"It's a lie. A vicious lie." Gwen Ellen's eyes were pools of angry chaos.

"I'm afraid it's not. They claim they can prove what they're saying. But they've gone back to Augusta, and I don't think they'll bother you again unless you make a fuss. Why don't you all go away for a week or two and rest— maybe to the Bahamas or the Virgin Islands? You enjoyed Nassau before. By the time you get back, everybody will be thinking about something else. Charlie was trying to·bluff you, to scare you. He knows you didn't kill Skye."

Gwen Ellen hadn't heard a word past my first sentence. "What kind of proof do they say they have? They can't have proof, because it isn't true."

I heaved a sigh and wished it could fill a sail and carry *me* to the Bahamas. "Skye paid for Nicole's birth and sent support checks to her every month until she turned eighteen." I didn't mention the life-insurance policy. I didn't want to drag in Joe Riddley. He could do what he had to and then wash his hands of the whole mess.

Laura gave a grunt of surprise and pain. Gwen Ellen lifted her chin. "Nonsense. They must have forged those checks, or stolen them. Maybe they found one of his checkbooks." She whirled to Laura. "Have you missed any checks from the motor-company account? I'd have noticed if any were missing from ours."

Laura's eyes met mine, and she gave her head a slight shake. We both knew Gwen Ellen never kept track of checks in her life. Skye used to joke that he got his exercise running down to the bank to keep their account a few dollars ahead of the checks she wrote. In recent years he'd given her a fistful of credit cards instead. He could have written all sorts of checks on their personal account and she'd never have known a thing.

Gwen Ellen was still waiting for Laura's answer. Laura shrugged. "I might be able to find them now that I know what to look for. Where did you say they lived?" Her last question was for me. I noticed she hadn't even considered her mother's theory that the checks were forged.

"Augusta. Your daddy opened an account in a bank over there for Nicole's support."

Gwen Ellen bent her head over her hands in her lap and twisted her large new diamond around and around. "I'd have known," she insisted. "I would have *known*. When was it this woman claims my husband was carrying on with her?"

"Back when you were so sick and Skye was . . . lonely." It wasn't Skye's coffin I was pounding nails into; it was hers.

"Lonely?" Her face twisted with pain. "Don't you think I was lonely, lying in that bed day after day? But Skye was here. He brought me roses and candy, and he rubbed my back. He called me his precious baby. . . ." Her voice sank to a whisper.

I reached for her nervous fingers and rubbed them to take away the chill. "You were, sweetie. You always were, and you still are."

She shook her head and said fiercely, "Everything we had is dirty, now. I won't share Skye with a tramp." She clutched her stomach, jumped up, and ran to the bathroom.

"She always throws up when she gets too excited." Laura's voice was weary.

I reached over and laid a hand on her arm. "I know, honey. I'd give my eyeteeth to have kept you from going through this. What happened back then is between your mother and daddy. It had nothing to do with the way he felt for you."

She nodded, but she did not say a word. She reached to her neck for a strand of hair, then gave me a wide, lopsided smile that nearly broke my heart. "I haven't learned yet how to suck my toes."

We both jumped when we heard the medicine-cabinet door slam shut. Laura's face went white with fear. "She's found pills. She's taking something. She could kill herself!"

I hurried to the powder-room door and grabbed the knob to rattle it, but the door wasn't shut. I literally fell into the room. Gwen Ellen's hand slipped, and pink lipstick went down her chin. I jerked open the cabinet and saw a bottle of foundation, a powder compact, blusher, mascara, and several bottles of perfume. No pills whatsoever. She reached for a tissue from the counter and asked as she scrubbed the smear, "What do you want?"

"I . . . uh . . . wanted to make sure you were all right." Prepared to rescue her from downing a fistful of medicine, I didn't know how to apologize for barging in on her while she was fixing her face. Thank goodness I used to baby-sit her. I don't think I could have stood the embarrassment if I hadn't.

Her eyes met mine in the mirror as she put the lipstick back in the cabinet and reached for a hairbrush on the next shelf. She pulled the brush through her hair and curled it under at the ends. "Did you all think I was killing myself in here?" Her laugh was high and brittle, but her eyes were genuinely amused. "I'm not. If that's why Laura hauled you over here when you ought to be in bed with that cold, you can go back home. I need to be alone. I've got a lot of thinking to do. I need to find out the whole truth; then I need to figure out how to live with it. I can do it, though." She set down the brush and turned to face me. "I'm not weak, you know. I know people used to say Skye treated me like porcelain—I've heard them. But I'm stronger than they gave me credit for. Go home, MacLaren. I am going to be fine. I just need a little time."

I backed from the bathroom and closed the door behind me, relieved.

I heard Laura at the front door; then she came back to the

living room with Ben. He'd changed his suit for a tan polo shirt and brown slacks, but he still looked handsome as all get-out. He also still looked like a totem pole—a totem pole with brown curls. It was hard to picture him laughing and talking up in Laura's apartment.

"Hello, Judge," he greeted me woodenly. "I . . . uh . . . stopped by to see if . . . uh . . . they needed anything. You all okay, Laura? Anything I can do for you folks this afternoon?"

She gave him a wide, sad smile. "No, but I appreciate you asking. Mama's had a rough time since the people all left. I got so worried about her, I called Mac."

"Why didn't you call me?" His voice was rough, almost angry.

She stared at him in astonishment. "I couldn't bother you. . . ."

His eyes were hard and morose. "We're friends, aren't we? I told you, anything you need, call me."

She looked away. "I know, but I hated to bother you." They towered above me like two awkward giants. Finally she asked, "Do you want to sit down?"

Ben was Laura's problem. I'd solved mine. I bent to pick up my pocketbook. "I'll go on home now. Your mother's freshening up her makeup and brushing her hair. Everything's going to be fine. I promise."

Mama used to say, "Never make promises you don't have the power to keep." I should have listened.

❧ 26 ❧

Sunday, I rested. I didn't see anybody, and I didn't call anybody, I ate the sandwich Joe Riddley put together and didn't even point out he'd forgotten the mustard. I did a lot of thinking, though, and my thoughts were real poor company. By the time I turned off my light, I was pretty sure I knew who had run over Skye MacDonald. I just wasn't sure what to do with what I knew.

Monday was sunny. I went back to work and paid bills while Joe Riddley went to the nursery for the morning. A new shipment of seed and fertilizer would occupy him awhile, because our forklift operator was out sick and Joe Riddley loved to operate the forklift. He also had to supervise our staff in shifting azaleas and other shrubbery, to make space for new ones that would come in later that week.

I waited until he and Joe pulled out of the parking lot before I called Laura to see how she was doing. With the funeral behind them, I figured she was beginning to think about how she and Skell could best work together as partners. I wanted to offer to sponsor her for our local business owners' association.

To my surprise, she was real subdued. When I asked about Gwen Ellen, she sighed. "She spent all day yesterday going through Daddy's things to give them away. She says he'd like for other folks to be getting use out of them."

"You think it's because of that Nicole thing? I hope she's not doing something she'll later regret." I'd have expected Gwen Ellen to keep Skye's closet, dresser, and den the way he'd left them for weeks or even months before she could face getting rid of them.

"I do, too." Laura sounded forlorn. "I told her to wait a little longer, at least, but she said I don't have to sleep in the same room with them and look at them all day long. She says they make her so sad she can't stand it."

"Well, honey, widowhood is funny. In my experience, it takes every woman differently, and we all have to deal with it in our own way. Your mama has a good head on her shoulders, and if she can bear to part with some of the things already, I wouldn't give her any grief over that. Just be sure to ask her for anything you particularly want to have."

"I took the mugs from his office, and his collection of Ford tie tacks. I'm going to have them framed. Skell asked for the furniture from his den."

"How is Skell today?"

She gave a huff of disgust. "Came strolling in late again this morning. Only half an hour, and I know he was tired, but still, we can't run a business like that. So I sat him down and told him we are now partners in this firm, and he needs to either start pulling his weight or, if he wants to go do something else, he and Mama can pay me a salary to run the place."

"That sounds fair. What did he say?"

"Said he'd think about it. Then Isaac James called, wanting one of us to come down to the station to talk about the mess over at Sky's the Limit, so I sent Skell. It's his problem—it wouldn't have happened if he'd kept an eye on his people."

"Good for you. Joe Riddley's daddy told us when we came in as partners that you have to start with people the way you mean to go on. But you sound awful gloomy. Is anything else the matter?"

"I'm fine." She paused, then added casually, "Ben's quitting."

"Quitting?" I felt like somebody had hit me in the midriff—which, now that I thought about it, is exactly how Laura sounded.

"Yeah. He came in while Skell and I were talking, and Skell told him right off that he and I are now coowners of the place. I wish he'd waited for us to talk about how to let people know, but Skell's mouth gets ahead of his brain sometimes."

"Occasionally," I agreed. "Around ninety percent of the time."

I wished she would laugh, but she sighed again instead. Laura wasn't usually a sigher, and they came out like little puffs of pain.

"Ben said he was real happy for us both," she continued, "and that he just wanted to know if any of the limos needed servicing before the weekend. He went on back to work then, but after Skell left, he came to my office again and said the reason he'd come in at first was to tell me that a mechanic down near Dublin is selling out, and Ben wants to buy his place. They talked this morning, and it looks like they can deal, so he wanted to give me a month's notice." She tried a laugh, but it fell flatter than a week-old hairdo. "I must be jinxed, Mac. Everybody's leaving me. Nicole, Ben—"

Daddy. She didn't say it, but I knew she was thinking it.

"Don't take it personal, honey. You said Ben has been wanting his own place."

"I know, but I hoped—" She stopped and rallied, trying so hard to sound cheerful she nearly broke my heart. "Yeah, that's what he really wants. I'm real happy for him, actually."

"Have you heard from Nicole?"

"No, and she's got a paycheck here and some personal
stuff in her desk drawers. You don't know how to reach her
do you?"

"No, but you could check the Augusta phone book.
There might not be too many Shandy families in town."

"Yeah." She still sounded lower than a crawling baby's
knees. When I didn't jump in to say something else, she
asked, "You think it would be all right to call her?"

"The way you two were giggling together last Monday, I
think she'd like to hear from you. She's probably feeling
pretty bruised right now, and embarrassed."

"I can't promise her anything until I talk to Skell—"

"You don't have to promise her anything, honey. I don't
want to tell your mama, but your daddy left her a little
something to get her started. Why don't you just call to see
how she is?"

As Laura hung up she sounded like at least one ray of
sunshine was peeping through her cloudy day.

Next I called her mother and, of course, got Tansy. Gwen
Ellen never answered her own phone.

"Hey, Tansy, it's MacLaren. How's Gwen Ellen this morning?"

"She's gone to get her hair washed again—she said they
put too much stuff on it for the funeral, and it was getting
all flat."

"If she's thinking about her hair, she must be feeling a bit
better."

"She's doin' all right," Tansy opined, "considerin' what
she's been through. She spent yesterday boxing up all of
Mr. Skye's things and had Skell carry them downstairs."
She echoed Laura's anxiety. "You think she's going to be
sorry later she gave them away so fast?"

"It seems soon to us, but she knows when she's ready to let the stuff go. Love has its own seasons."

"Her season has been helped a lot by having Skell here. This morning she had already started in on a little bit of cereal, but when he said, 'Tansy, can I have eggs and bacon?' she said, 'I think I'll have some, too.' That's the first real meal she's eaten since Saturday a week. It sure did me good to see it."

"Does me good to hear about it. When will she get back from the beauty parlor?"

"Too soon, I can tell you that. Her appointment was for nine. Before she left, she told me to call somebody to come pick up the boxes and suits before she gets back. I want 'em for the clothes closet down at my church, but I can't reach the reverend and I hate for her to come back and find 'em still here. I guess I'll try that secondhand place over on Bond Street."

"Why don't I send one of our trucks over to pick up the stuff and take it to your church? If nobody's there, the driver can leave a note for your preacher to call here, and we'll just leave everything in the truck until then."

"That would be so nice of you, Miss MacLaren. I can't tell you how much I'd appreciate that. We've got folks who can sure use all these fine suits and stuff."

"Glad to help." I was. It's nice to be appreciated, and Tansy might be the only one to appreciate me that day.

I hung up and spoke with one of our drivers, then sat trying to figure out how justice could best be served without my hurting people I loved. I finally concluded it could not be done. What Skye had thought was his own private business was oozing all over the place now that he was gone, becoming public and very messy. The Bible isn't kidding when it says the dark things we do in secret will one day be shouted from the housetops. The problem is, it is so often other people's housetops.

The person who would get hurt the most, once more, was Gwen Ellen, so I wanted to see her soon. When I called a second time, Tansy told me, "Your truck came and we just finished loading. Miss Gwen Ellen says I should go with him, to help him unload and put the things on hangers so they'll be ready for people who want them on Sunday. Then she says for me to go on home again. She's got an appointment later anyway, and will be busy all day."

"So she's back? I want to run over and see her."

"She's upstairs right now, but I'll tell her you're coming."

The courthouse clock chimed ten as I drove past. A minute later the Episcopalians chimed in with their spirited rendition of "Fight the Good Fight."

"I'm doing my best," I assured them as I drove past.

The truck and Tansy's car were both gone when I got there. Gwen Ellen answered the door, lovely in moss-green pants, a creamy silk top, and a green tweed jacket that brought out green flecks in her eyes. I would have known without being told that she had just been to the beauty parlor, because the lovely smells that go with pampering wafted through the screen, and her hair had that silky sheen that is hard to get at your own bathroom vanity. "That style sure suits you," I told her.

"Thank you. I can't talk long because I have an appointment, but I think we have time for a cup of tea. I've just put the kettle on. Shall we sit out on the sunporch? It's so pleasant today." She moved to lead the way, but we both turned as a red Jeep Cherokee crackled up the gravel driveway and pulled to a stop beside my car. Behind me, Gwen Ellen huffed daintily and muttered to herself, "She's too *early.*"

I certainly never expected Marilee Muller to get out and head toward us. She looked like a blazing candle in pants and a jacket as red as her car, her hair the yellow flame. She had a determined set to her head and a charming smile on her face.

She was already talking as she approached us. "Hello, Mrs. MacDonald. Judge Yarbrough." She added that as an afterthought, and gave me an odd, doubtful look. If she'd made this appointment for the showdown she'd threatened with Gwen Ellen, she couldn't be pleased to see me.

"Do come in." If Gwen Ellen's welcome wasn't warm, it was at least polite. The three of us went through the kitchen to the glass sunroom where Gwen Ellen had raised the bamboo blinds to catch the morning sun.

I claimed one of the green wicker chairs, took a deep breath of soft, fragrant air coming through a slightly open window, and decided to outstay Marilee. Surely she wouldn't have the nerve to do go through with a showdown with me right there. What could she hope to accomplish anyway? The person who said confession is good for the soul didn't mean the confession of a mistress to her lover's widow.

Marilee and Gwen Ellen each took a seat, and we sat there like the proper Southern ladies we were, all raised by mothers who sent us out into the world every morning with the warning, "Be sweet, now." We talked about the weather, the new Mexican restaurant, and whether global warming had been causing all that rain. In a lull, Gwen Ellen put up her right hand to smooth her hair. Her new diamond sparkled in the sunlight.

Marilee stared. Her tongue darted out to lick her upper lip. "Where did you get that ring?" Her voice had almost no breath behind it.

Gwen Ellen steadied the stone with the fingers of her left hand and held it out for our admiration. "Skye bought it for me. Last Sunday was the thirtieth anniversary of the day we got engaged. Isn't it lovely?"

"He never gave it to you."

"No, Laura found it in his safe Sunday afternoon."

Marilee lifted her chin. "He bought that ring for me."

I felt a shiver of fear climb my spine. Things could go dreadfully wrong here.

Gwen Ellen's eyes widened, and she pressed herself back in her chair. "I beg your pardon?"

"He bought it for me. He hadn't gotten around to telling you, but your husband and I were planning to be married. Ask Judge Yarbrough—I told her all about it. He bought that ring for me. He showed it to me last Friday, then put it in his safe until he could tell you about us and get his divorce."

Gwen Ellen turned so white I thought she'd faint, but she just sat there, staring at Marilee. Her eyes seemed larger and darker than usual.

I leaned toward Marilee and spoke firmly. "I think you ought to go. This isn't helping anybody."

She didn't budge. "See how loose it is on her finger? It fits mine." She held out her left hand with its large strong fingers. "It's the last thing I have from Skye. I want it."

Whatever Gwen Ellen was about to say, she was saved by the whistle. The kettle emitted a sound like an old-fashioned factory at quitting time. It was certainly quitting time for that conversation as far as I was concerned.

I started to stand. "I'll make the tea."

Gwen Ellen waved me back. "No, I'll do it." She rose unsteadily, putting out one hand to keep her balance.

"You don't have coffee, do you?" Marilee asked. "I've never been a tea person. If you don't, it's all right. A glass of water will do."

"There's coffee. It's no bother." Gwen Ellen moved out of the room like a woman negotiating her way underwater. I felt a little at sea myself.

"That was very cruel," I informed Marilee.

She gave a little shrug with one shoulder. "I didn't mean

to be, but there's no point in pretending. If something is true, it's true."

"Honey, if Southern women hadn't pretended for the last two hundred and fifty years, we'd all be snatched bald-headed by now. Pretending is the cornerstone of polite society."

We didn't say another word until Gwen Ellen came in with a tray holding a china teapot, the pot from her coffeemaker, and three cups. "I used the butterfly cups," she told me, adding to Marilee, "The butterfly stands for resurrection." She set the tray on the green wicker table and poured out. "Sugar?" she asked Marilee, holding a cube above her cup with silver tongs.

"Yes, please." Maybe Marilee would be nice after all. She leaned back in her chair, crossed her long legs, and seemed prepared to pretend this was a normal tea party. She didn't mention the diamond ring. Gwen Ellen had taken it off.

After Gwen Ellen dropped three sugar cubes in Marilee's cup and offered milk, which Marilee refused, she poured our tea and handed me a cup with lemon. She squeezed a slice of lemon into her own and raised it to her lips. "Poor Tansy," she said softly. "This past week has plumb worn her out. I told her not to bother coming back when she finishes at the church."

Instead of sitting down, she fussed around the porch, carrying her cup and taking occasional sips as she pinched yellow leaves off the potted geraniums and dropped them into the wastebasket. She bent to straighten a stack of magazines. "These are so old. I need to go through things in this house and throw stuff away. We've been here so long that all the closets are crammed and all the window seats are full. Remember, Mac, how you once said you'd bring your extra stuff over here to store because we had so much storage space? We don't have any extra space right now."

"This past week has worn us all out," I told her. "Sit down. Don't fool with those right now."

"I feel like I could sleep a hundred years," she admitted. But when she sat, she merely perched, still sipping her tea. "More?" she asked.

Marilee took another cup of coffee, and Gwen Ellen poured herself more tea. I didn't like this particular tea she was serving—it was one of those fancy new ones she was always trying—so I claimed that my cup was still half full, but kept sipping to avoid talking.

In all our years of friendship, I couldn't remember feeling so uncomfortable with Gwen Ellen. Normally she was a restful person to be with. Now she kept watching Marilee as if afraid she'd burst out again.

Marilee sipped her coffee and frowned, as if trying to decide what to say next. I still wondered why she had come.

I crossed my legs one way, decided that wasn't comfortable, and tried them the other. "Laura told me about what you are doing with the business, Gwen Ellen," I said. "I think that is grand. She loves it as much as Skye ever did."

Gwen Ellen nodded. "Skell never has, you know. I hope he'll let her run it and find something else to do, something he really likes."

"I'm sure he will."

We could have been actresses sitting on a stage. I just wished somebody had handed me my script ahead of time, so I'd know my part. I was so unaccustomed to sunshine that I was getting drowsy, too—or maybe that was my antihistamine kicking in. But I was determined to outstay Marilee. Was she hoping I'd leave? I crossed my legs again and prepared to wait her out.

At last she came to a decision. "Could we get to the point? I have an appointment this afternoon."

I looked from one to the other in surprise. Gwen Ellen had called this meeting?

She set down her cup with a dainty *click*. "Very well. You went with my husband to a ranch for a week, didn't you? You went as Mrs. Fergus MacDonald."

Marilee was startled but bold as brass. "Yes, I did. Did Skye tell you?"

"No. I saw an envelope in his office addressed to both of us, so I took it with me. I read it in the beauty parlor while I was waiting to get my hair cut. It said they hoped we enjoyed our week with them and would come again. But I'd never been there." Her face was very pale. "Can you imagine what it was like to have to sit there pretending my world hadn't just ended?"

For once, Marilee seemed embarrassed. "I'm real sorry about that. Skye and I wouldn't have hurt you that way for the world. He wanted to explain . . . to make it easy for you."

"To make it easy for me." Gwen Ellen did not make a question out of it, but Marilee answered anyway.

"He honored all the years you'd had together. He didn't want to hurt you. But we were so much in love, you see."

I put out a hand to stop her, but Gwen Ellen put her hand over mine. "No, I want to hear. When did you meet my husband?"

"We were on a committee together for the college. To raise funds from alums, you know?"

"Yes, he told me."

"We didn't mean for anything to happen, but it was like—electric." Her face lit up and she gave a happy little laugh; then she pressed one hand to her mouth. "I'm sorry. I shouldn't be saying things like that to you. But you asked," she added defiantly, "and we were going to get married. He'd bought me the ring."

"You think he would have actually married you?" Gwen Ellen's voice was remote, as if she were asking about two strangers. "He'd have lost the business, you know. Mac-

Donald's wasn't his; it was mine. I made him put it in my name after Nicole was born." She saw me jump, and spoke to me. "I knew about Nicole's mother. I just pretended Saturday for Laura's sake. Skye was so ashamed, he had to tell me. It made him feel better, I think."

She didn't say how it had made her feel. I stared at her in astonishment and admiration. Never in twenty years had she betrayed him, even to me, who knew her so well.

"Did you also pretend that Skye wanted Laura to have half the company?" I asked, hoping it wasn't true. Laura had been so touched by her daddy's change of heart.

"Oh, no. He really did change his mind. He told me on the way to the Mexican restaurant that he'd finally accepted that Laura would be better at running the business than Skell. He said he thought I should leave it to them jointly. Laura could run it and let Skell do something else." She turned back to Marilee. "Do you understand what I'm saying? If Skye married you, he'd have had to give up the company. Do you really think he would have done that?" She stifled a yawn.

Marilee leaped to her feet. "He *was* going to marry me. He was. You'll never make me believe otherwise." She stormed out of the room. "He loved me," she called back.

"He loved that motor company," Gwen Ellen called after her.

The back door slammed.

Only then did she turn to me, her eyes full of pain. "He *was* going to marry her, MacLaren. When he got home that evening after work, I showed him the letter and asked who he'd gone with. He admitted it was Marilee, and he said he couldn't help himself, he loved her. He wanted to marry her. You didn't know, MacLaren—nobody knew—but Skye's had other women through the years. He thought I didn't know, but I did. I put up with it because he always played out of town. This time, though, was different. He said he was real sorry to be hurting me, but he just had to be with her. He said she made him feel alive and young again." Gwen Ellen lightly touched the haircut that hadn't made her young enough. "That's why he told me on the way to the restaurant what he thought I ought to do with the business. He was giving it up. He was planning to *leave*." Tears filled her eyes and spilled down her cheeks.

"Oh, honey!" Tears stung my own eyes and clogged my throat. "I saw the letter, too. You left it on your dresser, and I was up there looking for Skell's ferret. But I didn't realize at the time that the dude ranch trip was the same week Skye was supposed to be in Denver and you and I went on our weekend retreat. Laura said she couldn't reach him there to get his approval for a new radio ad. That's because he was in New Mexico, I guess."

She wasn't paying attention to me. Her dark head was bent toward the window, listening. When we heard Marilee's car start, she gave a remote little smile. Then she turned to me and said the oddest thing. "MacLaren, I really wish you hadn't stayed so long."

"You killed Skye, didn't you?" I asked gently. "After you all left the restaurant, he went by some property he was thinking of buying for Hands Up Together. When he got out to look at it, you ran over him."

The tears that had stood in her eyes welled up and rolled down her cheeks. Slowly she nodded.

She started to talk in a dreary, toneless voice. "I didn't care a thing about that land, but he just had to show it to me. He was so excited about that project. But when he got out of the car and I saw him standing there looking at the fields, all I could think of was the letter in my pocketbook, and how no matter what he did to me and the children, everybody was still going to say what a fine man he was. Skye MacDonald, benefactor of Hopemore. They wouldn't care if he left me and married Marilee—not for long, they

wouldn't. They wouldn't care if he had more children. He
was killing our family, MacLaren. Yet people would still
think he was *fine.*" She pressed a hand to her mouth to
stem the torrent.

Do not destroy. That's what the last six commandments
are all about. Don't destroy yourselves by working too
hard. Don't destroy trust, love, life, natural boundaries, and
truth among you. The commandments aren't heavy-handed
Keep Out signs. Joe Riddley calls them "the manufacturer's
operating instructions for this computer we call life." Skye
violated those instructions. But oh, my dear God, so had
Gwen Ellen.

She spoke in a whisper. "I couldn't let him destroy us. I
slid over into his seat, put the car in gear, and ran right over
him. Then I backed up and drove away. The whole time I
drove back to town, I thought, 'I can't live without Skye. I
can't. God, let me die; let me die!' But I didn't have the
courage to kill myself. When I saw I was on Oglethorpe
Street, I decided to go to the church. I don't know why."

I did. Sanctuary. The refuge of lost and desperate souls
for centuries. "Oh, God, you are our fortress." The Psalm
left my lips in a murmur. I half rose in my chair, wanting to
take her in my arms like I used to when she was little, but
she waved me back to my seat.

"Let me finish. I have to tell you. I parked in back so nobody would see me, and I wiped the steering wheel real
good. Then I slid to my own side, because my prints were
supposed to be there. I got out and started for the door, but
just then it started to rain. Buckets and buckets, all at once.
I didn't want to track muddy water all over the church, and
I was already soaked, so I decided to walk home. This may
sound silly, but that walk in the storm felt like a cold,
cleansing shower. And I had lots of time to think exactly
what I would do and say the next morning. If it had just
been me, I'd have gone straight to the police station. But I

didn't want the children to suffer any more than they had to." For the first time I saw remorse and uncertainty in her eyes. "After I got inside, I threw my clothes in the drier and took a sleeping pill. When I woke up the next morning, I truly didn't remember for a few minutes what I had done. I thought Skye was just down at the motor company. And then, I remembered—"

Sobs finally came, terrible racking sobs that wrenched her shoulders and heaved up her grief. "I worked in the yard all morning and felt like I was burying my love under chicken manure. He did bad things, Mac, but I loved him. I truly loved him."

Finally I could go to her. Kneel down and hold her, murmur senseless things that seemed to comfort and quiet her.

"How did you know?" she whispered into my collar. "How did you figure it out?"

"The ground wasn't wet under him. It started pouring rain just as we got to Maynard's, and we left Casa Mas Esperanza not too long after you did. There wasn't time for Skye to come home, come inside the house with you, receive a phone call, and get back out there. When I thought about how little time anybody had to kill him, it had to be you." I shivered as I remembered that what had worried Gwen Ellen the day after Skye died was not who could have killed him, but that he had lain all night in the rain.

Outside the window, something crashed.

"That sounded like a car." I meant to jump to my feet, but I'd been kneeling, and at my age you don't jump the way you used to. My knees were stiff, my legs tottery.

"Marilee must have hit a tree." Gwen Ellen said it with no emotion whatsoever. I looked down at her, and she was smiling. "I laced her coffee with half a bottle of sleeping pills. I got a new prescription filled this morning."

The tea in my stomach rose up in protest. "Oh, honey." I pressed one hand to my lips, feeling very sick indeed.

"You'll never get away with that. You know I'll have to tell somebody."

She reached up and stroked my cheek with tender love. "I knew that, MacLaren. That's why I put the rest in our tea."

⇜ 27 ⇝

I staggered across the room and bent to grab my pocket-book for the cell phone, but my battery was dead. I'd for-gotten and left it on the whole time I was sick in bed. I turned toward the kitchen and hoped I could make it that far.

"Don't leave me," Gwen Ellen said sweetly, laying her head against the back of her chair. "Sit down and wait. We won't feel any pain. We'll just drift off and sleep forever."

Gwen Ellen had no notion how nasty a person is who has drifted off to that kind of sleep. She would never expect to be found with her bowels and bladder emptied into her chair. She probably expected Skye to meet her on the other side and wake her with a kiss.

I didn't believe in Prince Charming; I believed in God. "Help me. Help me," I muttered as I lurched toward the kitchen.

"Don't go, MacLaren," she whimpered. "Don't leave me alone. It's getting dark."

My own eyes were blurring, and I wasn't sure I could speak. It took three tries for me to punch in 911, and I could barely whisper, "Help, help, help," when somebody an-swered.

I leaned over the sink and thrust my finger as far down

my throat as I could get it. I gagged, but nothing came out. I've never been one to throw up when I'm sick.

What was it Mama used when I ate those pokeberries?

Mustard. I saw the picture in my mind's eye. Dry mustard. In water.

My legs were spaghetti, so I propped myself against the counter and used my elbow as a crutch, opening upper cabinets as I went. My ears were rushing, and the world was growing dim.

I found the dry mustard and emptied it into a glass by the sink. I didn't worry if the glass was clean; I had to summon all my energy to turn on the tap. I stirred with a knife from the drainer and downed the entire glass in one long swallow, then stood by the sink and waited for half an eternity.

I felt myself slipping to the floor when my stomach began to heave. With my last reserves of energy, I hauled myself against the sink and flopped over into it. That's the only time in my life I ever thanked God for the ability to vomit.

I felt only a little better. How much of the drug had entered my system?

I heard a siren wail down the street, turn into the drive, and stop.

"Oh, God," I groaned. They had stopped for Marilee. They didn't know we were there.

Again I dragged myself to the telephone. This time I had to sit before I could punch in 911. Three numbers were far too many. Two rings too far too long. When the voice came, I croaked hoarsely, "Please, another ambulance. Inside the house. Two of us—"

That's when everything went black.

"Come on, Little Bit. Come on. You can do it." Joe Riddley sounded like he thought I ought to be up and doing something, but I was far too weary.

"I can't." I turned my head away.

"That's my girl! Come on. Wake up!" He shook me.

Joe Riddley weighs twice what I weigh. He probably thought he was shaking gently, but my whole head rattled. I could feel my brains jiggling around in there. "Stop," I grumbled. "That hurts."

"Open your eyes. You can do it."

"Don't wanna." He didn't realize my eyelids had been attached to my eyes with glue. If I tried to open them, I'd pull out my eyeballs.

He bent down so close I could feel his whiskers on my cheek. First he gently kissed each eye. Then he took his finger and raised one lid. It went up slick as spit. "Hey. You in there?"

"Yeah. I'm in here." I just didn't know where here was. I didn't have a clue where I was until I recognized the color of the walls. I'd seen enough of that particular shade of pink when Joe Riddley was in the hospital. Everything came back like an enormous wave, knocking the breath out of me.

"Gwen Ellen? Marilee?"

He shook his head. "They didn't make it. When you feel better, you can tell us what went on. Marilee crashed into a tree and died instantly. Gwen Ellen was found on her sunroom with an empty pot of tea."

Empty? She must have drunk another cup after I left.

Hot tears squeezed through my closed lids and ran down the sides of my face. Joe Riddley gently swabbed them with his finger. "Don't cry, Little Bit. Don't cry." I could tell he was getting distressed, but I couldn't stop crying. I cried for Gwen Ellen. I cried for Skye. I even cried for Marilee. Underneath the barracuda suit was a plain little girl who wanted more cards than life had dealt her, and looked for them in the wrong deck.

Joe Riddley got up and left; then I felt a wet washcloth

flop onto my face. "Stop crying," he said urgently. "Stop it."

I pushed away the washcloth. "I've stopped. Get me a towel."

I dozed on and off for the next twenty-four hours. That afternoon, I knew when Ridd's wife Martha stopped by just before she went on duty. She squeezed my hand and whispered, "Thanks for sticking around. We all need you, you know."

I knew when Walker and Cindy came, because I could smell her expensive perfume and his aftershave. Walker leaned over my bed and muttered, "So help me, if she doesn't stop this detectin', I'm gonna—"

I opened one eye. "You're gonna do what?"

He grinned a bit shakily. "I don't know, but it will be terrible."

Cindy set a gorgeous white cattleya orchid on my windowsill and bent to give me a hug. I reached up and stroked her soft cheek. "Hey, honey. Good to see you." I was moved to see tears in her eyes. But I fell into a doze before they left.

I was surprised after dark, when my room was lit only by lights from the hall, to open my eyes and see Laura standing in my doorway. "Come in." I held out my hand. She clutched it and slipped into the chair by my bed.

"Are you all right? Really?" Her voice was gruffer than usual, and her eyes swimming.

"A little rocky still, but I'm going to be fine. I'm so sorry about your mother."

She shook her head and bit her lower lip so hard I feared she would draw blood. In the dimness, I saw tears shimmering in her eyes. "I don't know what happened, Mac. Nobody does. Will you tell me?"

I closed my eyes, took a deep breath, and tried to figure out how to tell it with the least expenditure of energy. "She killed your daddy. He—" At that minute I made a decision I have never regretted. "He got out to look at the land. She was sliding over the seat to join him and her foot hit the gas. She was so upset, she didn't know what to do. So she went home and took a sleeping pill, and when she woke up, she had forgotten what she'd done. When she remembered—" I had to stop for more air. "She couldn't live with that on her conscience." Finally I could open my eyes. Eyes are the windows of the soul. They proclaim when we are lying. "She loved him very much," I whispered. That part, at least, was true.

I'd have to figure out later what to tell Isaac and Charlie, because both Gwen Ellen and Marilee had been full of sleeping pills. But I'd think of something. I don't believe in lying, but I also believe grown-ups have a responsibility to carry the burdens of the young. I'd clean up Skye and Gwen Ellen's mess and do my best to keep their children from being contaminated by it for the rest of their lives.

"I know she loved him." Laura's face was grave and her voice thick with tears. "I just wish she'd told us. Daddy wouldn't have held it against her. You know he wouldn't."

I reached out and touched her cheek as her mother had touched mine. "Are you going to be all right?"

She sighed. "Eventually." A shadow passed over her face, and I wondered if she, like I, was thinking it sure would have been nice for her to have some broad shoulders to share the load. Shoulders like—

"You doin' all right?" Ben Bradshaw darkened my door and ducked as he came in to keep from hitting his head on the door lintel. He had his hands clasped tight in front of him. I suspected visiting the sick wasn't something he did very often.

"I'm going to be fine," I assured him weakly. "I figured the best way to see all my friends was to lie around a day or two and let you all come to me."

A smile flickered on his lips and even touched his eyes.

"Sit down," I suggested, waving him to my other visitor's chair. "What's this I hear about you desertin' us in our hour of need?"

He frowned. "I'm not . . . I need to . . ."

"Laura sure needs you right now." I ignored Laura's gasp and frown. "Skell's not going to be much help. I wouldn't be surprised if he left Hopemore before long."

Laura nodded. "You know what he wants to do?" She talked fast, and with an enthusiasm I knew she didn't feel. Anything to shut me up. "He wants to go to law school. He said he wants to defend people who are wrongfully imprisoned, and to prosecute drug lords."

I wasn't clear how he planned to be both a prosecutor and a defense attorney, but we didn't need to settle that at the moment. Laura was babbling on. "He says I can run the place and we'll pay me a salary. And you know, I think he'll be a good lawyer. He's certainly a motormouth."

"He's not the only one," I teased her. Then I gave her an appraising look. "Have you ever considered selling your service department? Looks like if somebody else owned that—somebody you trusted to keep up the high standards Skye set and maybe even take them a little farther—"

That's when I ran out of steam, but it didn't matter. Laura looked at Ben, and Ben looked at Laura. I saw the first shy shoots of the seed I'd planted spring up between them.

"I don't know anything about running the service department," Laura said thoughtfully. "Daddy did that—and Ben here."

"I always liked Hopemore," Ben acknowledged. "It's a nice little town."

She stood. "We can talk about that later. Mac looks worn out. Go to sleep," she said softly, squeezing my hand. "We'll check on you again tomorrow."

They walked out the door, a tall brave young woman

with a heavy load to carry and a pair of broad, strong shoulders beside her.

The next morning I had three sets of visitors between naps. Selena and Maynard came in, bringing enough sunshine between them to supply our town's needs for a month. "Not exactly your run-of-the mill honeymoon," I told them.

Maynard grinned. "But not one we're likely to forget."

They didn't stay long—she was due in the emergency room and he had a shipment of antiques coming in from Charleston.

"I'm glad your night in jail didn't permanently scar you," I said weakly as they got ready to leave.

"No, but we're gonna volunteer in your church's prison ministry," Selena told me. "When I think of the sad stories some of those women told me . . ."

I smiled. "I'm so proud to know you, honey."

My next visitors were the whole Garcia family, bearing an enormous bouquet of red roses. "The judge dismissed all charges," Mr. Garcia told me happily. "And would you believe our restaurant has not suffered while I was away? My wife and Rosita here have kept it going just fine, and last night I think everybody in town came to eat dinner and tell me how sorry they were about the mistake. I am famous in Hopemore!" He beamed at me.

His wife pushed him aside and smiled shyly down at me. "When you get well, come to eat. Dinner for you and your husband, on the house."

Rosa gave me one of her brilliant smiles. "And I want you to come address my class on how to be a magistrate. Will you?"

"I'd be happy to," I informed her. But I could feel myself slipping into a doze again.

When I woke, I saw sunlight streaming through my window, but my spirits were lost somewhere in stormy clouds.

Everything that had happened seemed to pour down on me like the rain had poured over Hopemore that dreadful week. Tears started sliding down my cheeks.

"Looks like you need this," said a deep voice at the door. Isaac James crossed the room and handed me an odd-shaped package wrapped in white tissue paper. "It's a blue-bird of happiness, so my wife tells me."

I unwrapped a small bird molded of deep blue glass. The sun poured through him and made a river on my wall. I set it gently beside the bed where it would hold the light.

"I could use some happiness," I admitted as Ike lowered his bulk into my visitor's chair.

"You ready to tell me what happened over at MacDonald's?"

I hesitated. "What do you already know?"

"Sleeping pills in Ms. Muller, Mrs. MacDonald, you, the tea, and the coffee, and an empty bottle on the counter that had been full a couple of hours earlier when it left the pharmacy. What I don't know is who put them in the tea and coffee. I'm betting on Ms. Muller—she always did have a temper. But I'd better warn you what Chief Muggins says: he'd originally figured Mrs. MacDonald for the killer, but now he thinks it peculiar that you were the only one who survived."

I sighed. "If you'll promise not to let it leave this room, I'm going to tell you exactly what happened. You and I will have to live the rest of our lives with the lowering knowledge that for once in his life, Charlie Muggins was right."

I got home Wednesday in time for dinner. As soon as I stepped into the kitchen, I could see Clarinda was fixing to have a conniption.

"Who put ants between your sheets?" I demanded, collapsing into my chair.

"Not to worry. Not to worry," Joe assured me from the curtain rod.

I looked up at him in surprise. "Did Joe Riddley leave him in here while he came to get me?" Ever since Joe came to live with us, Clarinda had refused to "parrot-sit."

She flapped one hand. "He's no bother. But Miss Mac-Laren, you won't believe what those boys are doin'."

"Which boys are those?" I laid my cheek against the hard cool table. The doctor said it could take me a couple more days to fully wake up. It wasn't just the sleeping pills. Between the cold and the week I'd just had, I was pure-T exhausted. He recommended a week in the Caribbean. I was planning to work on that.

Meanwhile, Clarinda stood over me like a dark angel of judgment. "First, Maynard's gone and bought himself another expensive car, just like the first one, except green this time. He don't need no fancy car. And that Skell—you know what he's fixin' to do? He's gonna leave his sister and go up to Athens to become a lawyer. She needs him. He could live here and commute. . . ."

"He doesn't want to commute," I informed her drowsily. "He wants to go somewhere exciting where things happen."

"Well, he sure won't find that in Hopemore," she agreed. "Not much ever happens 'round here. You look bushed. You want me to fix you a nice cup of tea?"

I shuddered. "No, Clarinda. I want a nice cold Co-cola. In an unopened can."

Kate Collins

The Flower Shop Mystery Series

Abby Knight is the proud owner of her hometown flower shop. She has a gift for arranging flowers—and for solving crimes.

Acts of Violets
Mum's the Word
Slay It with Flowers
Dearly Depotted
Snipped in the Bud
A Rose from the Dead
Shoots to Kill

"A spirited sleuth, quirky sidekicks,
and page-turning action."
—Nancy J. Cohen

**Available wherever books are sold or at
penguin.com**